"Lourey pulls out all the stops in this eighth case."

—*Library Journal*

PRAISE FOR *NOVEMBER HUNT*

"It's not easy to make people laugh while they're on the edge of their seats, but Lourey pulls it off, while her vivid descriptions of a brutal Minnesota winter will make readers shiver in the seventh book in her very clever Mira James mystery series."

—*Booklist* (starred review)

"Clever, quirky, and completely original!"
—Hank Phillippi Ryan, Anthony, Agatha, and Macavity Award–winning author

"A masterful mix of mayhem and mirth."
—Reed Farrel Coleman, *New York Times* bestselling author

"Lourey has successfully created an independent, relatable heroine in Mira James. Mira's wit and fearlessness enable her to overcome the many challenges she faces as she tries to unravel the murder."

—*Crimespree Magazine*

"Lourey's seventh cozy featuring PI wannabe Mira James successfully combines humor, an intriguing mystery, and quirky small-town characters."

—*Publishers Weekly*

"Lourey has a knack for wholesome sexual innuendo, and she gets plenty of mileage out of Minnesota. This light novel keeps the reader engaged, like one of those sweet, chewy Nut Goodies that Mira is addicted to."

—*The Boston Globe*

PRAISE FOR *OCTOBER FEST*

"Snappy jokes and edgy dialogue . . . More spunky than sweet; get started on this Lefty-nominated series if you've previously missed it."

—*Library Journal* (starred review)

"I loved Lourey's quirky, appealing sleuth and her wry-yet-affectionate look at small-town life. No gimmicks, just an intriguing plot with oddball characters. I hope Mira's misfortune of stumbling over a dead body every month lasts for many years!"

—Donna Andrews, *New York Times* bestselling author of *Stork Raving Mad*

"Funny, ribald, and brimming with small-town eccentrics."

—*Kirkus Reviews*

"Lourey has cleverly created an entertaining murder mystery . . . Her latest is loaded with humor, and many of the descriptions are downright poetic."

—*Booklist* (starred review)

PRAISE FOR *SEPTEMBER MOURN*

"Once again, the very funny Lourey serves up a delicious dish of murder, mayhem, and merriment."

—*Booklist* (starred review)

"Beautifully written and wickedly funny."

—Harley Jane Kozak, Agatha, Anthony, and Macavity Award–winning author

"Lourey has a talent for creating hilarious characters in bizarre, laugh-out-loud situations, while at the same time capturing the honest and endearing subtleties of human life."

—The Strand

PRAISE FOR *AUGUST MOON*

"Hilarious, fast paced, and madcap."

—*Booklist* (starred review)

"Another amusing tale set in the town full of over-the-top zanies who've endeared themselves to the engaging Mira."

—*Kirkus Reviews*

"[A] hilarious, wonderfully funny cozy."

—*Crimespree Magazine*

"Lourey has a gift for creating terrific characters. Her sly and witty take on small-town USA is a sweet summer treat. Pull up a lawn chair, pour yourself a glass of lemonade, and enjoy."

—Denise Swanson, bestselling author

"A fun, fast-paced mystery with a heroine readers will enjoy."

—*The Mystery Reader*

"Don't miss this one—it's a hoot!"
—William Kent Krueger, *New York Times* bestselling author

"With just the right amount of insouciance, tongue-in-cheek sexiness, and plain common sense, Jess Lourey offers up a funny, well-written, engaging story . . . Readers will thoroughly enjoy the well-paced ride."
—Carl Brookins, author of *The Case of the Greedy Lawyers*

PRAISE FOR *MAY DAY*

"Jess Lourey writes about a small-town assistant librarian, but this is no genteel traditional mystery. Mira James likes guys in a big way, likes booze, and isn't afraid of motorcycles. She flees a dead-end job and a dead-end boyfriend in Minneapolis and ends up in Battle Lake, a little town with plenty of dirty secrets. The first-person narrative in *May Day* is fresh, the characters quirky. Minnesota has many fine crime writers, and Jess Lourey has just entered their ranks!"
—Ellen Hart, award-winning author of the Jane Lawless and Sophie Greenway series

"This trade paperback packed a punch . . . I loved it from the get-go!"
—*Tulsa World*

"What a romp this is! I found myself laughing out loud."
—*Crimespree Magazine*

"Mira digs up a closetful of dirty secrets, including sex parties, cross-dressing, and blackmail, on her way to exposing the killer. Lourey's debut has a likable heroine and surfeit of sass."
—*Kirkus Reviews*

PRAISE FOR *THE TAKEN ONES*

Short-listed for the 2024 Edgar Award for Best Paperback Original

"Setting the standard for top-notch thrillers, *The Taken Ones* is smart, compelling, and filled with utterly real characters. Lourey brings her formidable storytelling talent to the game and, on top of that, wows us with a deft stylistic touch. This is a one-sitting read!"

—Jeffery Deaver, author of *The Bone Collector* and *The Watchmaker's Hand*

"*The Taken Ones* has Jess Lourey's trademark of suspense all the way. A damaged and brave heroine, an equally damaged evildoer, and missing girls from long ago all combine to keep the reader rushing through to the explosive ending."

—Charlaine Harris, *New York Times* bestselling author

"Lourey is at the top of her game with *The Taken Ones*. A master of building tension while maintaining a riveting pace, Lourey is a hell of a writer on all fronts, but her greatest talent may be her characters. Evangeline Reed, an agent with the Minnesota Bureau of Criminal Apprehension, is a woman with a devastating past and the haunting ability to know the darkest crimes happening around her. She is also exactly the kind of character I would happily follow through a dozen books or more. In awe of her bravery, I also identified with her pain and wanted desperately to protect her. Along with an incredible cast of support characters, *The Taken Ones* will break your heart wide open and stay with you long after you've turned the final page. This is a 2023 must read."

—Danielle Girard, *USA Today* and Amazon #1 bestselling author of *Up Close*

PRAISE FOR *THE QUARRY GIRLS*

Winner of the 2023 Anthony Award for Best Paperback Original

Winner of the 2023 Minnesota Book Award for Genre Fiction

"Few authors can blend the genuine fear generated by a sordid tale of true crime with evocative, three-dimensional characters and mesmerizing prose like Jess Lourey. Her fictional stories feel rooted in a world we all know but also fear. *The Quarry Girls* is a story of secrets gone to seed, and Lourey gives readers her best novel yet—which is quite the accomplishment. Calling it: *The Quarry Girls* will be one of the best books of the year."

—Alex Segura, acclaimed author of *Secret Identity*, *Star Wars Poe Dameron: Free Fall*, and *Miami Midnight*

"Jess Lourey once more taps deep into her Midwest roots and childhood fears with *The Quarry Girls*, an absorbing, true crime–informed thriller narrated in the compelling voice of young drummer Heather Cash as she and her bandmates navigate the treacherous and confusing ground between girlhood and womanhood one simmering and deadly summer. Lourey conveys the edgy, hungry restlessness of teen girls with a touch of Megan Abbott while steadily intensifying the claustrophobic atmosphere of a small 1977 Minnesota town where darkness snakes below the surface."

—Loreth Anne White, *Washington Post* and Amazon Charts bestselling author of *The Patient's Secret*

"Jess Lourey is a master of the coming-of-age thriller, and *The Quarry Girls* may be her best yet—as dark, twisty, and full of secrets as the tunnels that lurk beneath Pantown's deceptively idyllic streets."
—Chris Holm, Anthony Award–winning author of *The Killing Kind*

PRAISE FOR *BLOODLINE*

Winner of the 2022 Anthony Award for Best Paperback Original

Winner of the 2022 ITW Thriller Award for Best Paperback Original

Short-listed for the 2021 Goodreads Choice Awards

"Fans of *Rosemary's Baby* will relish this."
—*Publishers Weekly*

"Based on a true story, this is a sinister, suspenseful thriller full of creeping horror."
—*Kirkus Reviews*

"Lourey ratchets up the fear in a novel that verges on horror."
—*Library Journal*

"In *Bloodline*, Jess Lourey blends elements of mystery, suspense, and horror to stunning effect."
—*BOLO Books*

"Inspired by a true story, it's a creepy page-turner that has me eager to read more of Ms. Lourey's works, especially if they're all as incisive as this thought-provoking novel."

—Criminal Element

"*Bloodline* by Jess Lourey is a psychological thriller that grabbed me from the beginning and didn't let go."

—*Mystery & Suspense Magazine*

"*Bloodline* blends page-turning storytelling with clever homages to such horror classics as *Rosemary's Baby*, *The Stepford Wives*, and *Harvest Home*."

—*Toronto Star*

"*Bloodline* is a terrific, creepy thriller, and Jess Lourey clearly knows how to get under your skin."

—Bookreporter

"[A] tightly coiled domestic thriller that slowly but persuasively builds the suspense."

—*South Florida Sun Sentinel*

"I should know better than to pick up a new Jess Lourey book thinking I'll just peek at the first few pages and then get back to the book I was reading. Six hours later, it's three in the morning and I'm racing through the last few chapters, unable to sleep until I know how it all ends. Set in an idyllic small town rooted in family history and horrific secrets, *Bloodline* is *Pleasantville* meets *Rosemary's Baby*. A deeply unsettling, darkly unnerving, and utterly compelling novel, this book chilled me to the core, and I loved every bit of it."

—Jennifer Hillier, author of *Little Secrets* and the award-winning *Jar of Hearts*

"Jess Lourey writes small-town Minnesota like Stephen King writes small-town Maine. *Bloodline* is a tremendous book with a heart and a hacksaw . . . and I loved every second of it."
—Rachel Howzell Hall, author of the critically acclaimed novels *And Now She's Gone* and *They All Fall Down*

PRAISE FOR *UNSPEAKABLE THINGS*

Winner of the 2021 Anthony Award for Best Paperback Original

Short-listed for the 2021 Edgar Awards and 2020 Goodreads Choice Awards

"The suspense never wavers in this page-turner."
—*Publishers Weekly*

"The atmospheric suspense novel is haunting because it's narrated from the point of view of a thirteen-year-old, an age that should be more innocent but often isn't. Even more chilling, it's based on real-life incidents. Lourey may be known for comic capers (*March of Crimes*), but this tense novel combines the best of a coming-of-age story with suspense and an unforgettable young narrator."
—*Library Journal* (starred review)

"Part suspense, part coming-of-age, Jess Lourey's *Unspeakable Things* is a story of creeping dread, about childhood when you know the monster under your bed is real. A novel that clings to you long after the last page."
—Lori Rader-Day, Edgar Award–nominated author of *Under a Dark Sky*

"A noose of a novel that tightens by inches. The squirming tension comes from every direction—including the ones that are supposed to be safe. I felt complicit as I read, as if at any moment I stopped I would be abandoning Cassie, alone, in the dark, straining to listen and fearing to hear."

—Marcus Sakey, bestselling author of *Brilliance*

"*Unspeakable Things* is an absolutely riveting novel about the poisonous secrets buried deep in towns and families. Jess Lourey has created a story that will chill you to the bone and a main character who will break your heart wide open."

—Lou Berney, Edgar Award–winning author of *November Road*

"Inspired by a true story, *Unspeakable Things* crackles with authenticity, humanity, and humor. The novel reminded me of *To Kill a Mockingbird* and *The Marsh King's Daughter*. Highly recommended."

—Mark Sullivan, bestselling author of *Beneath a Scarlet Sky*

"Jess Lourey does a masterful job building tension and dread, but her greatest asset in *Unspeakable Things* is Cassie—an arresting narrator you identify with, root for, and desperately want to protect. This is a book that will stick with you long after you've torn through it."

—Rob Hart, author of *The Warehouse*

"With *Unspeakable Things*, Jess Lourey has managed the near-impossible, crafting a mystery as harrowing as it is tender, as gut-wrenching as it is lyrical. There is real darkness here, a creeping, inescapable dread that more than once had me looking over my own shoulder. But at its heart beats the irrepressible—and irresistible—spirit of its . . . heroine, a young woman so bright and vital and brave she kept even the fiercest monsters at bay. This is a book that will stay with me for a long time."

—Elizabeth Little, *Los Angeles Times* bestselling author of *Dear Daughter* and *Pretty as a Picture*

PRAISE FOR *SALEM'S CIPHER*

"A fast-paced, sometimes brutal thriller reminiscent of Dan Brown's *The Da Vinci Code*."

—*Booklist* (starred review)

"A hair-raising thrill ride."

—*Library Journal* (starred review)

"The fascinating historical information combined with a storyline ripped from the headlines will hook conspiracy theorists and action addicts alike."

—*Kirkus Reviews*

"Fans of *The Da Vinci Code* are going to love this book . . . One of my favorite reads of 2016."

—*Crimespree Magazine*

"This suspenseful tale has something for absolutely everyone to enjoy."

—*Suspense Magazine*

PRAISE FOR *MERCY'S CHASE*

"An immersive voice, an intriguing story, a wonderful character— highly recommended!"

—Lee Child, #1 *New York Times* bestselling author

"Both a sweeping adventure and race-against-time thriller, *Mercy's Chase* is fascinating, fierce, and brimming with heart—just like its heroine, Salem Wiley."

—Meg Gardiner, author of *Into the Black Nowhere*

"Action-packed, great writing taut with suspense, an appealing main character to root for—who could ask for anything more?"
—Buried Under Books

PRAISE FOR *REWRITE YOUR LIFE: DISCOVER YOUR TRUTH THROUGH THE HEALING POWER OF FICTION*

"Interweaving practical advice with stories and insights garnered in her own writing journey, Jessica Lourey offers a step-by-step guide for writers struggling to create fiction from their life experiences. But this book isn't just about writing. It's also about the power of stories to transform those who write them. I know of no other guide that delivers on its promise with such honesty, simplicity, and beauty."
—William Kent Krueger, *New York Times* bestselling author of the Cork O'Connor series and *Ordinary Grace*

JANUARY
THAW

OTHER TITLES BY JESS LOUREY

MURDER BY MONTH MYSTERIES

May Day

June Bug

Knee High by the Fourth of July

August Moon

September Mourn

October Fest

November Hunt

December Dread

January Thaw

February Fever

March of Crimes

April Fools

STEINBECK AND REED THRILLERS

The Taken Ones

The Reaping

THRILLERS

The Quarry Girls

Litani

Bloodline

Unspeakable Things

SALEM'S CIPHER THRILLERS

Salem's Cipher

Mercy's Chase

CHILDREN'S BOOKS

*Leave My Book Alone! Starring Claudette,
a Dragon with Control Issues*

YOUNG ADULT

A Whisper of Poison

NONFICTION

*Rewrite Your Life: Discover Your Truth
Through the Healing Power of Fiction*

JANUARY THAW

JESS LOUREY

THOMAS & MERCER

Text copyright © 2013, 2018, 2024 by Jess Lourey
All rights reserved.

Published by Thomas & Mercer, Seattle

www.apub.com

Amazon, the Amazon logo, and Thomas & Mercer are trademarks of Amazon.com, Inc., or its affiliates.

ISBN-13: 9781662519390 (paperback)
ISBN-13: 9781662519383 (digital)

Cover design and illustration by Sarah Horgan

Printed in the United States of America

To Catriona, for being such a gallus besom herself

A special thanks goes to the Prospect House & Civil War Museum for letting me set major portions of the novel in their amazing mansion and on their grounds. A particular shout-out to Jay Johnson and Abby Bizzett Johnson for the private tour. They have allowed me to cherry-pick from the Prospect House's history (and a little bit from their personal lives) and twist where necessary to fit my narrative. Everything good I wrote about the Prospect House and the dedicated, incredible people who care for it is true; everything dark is entirely a work of fiction. If you're in the Battle Lake area, I encourage you to stop by and visit this impressive piece of history. Heck, I think you should make a special trip just to check it out. It's that cool. Find out more at their website: www.prospecthousemuseum.org.

Chapter 1

The world was safely tucked in under blankets of snow. I navigated Battle Lake's well-lit main street, pushing against the weather with hands shoved deep into fleece mittens and chin tucked into my neck. This was my favorite kind of snowfall—the flakes drifting down lazy and white like dandelion fluff. The outdoors felt cozy, the air scrubbed clean by ice crystals, all sound muffled in soft white snow.

Earlier today, a library patron had mentioned that a January thaw was on its way. I believed that about as much as I bought into the covers of the pulp fiction books he checked out weekly. It was currently six below, not counting the windchill. The glittering Christmas garlands had been removed from the light posts only a week earlier.

Plus, this was Minnesota. If the thermometer topped zero in January, we referred to that as a "warm snap." I didn't expect to see above-freezing temps until March, and that was fine by me. Winter was a magical season, if you had the heart and cojones for it.

I took another step, admiring how the snow dusted up like smoke. If you'd told me a year ago that I'd be admiring the winter weather in Battle Lake, Minnesota, population 747 (according to the sign you passed on the way in) and dropping, I'd have laughed in your face. But sometimes, life steers and all we can do is hang on. For my part—

"Are you writing a book in your head or just trying to hold in a fart?"

I glanced over at Mrs. Berns. I'd almost forgotten she was walking with me. *As if.* She was ninety, sharper than me on my best day, and my closest friend. She also possessed a wicked tongue, blended in nowhere, and courted trouble with the same single-minded focus that she chased men.

"Because if it's the latter," she continued, "I suggest you let 'er rip. The only people stupid enough to step outside in this weather wouldn't complain about the extra heat." She blew on her mittened hands. "That includes me, by the way. Remind me again why we're walking?"

"It's a gorgeous night." I kicked up another puff of snow. "And you didn't have to come with, you know."

My plan for the evening had been to close up the library and grab a bowl of Nancy's famous firehouse chili and a bagel to go. I could visit with Nancy while Sid readied my order, then shuffle back to the library to grab my car and head on home to enjoy a quiet dinner with my cat, dog, and TV. I normally enjoyed cooking, but the library had gotten so busy today that I'd had to skip lunch and work well past normal closing hours. My stomach was burbling like a tar pit. The Fortune's food was some of the best in town, and it turned out that was only one of the unexpected rewards of moving to Battle Lake, the teeny-tiny town I'd relocated to last April. Previously I'd been living in Minneapolis, doing a half-assed job earning my master's in English and paying the bills with tips from my waitressing gig at a Vietnamese restaurant on the West Bank. My boyfriend at the time was a musician who turned out to be a little too free with his "flute." On top of all that, I drank too much every chance I got.

Still, I was hanging in there.

Until the fateful day when I'd gotten flashed by a vagrant whose business looked like a sad little green bean that had sat in the microwave for too long, followed by a phone call from Sunny asking me to house-sit for her in Battle Lake.

Voilà. The scales had tipped.

What was supposed to have been only a few months of house-sitting had grown into an open-ended appointment. Despite having lived in Battle Lake for nearly a year, however, I was and always would be "not from around here." Plus, I'd developed a distasteful habit of dealing with at least one corpse a month since May. A lesser woman would think herself cursed. I'd been raised by a codependent mother eligible for sainthood and an alcoholic father who'd killed himself and the occupant of an oncoming car in a drunk-driving accident when I was a junior in high school, and so I had a different perspective on life.

I was an optimist always waiting for the other shoe to drop.

The inaugural dead body appeared about the time I landed my first job in town. Both the job and the corpse were located at the Battle Lake Public Library. When the head librarian disappeared shortly after the murder, the city council promoted me to fill in for him until they could find someone qualified; a budget cut (plus the fact that I regularly "lost" applications) kept that possibility at bay.

The most recent carcass had nearly been mine. Not even a month ago, an honest-to-goodness serial killer—dubbed the Candy Cane Killer by the press—had hunted me like an animal, stalking close enough to leave scars that I'd carry for the rest of my life. I hadn't slept a full night since, though I refused to reveal that when anyone asked how I was.

Admitting it out loud would make the fact that I'd trusted someone who turned out to be a killer too real. Besides, to whom could I confess that I'd started sleeping under my bed instead of *on* it—that every evening before I drifted off for an hour or two, my nose inches from the box spring, I wondered if I'd witnessed too much to ever feel safe again?

And so I kept my mental state to myself.

I worked, I laughed, I played, and I watched the shadows.

On a positive note, I'd moved my life forward in Battle Lake in ways I never could have imagined. My drinking was mostly in check, I'd begun to repair my relationship with my mom and make peace with the memory of my dad, I was pursuing my PI license based on the belief that the Universe was telling me it was that or become a mortician, and I'd even fallen in love with a guy who walked upright. His name was Johnny Leeson, and he was a horticulturist and the lead singer for a local band.

If Johnny were food, he'd be chocolate, and if he were a drink, he'd be a rare red wine. I still didn't entirely trust that somebody as amazing as him was all mine, but I was willing to work on it. We'd been dating exclusively for a few months. And over Christmas, the file I'd started on Johnny had finally gotten indexed, if you know what I mean. It was everything I'd imagined, except for the location: my childhood bedroom.

Argh.

He'd been busy since then, starting the spring seedlings at the local nursery and playing gigs all over the Midwest with the Thumbs. Subsequently, we hadn't gotten to repeat the glory we'd first discovered under the Jimmy Page and Kevin Bacon posters still hung in my room, though we did have a date planned for tomorrow night.

"You're thinking about Johnny now, aren't you?" Mrs. Berns asked, interrupting my thoughts for the second time. "You better not take up poker. You're easier to read than a comic strip. With large print."

I realized I'd been grinning as I walked through the fairy snow, and that made me beam even wider. "He's pretty cute, isn't he?"

She tried to scowl, but her reluctant smile undermined the expression. "You could do worse."

An occasional car burred past as we walked, but it was almost seven at night and all the businesses except for the apothecary and the Rusty Nail were closed in accordance with their winter hours. Theadora, manager of the apothecary, glanced up from rearranging her Valentine's Day window display as Mrs. Berns and I strolled past. She waved, and we returned the gesture before crossing the street. We'd nearly reached the end of the block, encased again in our own thoughts and body heat, when I heard what sounded like a child crying.

I stopped and cocked my ear. When the snowflakes grew this big, they sometimes warped sound.

"Hear that?" I asked.

Mrs. Berns kept walking. "My feet crying out from the cold? My stomach growling from starvation? Yep and yep."

"No, it's definitely something." I pointed at the alley entrance between the post office and an abandoned building that used to house a movie rental store. "From down there. I can't tell if it's a person or an animal."

Mrs. Berns returned to my side to listen.

The plaintive cry repeated itself, high and whining, at a pitch that thrummed a deeply instinctual fear chord. The six-below temperature suddenly felt ominous, and my blood turned sluggish. The Candy Cane Killer's leering face returned to me, unbidden: banal, deadly. *Familiar.* I forced myself to breathe, repeating like a mantra the fact that the police station was only two blocks away.

"Should we run for help?" I asked. I was grateful that my voice worked.

"Excellent idea," Mrs. Berns said. "Nothing Chief Wohnt would prefer to do tonight than check on a rabbit stuck in a snowy alley. Unless you broke a nail? Because he'd want to hear about that as well."

I realized I'd been holding my breath. I released it in a sharp gush. Mrs. Berns was right. The Candy Cane Killer was in a maximum-security prison in Chicago—no way for them to get me. There was nothing horrible down that alley. It was only a hurt animal. And I'd feel like an ass if I called out the guards for a rabbit, not to mention Gary Wohnt and I didn't have the best relationship.

Ultimately, though, what spurred me to check on the sound was this: I was tired of being so afraid. I'd been wearing it like a shock collar since the killer put me in the hospital, and I could already feel the conditioning settle in. *Don't take chances. Stay in your routine. Don't step out of line, and you won't bring any more bad on yourself.*

I glanced around. Theadora was still busy in the apothecary's display window, though she looked far away and pieced-up through the falling snow. The Fortune Café was just ahead, the streets mostly well lit. A rusty Ford pickup with a snowplow wedge mounted on the front drove past, the snow muffling the engine's rattle. The driver honked a greeting at Mrs. Berns and me. I held up a hand. He kept driving.

I sighed. It was now or never: confront my fear or forever wear the yoke. If the boogeyman was down the alley, I could yell and Mrs. Berns would have someone here in two minutes. If it was an injured animal, I could carry it back to my car and drive it to the emergency vet. If it was a scared child or, worse, an injured one, I was a monster for even debating this long.

"I'm going in," I said. "You wait here."

I held my hands loose at my sides like I'd learned in a recent self-defense class and strode resolutely down the alley.

Right into the devil's mouth.

Chapter 2

"Hey, what're you doing walking down dark alleys? Didn't your mama warn you?"

My heart pounded on the back of my throat, looking for escape. Even in the dim light, I could see that the brute was younger than me, maybe early twenties, an ogre of a man with a heavy forehead and eyes that squinted under its weight. His jean jacket was far too light for the weather, even with the hoodie underneath.

I sensed another person move behind me, certainly male. I couldn't see him, knew he was blocking my escape, but I was too scared to turn away from the ogre. Whoever was behind me made a sound, a replica of the mewling that'd drawn me into the alley in the first place.

"He sounds like that when he gets tweaked. Says he can't hear it himself, but I tell him he sounds just like a damn trapped kitten." The ogre reached forward and plucked my hat off my head and shoved it onto his. "And that's exactly what I feel like: a stuck animal. This weather is inhumane, you got that? It's like someone left the goddamn freezer door open in this state."

White spots floated across my eyes. I wanted to see who was behind me but couldn't drag my eyes off the immediate threat. I prayed fervently that Mrs. Berns wouldn't follow me down here, that she would instead intuit I needed help and take off for the police station. I considered yelling, but I knew she'd come if I did, and the only thing that would make this situation worse was if there were two of us stuck in it.

The ogre stared me down. If there'd been more light, his flat black shark eyes would have reflected it back at me. I could barely see around his hulking form, the post office on one side of him, the three-story wall of an apartment building on the other. Behind was the alley leading to the opposite street, a streetlight flickering at the end through the deepening snow, forty eternal feet away.

"How 'bout those mittens, baby? They look like they'd be mighty warm to slide into."

Behind me, the soft animal cry took on a wheezing quality that made my stomach tighten. I was aware of each hair on my head.

I slipped off my mittens, every nerve in my body keening. I needed to escape. My best bet was to run through the ogre, but I'd have only one chance. I held out the mittens, visibly trembling. As he reached forward, I pretended to drop them. He bent down, and I charged to his right. I made it all of two feet before the person behind me jumped onto my back and crashed us both into the icy ground.

The fall knocked the wind out of me and twisted the newly healed knife wound in my right arm. The pain burned all the way to my teeth. I so wanted to play possum until all this went away, until the bad guys were gone and I was back safe on a well-lit street, but I didn't have that luxury. The man who'd dropped me rolled off, and I gasped for breath, taking stock of my ribs and wrists, feeling for breaks. The ogre toed me with his boot.

"Where were you going, baby? Doncha know there's nothing to see around here? This place is about as interesting as bread. Everyone looks the same, nothin' to do."

I winced as I pulled myself into a sitting position. In a different life, I might have agreed with his assessment. I tried out my voice, not liking how small it sounded. "What are you doing here if you dislike it so much?"

"She talks!" said the ogre. "You hear that, Ray? She's got a voice."

My back to an apartment dumpster, I finally risked a look at the ogre's partner. He was lean and hungry-looking, also underdressed for the weather, with a lick of a tattoo showing on his neck. Where the big one looked like he was from eastern European or Russian stock, Ray had the wide face and blond hair of a Scandinavian.

Rather than answer the ogre, Ray kept glancing furtively down the alleyway behind him, then over the other guy's shoulder, as if expecting someone. Jumping on me had ramped up his baby-animal noises, and he seemed ready to crawl out of his own skin.

I pushed myself to my feet. My hands were ice-scraped from trying to brace my fall, and likely my knees were as well, but I was alive. From this angle, I noticed a crowbar and duffel bag at the ogre's feet, and I added these to what I knew. That meant I now had three bits of knowledge, the other two being that the man who had pounced on me was quick and that running clearly wasn't going to work.

Which left talking.

Mrs. Berns had surely gone for help, right? I just needed to keep them from hurting me until the police showed up. It was a long, desperate shot, which felt just about right.

I rubbed at my palms, checking for ice shards and gravel. "I have plenty of other hats and mittens. I could bring you some if you like."

Ray's fidgety glance stopped on me for a moment, then kept traveling.

The ogre tried to stretch one of my mittens over his meaty paw. It covered three fingers. "Naw, baby, I don't think your winter gear is worth crap. What else you got that might be worth somethin'? You got a purse? Why don't no ladies here carry purses?"

It was true. When the temperature dropped, Minnesota women tended to store everything close to their bodies. It just made sense. My money was housed in the interior pocket of my down jacket, along with peppermint lip balm, keys, and three pieces of cinnamon gum. I could live without any of it.

I held up my cold hands. "I've got about thirty bucks. You're welcome to it. It's inside my pocket."

I started to reach in, but before I could unzip my jacket, Ray had me pinned to the icy ground again, this time flat on my back. Sharp air rushed out, scraping my lungs. And here I'd just gotten the hang of breathing again. I willed myself to keep calm, to ignore the hot trickle of blood that had begun seeping out of the freshly opened wound on my arm. If I didn't have my wits, I had nothing.

"I don't like this, Hammer! I don't like her, I don't like this town, I don't like any of it." The mewling came rapidly now, like a heartbeat.

Hammer seemed unsurprised by his partner's jittery outburst. "Do what you need to, man."

"Wait, what?" I asked. "No one has to get hurt here."

Ray leaned in. His shivering pupils were so dilated that his eyes looked like two bullet holes. His breath smelled cough-syrup sweet. His exact intentions were unclear, but he wore his unhinged state like a sign. A distant part of me could not believe this was how I was going to go, in a small-town alley, one block and a million miles away from friends and warm food. My eyes felt hot, but I'd rather fight than cry.

Gathering my strength, I punched Ray's stomach and twisted my hips at the same time, hoping to unbalance and then buck him. The force of my thrust knocked him off, but he landed on his feet and clenched, ready to pounce back on me.

"What the goddamned hell is going on here?"

All three of us froze and turned to the voice.

It was Mrs. Berns. She was alone.

My heart plummeted.

Ray glanced from Mrs. Berns to Hammer, his eyes agitated, his fingers curled into claws. Mrs. Berns stood her ground, one hand on her hip and the other stuffed in her pocket as if she might be hiding a gun. She looked like the angriest grandma you ever met.

Why had she come down here? Had she gone for help first?

"Run!" I yelled to her.

Too late.

Ray pounced.

Chapter 3

I lurched forward, my strength superhuman. It was one thing to hurt me but a whole nother to hurt my friends. I flew at Ray, who had Mrs. Berns's beautiful bony arm twisted behind her back. I fully intended to take a pound of flesh. Before I had a chance, though, he was yanked backward, a shocked expression on his face. Free of his grip, Mrs. Berns fell forward and into my arms. I pulled her close.

Another man, a new one, had Ray pushed against the rear wall of what used to be the video rental store, his forearm against Ray's throat. This third man wasn't large, but Ray's feet weren't touching the ground. My eyes raced between the three strangers as I inched Mrs. Berns and myself toward escape.

"What're you doin', Maurice?" Hammer asked, not moving from his original position. "We were just having some fun."

The man named Maurice shot me a dismissive glance, not letting go of Ray. I recognized him immediately. He was midtwenties, African American, a cap pulled tight over his head. His jacket, gloves, and boots looked warm. He'd been in the library maybe a half dozen times in the past week, spending a lot of time in the local history section but never checking anything out.

"Stupid chuckleheads," he said. "I told you to sit tight. Why do you have to make trouble?"

"Shit, we was only playing," Hammer said, his voice whiny. "Killin' time. When did you get so soft?"

Maurice stepped back. Ray dropped to the ground, his hand on his throat as if he hoped to reinflate it. His mewling returned to a steady rhythm, but his eyes grew busier. Hammer's heavy brow drooped even farther.

"Go," the man named Maurice ordered us. He flashed me another look, his expression indecipherable.

We didn't need to be told twice. I pushed Mrs. Berns toward the light at the end of the alley, leaving my hat and mittens behind.

Chapter 4

"Tell me again why the two of you went down an alley alone."

I didn't care for Battle Lake police chief Gary Wohnt's tone of voice any more than I liked the way his deep-blue uniform hugged his chest and arms. When Gary and I'd first crossed paths last May, he'd been paunchy, crabby, and perennially concealed behind mirrored sunglasses. We were instant enemies. I didn't like him because he was arrogant and seemed always on the verge of catching me with my hand in the cookie jar. I had no idea why he disliked me.

I had him perfectly pigeonholed—until he left town with a born-again lady, got dumped, and returned to Battle Lake lean, dark, and handsome. My brain and heart knew the score. I was working on the other parts. When he made me this angry, though, all I wanted to do was fry him like an ant under a magnifying glass.

"Like I told you," I said through gritted teeth, "we thought we heard an injured animal. Or a person. I went ahead to check, and when I didn't come out after a few minutes, Mrs. Berns came in after me."

"Definitely sounded like a baby," Mrs. Berns hollered from the other side of the room, where the new officer was examining her arm. He'd sworn there was no need for her to remove her sweater, but she'd demurred, arguing it was better to be thorough. She'd recently joked that her boobs were now 32 Longs instead of 32 Cs, but they looked pretty good in the lavender silk bra she was wearing.

I'd already checked out her arm and knew it was fine, if a little bruised. My arm would also be all right. The fight had ripped the last scab off the scar, but the rest of the stitched skin had stayed intact. The only casualty was what had been left of my personal security.

"That Maurice guy saved our biscuits," Mrs. Berns continued loudly.

Gary ignored her and studied me over the steeple of his fingers. His eyes were inky, and they gave away nothing. They also made me want to blurt out the fact that I had stolen two pencils from work today and didn't always wash my hands after using the bathroom.

"Look," I said, when the silence became painful. "Am I the one on trial? Because last I checked, going down an alley intending to help the vulnerable is a *good* thing. It's attacking people and stealing mittens that's the crime."

He leaned forward, grabbed a pen and a slip of official-looking paper off his desk, and began writing. Finally, he was going to take me seriously. I sat forward.

"You say they stole your mittens," he said with gravitas, "but were you able to get away with your lunch money intact?" He didn't pause in his writing.

Was that a smile tugging at the corner of his mouth? I wanted to punch him so badly. But then, suddenly, I just wanted to cry. "The one guy was *huge*. The second one jumped me from behind. He was all hopped up, making the noises. Who knows what they would have done if that Maurice person hadn't shown up? Do you really want these guys walking around in your town, robbing people—or worse—right under your nose?"

He laid down the pen and paper, and his jaw clenched in a gesture I was familiar with. Any levity that might have been present was now completely erased. "I have all your information. Is there anything else?"

I studied him, noting the abrupt change in his demeanor. "You already knew about them, didn't you?"

He opened a drawer, dropped the pen in, and slammed it closed. "Like I said, is there anything else you want to tell me? If not, I've got work to do."

I reflected on the men's clothes and the rhythm of their language. They weren't from this area, maybe not even from the Midwest. Hammer and Ray had *dangerous* written all over them, but Maurice seemed cut from different cloth. He'd still been rough around the edges, no doubt, but he'd saved us when he could have just as easily walked away. I shuddered to think what would have become of us if he hadn't shown up when he did. "You're watching them, aren't you? Who are they? What're they doing in Battle Lake?"

Wohnt grabbed a brochure off the top of his desk and began reading it.

I leaned forward. "Minnesota fishing regulations? Fascinating. You're not going to tell me anything about the Hulk and his sidekick, are you?"

No answer. I scowled. I sat there for another full minute watching him pretend to read, but then my stomach growled. I sighed. I knew Gary well enough to realize I couldn't squeeze anything out of him that he didn't want me to know. I also knew I would get even less sleep than usual unless I had some reassurance that he already had an eye on the bad guys. "Fine. I won't tell you about their tattoos, then."

"Hammerhead shark across the back and shoulders of the large one, stingray on the neck of the other."

I grinned. I'd only been guessing about the ogre having a tattoo and hadn't gotten a good look at Ray's. "Thank you."

He never removed his eyes from the brochure he was pretending to read, but a brief, rare smile moved across his face. "You're welcome."

Chapter 5

Despite his apparent nonchalance, Gary had immediately sent a car to check the alley as soon as Mrs. Berns and I spilled into his station. I suspected the goons were long gone, and my hunch was confirmed when the police car rolled into the parking lot just as I exited the station without Mrs. Berns, who said she was going to stay and practice some "stretches" with the new deputy.

I waved at the officer to stop and jogged over. He rolled down his window as I approached.

"Did you find anyone?" I asked.

"Nope. Just these." He held up my hat and mittens. "Yours?"

I nodded and accepted them gratefully. "Gary seems to know the culprits. Have they been causing trouble around here lately?"

The officer, a bearded man named Diego who was the middle guy on the three-man force, glanced over my shoulder toward the cop shop. His breath puffed out in tiny cumulous clouds.

"Let me guess," I said. "Gary told you not to tell anyone?"

He shrugged apologetically. "He specifically warned against saying anything to *you*. Said you stumble into enough trouble all on your own."

I held up my hands. "I don't go looking for it."

All he had for me was a smile. I sighed. "Thanks for my hat and mittens, anyways."

"Be safe." He rolled up his window and finished parking the car.

I glanced toward the sky. Snow was still falling, but it had lost its magic. I was cold and tired and hungry. The library and therefore my car were nearer than the Fortune Café, and my craving for a bagel and chili had been replaced by a strong desire to be home, behind locked doors, under my bed with my cat and dog nearby. I should have asked Diego to give me a ride to my car. It was only three blocks away, but in my current state of mind, it felt like three miles.

"Yoo-hoo!"

I immediately recognized the voice coming from the far end of the parking lot. I scrunched my shoulders and hoofed it in the opposite direction, following the tried-and-true axiom "if you can't see them, they can't see you."

"Mira James! I can see you plain as the nose on my face. Now turn around and say hi to my new sidekick."

So help me, I was powerless to deny Kennie Rogers's command, such was my complete submission to curiosity. I'd met Kennie about the same time I'd been introduced to Gary Wohnt—which was no coincidence, as they'd been dating at the time. Both were in their forties and graduates of Battle Lake High School. Neither had escaped their hometown, with Gary becoming police chief and Kennie mayor. Their past was sordid, as far as I could suss out, and since Gary had left Kennie cold when he'd skipped town with his Jesus-loving floozy, their relationship had been strained, to say the least.

They had to work together, though, and both were masters of the passive-aggressive game, a skill most Midwesterners come by naturally but that the two of them elevated to an art form.

It was funny, almost, to think that they'd ever been a couple. Gary was stoic and Kennie pathologically outgoing with an intermittent southern accent, despite being born and raised in west-central Minnesota. Gary favored dark colors, and Kennie was hard-pressed to leave the house without a tiara. Gary possessed all of two facial expressions—annoyed and suspicious—whereas Kennie wore makeup like a wedding cake wore frosting.

My natural aversion to Kennie had been nearly as strong as my dislike of the police chief, but god help me, the woman had grown on me. She was a fighter, and I liked my women strong.

So I stopped.

And I turned.

Which was how I came face-to-face with Kennie jogging toward me in a sequined, pink snowsuit, a wiener dog wearing a matching sweater trundling along behind her, its stubby legs pumping like pistons in the accumulating snow. The wiener dog also wore a pointy elf hat that fastened under its neck, its ears poking out of the pink yarn. The dog's eyes were impossibly big, wet, and brown.

"Awwww," I said. It really was that cute.

"Thank you," Kennie said, stopping a few feet away. Her breath was short—it couldn't be easy to jog across fresh-fallen snow in pink stiletto boots—but she covered by fluffing the crispy platinum hair that curled around her earmuffs. "I just got it done."

"I was referring to the puppy. When did you get her?"

"Him," she corrected. "His name is Peter. He's been living with me for two weeks."

"You named your wiener dog Peter?"

She ignored the question as Peter pitter-pattered over to sniff my ankles. "I adopted him from the humane society. I stopped by to see if they had any teacup poodles because they're the latest must-have accessory. Lord knows if I don't keep pushing the fashion envelope in Battle Lake, who will?"

I shrugged. It was one of those questions.

"Well, of course they didn't have any itty-bitty poodles," Kennie complained, "but then I met Peter. I didn't think much of him at first, until he had one of his spells. That was when I heard The Calling."

The capital letters were audible, but I stuffed my fingers into curiosity's ears and lalala'd. Kennie was notorious for her start-up businesses, from coffin tables that could be converted to your place of eternal rest, to Come Again, her online used marital aids company. Just two months ago, she'd sold me questionable vitamins that had nearly destroyed my dating life. I'd pass on finding out about her "Calling," I say.

Instead, I knelt to pet Peter. "Hey, sweetie, come here. That's right. Aren't you a honey? Aren't you a doll?" I started scratching his ears, and his back right leg thumped in joy. I reached under his chin to get at the sweet spot that my foster dog, Luna, loved. Peter's eyes rolled up in ecstasy. I was smiling when he fell over on his side, stiff as a stick.

"Oh my god!" I put my hand on his chest, feeling for a pulse. "Did I kill your dog?"

"No, silly," Kennie said, kneeling down to scoop him into her arms. "I was trying to tell you. I was in the kennel with Peter when he had a spell. He's narcoleptic. That's when the Lord came down and called me to help. He said I was to aid the silent by becoming an animal and plant psychologist."

"Animal *and* plant?" I asked, suspicious, and probably about the wrong thing.

"The Lord works in mysterious ways," Kennie said, shrugging. "Who can explain His thoroughness?"

I suspected the dual-career idea had more to do with Kennie's constant marketing machine than divine intervention. "Doesn't that require some training?"

"Turns out it doesn't," she said. She whispered into Peter's ear, and he began to wiggle. He blinked twice, then sat up in her arms and began thumping his back right leg again, rejoining us exactly where he'd left off.

The mini-miracle gave me pause. Had Kennie finally discovered her real deal? Could she actually be an animal whisperer? I gave that line of thinking a full twenty seconds. *Nope, not possible.* Surely Peter had woken up on his own.

"How's business?" I asked.

"That's what I wanted to talk to you about. Can I put some flyers up in the library? You know, spread the word?"

"Sure," I said. It wouldn't cost me anything.

"Can I also use you as a referral?"

"But I haven't used your services."

"Not yet, but I'm offering you a free consultation." She dug into her front pocket and came out with a business card that appeared printed from a home computer. The word *Serenity* was scrawled across the top in an ornate script, and below that in increasingly smaller print, PET AND PLANT PSYCHOLOGIST, and beneath that, KENNIE ROGERS, PHD.

"You don't have a PhD."

She drew herself up. "I don't *have* a PhD. I *am* a PHD. 'Plant/Pet Helper and Doer.'" She winked. "So what do you say? I'll come by your house tomorrow morning, maybe around eight? I can visit with your pets, perk up your plants a little?" She leaned her head back, studying me. "While I'm there, I could give you makeup tips, too. You look like a potato farmer on a death march. That's just my two cents, of course."

I wanted to tell her I had change for her, but suddenly I was exhausted. The full stress of the evening had finally caught up with me, landing on my shoulders like vultures, digging into my flesh and weighing me down. "Can I get back to you on that? It's been a long day."

"Fine. I'll mark you down as 'appointment pending.'"

Looking back, I still wouldn't be sure if allowing her to come by that next morning would have made any difference, as the pawns leading to the latest and most brutal murder I was to uncover were already in play.

Chapter 6

The first time I met Maurice, I had no idea I'd be running into him in a dark alley in a week.

"You got anything on Battle Lake?" he'd said.

I was kneeling at the bottom of the H–Ki shelf of the fiction section, where I'd been scraping fossilized gum from the metal rack. If Stephen King's *The Stand* was shelved, I couldn't see the gum, but the book had been on a steady checkout for three weeks, and I was sick of looking at the liver-colored blotch.

I turned toward the voice, paused for a nanosecond, and then answered, "The history of Battle Lake, you mean?"

I'm not proud of the pause, as short as it was, but the truth was that in this part of Minnesota, nearly everything was white: the food, the weather, and especially the people. I could count on two fingers the number of people of color who'd come into the library, and I was looking at the second. Early to midtwenties, five foot nine (maybe ten), hair cut close to his head.

"Yeah," he said. "The history." His tone was matter-of-fact, though his stance was uncomfortable, his hands shoved deep into his pockets.

"Mm-hmm," came the sound of a deliberate throat clearing from behind Maurice.

I rose to my feet, leaving the butter knife and paper plate of bubble gum shards on the floor. I tipped so I could see around Maurice. "Yes,

Jack?" He was a regular in his sixties who knew everything about the weather, trains, and guns, and loved to read pulp fiction.

"Everything OK here?" Jack asked.

I was momentarily puzzled, until he pointedly looked at Maurice, then back at me. Maurice kept his hands shoved in his pockets, his back to Jack. I guessed he'd been through this before.

"I'm fine. Just helping a patron."

Jack stood his ground for a moment, his eyes trained on Maurice, then pursed his lips and stepped away.

"Sorry." I wasn't sure who I was apologizing for. "The local section is right over here."

Maurice followed me. The library had maybe fifteen people in it. With the exception of Jack, and maybe a stray glance or three, they all kept to what they were doing. We reached the rear of the library, and I pointed at the two shelves I'd devoted to Battle Lake materials. "Any specific time period you're interested in?"

"Hey, it's about Battle Lake." His eyebrows lifted. "It's all got to be interesting."

It took me a beat to realize that he was joking. I smiled. "This must be your first time to the area."

He shrugged, and the gesture was oddly endearing. "Naw. My grandma used to rent a place near here. A cabin. Stopped by and it's nothin' but rotten wood now, but I used to come when I was a kid, a couple weeks each summer."

He looked like he was going to say more but stopped himself. I stood a moment longer, giving him a chance to continue. He didn't.

"If you need anything, I'll be scraping gum."

He flashed me a lopsided grin. It was quick, but brilliant. I smiled back before returning to my dirty chore.

Maurice came in a few more times after that, always walking straight to the local shelves, sometimes with a camera, other times carrying a shabby, spiral-bound notebook and a pen, never checking anything out. He'd sometimes make light conversation with me, but mostly he worked like a man on a mission. I was used to giving people space in the library, so I never asked any questions.

After the altercation in the alley, I wished I had.

At least, that's what I told myself, as I drifted in and out of uneasy sleep, curled against the wall under my bed. I'd slept forty-five minutes altogether, every muscle in my body aching from the uncomfortable position and the aftermath of the previous night's adrenaline clench. I finally dragged myself into the murky sunlight a little before 7:30 a.m., my hands, knife scar, and knees sore from the alley attack.

Luna rushed in through the bedroom door when she heard me moving, licking my face and wagging furiously. She didn't like that I was sleeping under the bed, whined at the edges of the mattress when I went in, and acted like it was Christmas in January when I came out.

"Hey, sweetie. How're you?"

She wagged some more and followed me around the house as I poured fresh food and water for her and Tiger Pop and prepped myself for work. The healing knife wound and my left knee needed salve and a bandage. The rest of my body would be fine after I washed down a handful of ibuprofen with yesterday's strong coffee heated up in the microwave.

I was out the door in under thirty minutes. When the sound of the ice cracking on the lake made me jump out of my hair on my way to start my car, though, I headed back into the house for my fully charged stun gun, which I slipped into the back seat. If I didn't have the library to go to this morning and instead had to be alone with my thoughts, I would've cracked louder than the lake.

I loved working at the library. The books were wonderful, of course, and I'd stuffed juicy, leafy green plants in all the windows and corners when I took over and was currently keeping up the Christmas twinkle lights past their season, but it was the people who walked through the door that made the job such a perfect fit. They were mostly quiet, first of all. Second, they liked books, so they were guaranteed smart. I had romance readers who reread the same book a dozen times and could remember every character's name in a ten-book series, fans of nonfiction who regularly checked out books thick enough to press flowers and who would tell me everything I didn't want to know about history if I stood still for too long, and literary fiction readers who always wore a secret smile. My favorite of all were the kids. I read to a regular group of them every Monday, and without fail, they were a squirming, burping, giggling pile of warm puppy love.

That made the library my life raft. Unfortunately, thanks to budget cuts all over the state, the limited Saturday hours meant I was off at noon. The only upside of the slashed hours was that it gave me more time for my second job, which I'd landed shortly after being hired by the library. I was a very part-time reporter for the *Battle Lake Recall*, an essentially one-man show known for its coverage of local church happenings, updates on city council meetings, high school sports scores, and my food column, Battle Lake Bites.

When I'd started the column, I was feeling a tad passive-aggressive about living my nowhere life in another small town—I'd graduated from a very similar one eleven years earlier—and I'd vowed to take editor / layout supervisor / sales director / owner Ron Sims's suggestion that I find dishes representative of central Minnesota. Hence "Deer Pie," "Twinkie Sushi," and "Phony Abalone," among others.

In addition to that column, Ron occasionally tossed me articles, including the latest: he wanted me to follow up on a report that Gilbert Hullson's chihuahua had accidentally slipped into an ice-fishing hole last week while Gilbert was looking the other way. According to the rumor, Gilbert had leaped forward to save his dog, but his reflexes weren't what they used to be, and she disappeared.

Distraught, he stumbled from his fish house just in time to see Jiffy pop up out of an uncovered hole thirty feet away like a rat shot out a geyser. She was reportedly a little shaken but happy to be topside.

Being as it was a rare news-heavy week, Ron also had me covering this weekend's Winter Wonderland festivities, Battle Lake's premier cold-time celebration. Today was day one of the two-day festival.

The kickoff was the grand opening of the Prospect House's Civil War Museum.

I closed the library at noon and headed to the museum. The temperature hovered around ten degrees with a crisp lemon sun shining heatless rays off a world of snow crystals, lighting up the landscape like a dragon's treasure. The air smelled of cold metal with the tiniest hint of green in it, and I wondered if there really was something to that talk of a January thaw.

I'd driven only half a mile before the traffic started backing up. Parking would be a bear. Just ahead, a white four-door pulled away from the curb and I thanked the Universe and glided the Toyota into the vacated spot. The Prospect House was still two blocks up, but I was lucky to have parked this close. I stuffed the newspaper's digital camera into the pocket of my puffy jacket, pulled my hat down tight over my ears, and hopped into the stream of festivalgoers.

I was excited to tour the mansion, which perched on a hill on the edge of town like aging royalty, hidden behind ancient hardwoods and thick, gnarled ivy branches, closed off from the public for decades and fodder for tales of hauntings and buried treasure. The official press tour wasn't scheduled for another hour, so I made my way to the lake across County Road 78 from the Prospect House, enjoying the buzz of a large crowd, the monolithic noise occasionally punctuated by laughter or an enthusiastic greeting.

The West Battle Lake beach became the public ice rink in the winter, and its gray-blue surface was already packed with families enjoying the sunny day. The warming house door was constantly opening and closing, letting in and out smiling people exchanging skates for boots and vice versa.

Beyond the skating rink, the Battle Lake ice castle soared toward the sky, her two gorgeous spires catching the sunlight and reflecting it back as a deep cobalt blue. It was not much larger than a three-bedroom bungalow, but its glowing ice and delicate turrets made it enchanting, drawing skating children to it like moths to a flame, despite the yellow tape marking its perimeter.

This was Battle Lake's first ice castle. The structure was sponsored by O'Callaghan's, the microbrewery that'd recently opened outside of town. They'd hired the workers, who'd taken eight days to build the hollow castle replica, using plans drawn by an architect from Saint Paul and enormous ice blocks cut from the center of the lake. The official lighting ceremony was tonight, and I bet the castle was a million times more magical glowing with twinkle lights. If I didn't have a date with Johnny, I'd have been in the front row. As it was, I couldn't wait to be in his arms.

Even farther behind the ice castle and to the left was a roped-off area designated to be the site of tomorrow's Darwin's Dunk. O'Callaghan's was also sponsoring that Winter Wonderland feature, though the Dunk was an annual tradition. It'd been jokingly developed as a rebuttal to naturalist Charles Darwin's theory of evolution of the species. Participants signed up for a time slot in which to jump into a hole carved in the twenty-six-inch-thick ice of the lake, and then leaped out about as fast as I imagined Jiffy had after she'd slipped into her little ice hole.

The jumpers raised money for the charity of their choice, and the Dunk motto was "Survival of the Littest." To that end, O'Callaghan's had installed a walk-up bar between the roped-off Dunk area and the ice castle. I'd heard it would open up for business an hour before the lighting ceremony began, after the children had cleared off the ice but well before tomorrow's annual Dunk.

The closer I got to the ice rink, the stronger the smell of hot chocolate grew. I smiled, captivated by the clean, slicing sound of hundreds of skate blades against ice and the sight of people gliding along at various skill levels.

"Mira!"

I glanced toward the warming house. Jed, a local friend, had popped out. Jed was a harmless stoner, the local Shaggy always in search of Scooby-Doo. His parents owned the Last Resort on the edge of town, and Jed was the local handyman. He'd tried to get a glassblowing business going in November, but that hadn't panned out as expected. Since then, he'd gone back to working odd jobs. This must have been one of them.

"You're running the warming house?" I asked as I walked toward him.

"Just for the Wonderland." He smiled his wide grin and nodded agreeably, the tassel on his Nordic winter cap bobbing. A riot of light-brown curls exploded from the base of it. He seemed to be trying to grow a beard and mustache, though both were wispy, with more than a little Fu Manchu to them. "Are you gonna skate?"

A father and his daughter teetered down the carpeted path from the warming house to the ice. "I don't know," I said. "I'm not very good. It's been years."

"If you can walk, you can skate," Jed said, motioning me into the warming house.

The blast of heated air and the heavy scent of wet wool were impossible to resist. Within ten minutes, Jed had me suited up and hobbling toward the ice. At least fifty people were already on the lake, which reminded me of a saying in these parts: *You know who walks on water? Jesus, and every Minnesotan.*

I tentatively stepped onto the lake. I was shaky at first, sticking to the edges so as not to mow over children and the elderly. As I gained confidence and grew less wobbly, I swirled in and out of people, remembering my father teaching me how to skate when I was eight.

He'd brought an old kitchen chair onto the ice for me to balance with. We spent a whole afternoon on the slough behind the farmhouse, and when we were done, I was bruised but happy, not to mention a decent skater. The memory was bittersweet—more sweet than bitter, as

I'd recently started to let go of resentments toward him and accept him as the whole, flawed man he'd been when he was alive.

The mental shift was hard, and I figured it would be an eternal work in progress, but it turned out to be a lot easier to love his memory than to judge it. Go figure. And once I opened up all that real estate where before I'd been holding anger and regret, I found a lot of things were simpler than I'd made them.

"Oh, sorry!" I said, narrowly missing a teenage couple holding gloved hands as they skated.

They rolled their eyes at me, but I didn't care. Skating felt like flying. I could almost hear the stress of yesterday fall away. Sure, it revealed another layer of stress immediately below it, but it was a start. I didn't even mind when I took a spill to avoid colliding with a chain of skaters playing Crack the Whip.

"Whoops!" one of them yelled as they flew past.

I shrugged and smiled, getting to my knees so I could hoist myself up using my hands and the toe of a skate. It was from this position that a flash drew my attention. I looked up, across the road, and toward the Prospect House.

This was a perfect angle from which to see the mansion a few hundred yards away. The grounds were crawling with people dressed in red, blue, green, and patterned parkas, but what had caught my eye was higher. I followed the grain of the house to the second floor, and then to the attic. There it came again, a flash from the round window below the chimney, like a piece of jewelry had caught the glare of the sun. I squinted. Were people up there?

Then, like a jack-in-the-box, a face appeared in the window, staring directly at me.

My heart jumped. Surely I was imagining that she could see me in this crowd, but the girl in the window seemed to be gazing right into my soul. She had the round cheeks of a child, and something about her stare left me icy inside.

"Beep beep!"

My attention broken, I glanced around. The voice making the honking noise sounded familiar. Mrs. Berns?

Before I could locate her in the crowd, my attention was drawn to the roar of a giant engine firing to life. I twisted around toward the ice castle and swallowed my own tongue.

Chapter 7

Mrs. Berns was rolling toward the skating rink on a Zamboni that lumbered as relentlessly as a dinosaur. It must have been parked behind the ice castle. She had one hand on the steering wheel and was pumping the air with the other, a grin of pure joy on her lovely lined face. She was wearing an old-fashioned aviator's cap and goggles, and a white scarf unfurled in the wind behind her.

"Mrs. Berns!" I yelled, scrambling to stand and waving my arms at her. "Put on the brakes!"

Her eyes landed on me, and her smile grew even wider. She stood, hoisting both hands in the air. The words "I'm the Zamboni queen!" drifted above the grumbling roar of the giant machine.

Families were gathering up their children as a mass exodus began toward the relative safety of land. A few people screamed as the Zamboni methodically ate up the two hundred yards of ice between the castle and the rink. I skated away from the crowd, trying to lead Mrs. Berns to an unpopulated spot.

"Turn it off!" I yelled over my shoulder.

She cupped a palm to her ear in the universal gesture of *I can't hear you*, but at least she steered the Zamboni toward me.

"I'm just going to clear a wider rink!" she yelled back. "Get everyone off of the ice!"

I glanced toward the shore. The sensible people of Battle Lake were taking care of that just fine by themselves. When I turned back toward Mrs. Berns, the Zamboni had grown uncomfortably close.

"Turn it off!" I screamed.

She nodded and reached below the steering wheel. Then her head shot back up. Was that a look of panic in her eyes? I kept skating away, and the Zamboni kept drawing nearer.

The ice was rough out here, covered in crusty snow, and I went from skating to high-stepping, trying desperately to put distance between me and her. This lasted all of four paces, until the toe of my skate caught on an ice shear and I pitched to the ground like a four-legged creature who'd been putting on airs.

Heart racing, I levered myself back to a standing position and took mad, mincing steps away from Mrs. Berns. Whichever direction I went, though, the relentless, hulking Zamboni seemed to follow. In the periphery, I spotted two men in winter overalls running across the ice toward Mrs. Berns.

Would they make it here in time?

I fell again, and the Zamboni continued to rumble toward me.

"Move!" Mrs. Berns hollered. "I can't figure out how to turn it off!"

"Can you figure out how to steer it?" I screamed, crawling forward as fast as my cold, sore knees could take me.

The caution ropes surrounding Darwin's Dunk were straight ahead. I scuttled under the rope and found myself gliding down the indent toward the center of the Dunk, where the crew must have begun the time-consuming work of cutting the hole the night before.

My pulse hammering, I swiveled, still on my knees, and tried to return to the safer ice, but gravity pulled me toward the thin center. Was I going to go the way of Jiffy, disappearing into an icy hole?

My soft mittens and wet knees gave me zero traction. I kept my eyes on the Zamboni, hoping against hope that it would stop and that last night's fresh ice would hold. Unable to fight gravity, I slid slowly to dead center of the Dunk and held my breath, thinking light, light thoughts.

The Zamboni growled closer.

The weakened ice beneath me made a gentle cracking sound, and I spread myself flat, my eyes closing involuntarily.

I waited for the inevitable impact of the Zamboni or the icy rush of West Battle Lake.

And then the world grew quiet.

I opened one eye. The Zamboni was on the lip separating the thick lake ice from the prepared Dunk ice. A man in overalls lay stomach down across Mrs. Berns's lap with the expression of someone who'd just swallowed a goldfish.

Mrs. Berns, on the other hand, looked completely exhilarated and ready for round two.

I opened my other eye and breathed in the heavy, oily scent of diesel, grateful I was still around to smell. "What were you doing? You almost killed me!" I didn't know if she'd be able to hear my shrill voice above the pounding of my heart.

Mrs. Berns rested her hands on the man lying across her lap. "You're the one who kept skating into my path."

The man sprawled across her raised the Zamboni keys into the air. His hand was shaking. "Got 'em," he said weakly, sliding to the ground.

I shook my head, fear turning to anger. I gently pulled myself onto my knees, intending to very carefully hoist myself up and off the ice so I could go give Mrs. Berns a piece of my mind. I was balanced on all fours, the roar of the Zamboni still echoing in my head, when something beneath the ice caught my eye.

I glanced down and into a dead man's eyes.

I was suspended above his frozen corpse, his blank gaze staring into mine, his open mouth and clutching hands mirroring my gesture, only a thin skin of ice separating us.

Chapter 8

"You were just . . . *skating* along," Police Chief Wohnt stated.

The disbelief sounded like it had less to do with the veracity of my story and more to do with the sheer variety of ways in which I'd discovered bodies.

I was sitting on the bumper of his car, my head between my knees. I hadn't stopped shivering since I'd been pulled off the dunk hole. Jed stood to the side, where he'd been begging me to drink hot chocolate for several minutes. Mrs. Berns was on the other side shooting me the stink eye, a cross between "Don't tell him about the Zamboni" and "Really?! *Another* dead body?"

I sat up. The blood rushed to my head. The ice had blurred the corpse's face, but not so much that I couldn't stare right into his brown eyes, his mouth open in a silent cry. It was impossible to make a positive ID, but he looked an awful lot like Maurice, my recent library regular and the guy who'd rescued us just last night. My stomach had been greasy since, my brain on overload.

The entire lake had been cleared, the mood gone from festive to shocked, children quickly herded to cars, conversations dropped to whispers. Only twenty or so people remained, milling on the edges of the lake, a handful talking to the waiting EMTs as the police cordoned off a wider area around Darwin's Dunk in preparation for removing the body.

"Did he drown?" I asked Gary.

He glanced over my shoulder, his breath showing up big and bold in the frozen air. He wore a trim blue winter coat and a fur-lined cap. His face was sunglass-free.

"We'll do an autopsy," he said.

"But what do you *think*?" I asked. The horror of that sort of death—being trapped and suffocating under the ice with freedom so close by—was overwhelming. It didn't help that I'd liked Maurice, at least what I knew of him. My shaking grew so strong that I had to tuck my hands into my armpits to contain myself.

Gary's jaw clenched. "I think you should go home."

He strode off toward the lake, leaving me to wonder why he'd interviewed me in the first place. One of his officers could have handled the duty.

His absence also left me wanting Johnny, though I didn't want to think too much about that. I dragged in a deep breath, relieved to discover that I wasn't shivering as much.

"I can see your hard-on," Mrs. Berns said.

"What?"

"You. Remember you've got the poker face of a kindergartner? Are you thinking about Johnny or the chief?"

For a moment, I thought she meant Chief Wenonga, the twenty-three-foot-tall fiberglass statue that resided just over the hill from our present location. He was shirtless and sculpted. In my lower moments, I'd harbored some adult thoughts about him, but I'd thought I'd played those cards closer to my chest. A full-on blush warmed my cheeks before I realized who she was really talking about. "Gary Wohnt?! I'd sooner eat a toe."

She nodded sagely. "I know how confusing it can be to the lady parts when we realize an officer of the law is one of the hottest tamales in town."

"Please," I scoffed. I stood and turned, just catching sight of Gary's back before he disappeared into the ice castle with a deputy. What were they doing over there? Darwin's Dunk was a good hundred yards away.

"Is that a request?" Mrs. Berns asked, smirking.

I shook my head. "I'm begging you to stop. I need to get out of here, take a shower, and wash the dead-body juju off of me."

"I recommend steel wool for that," Mrs. Berns said, patting my shoulder before tipping her head toward Jed. "Since you're in good hands, I'm going to leave you and go find out some more about that Good Samaritan who saved you from throwing yourself under a Zamboni, starting with his phone number."

She strode off before I could reprimand her for driving the Zamboni in the first place. A shudder ran down my body as I thought of Maurice's silent, screaming face. Away from the shock of it, more details came to me, like his one shoeless foot, so oddly vulnerable below the ice.

"You sure you don't want the hot chocolate?" Jed asked worriedly.

I realized he'd been standing next to me in the cold for nearly half an hour, leaving his post at the warming house.

"Thank you," I said appreciatively. I took the hot chocolate, but it was his friendship that I was grateful for.

"Do you want me to drive you home?" He was focused on me, but I could tell he wanted to check back at the warming house. At this very moment, a gaggle of adults milled around the door of the little hut, unreturned skates in hand. The children and most everyone else had been cleared off the lake. I could feel those who remained staring at me.

"I'm fine. Really."

"You positive?"

I smiled reassuringly. "Positive."

It was a lie.

Chapter 9

Although I'd told Jed I was driving directly home, I was too unsettled to be confined to my house. I'd probably drive Luna and Tiger Pop up a wall with all my nervous energy. I also wasn't quite ready to tell Johnny I'd skated upon a dead body, either. I'd have to come up with a story before our date tonight.

He'd always been sympathetic to my bad luck, but even someone as amazing as him must have limits. It wasn't like I needed to quit smoking or snore more quietly. I had to stop finding *dead bodies*. It was honestly a surprise I had friends left. Or, I mused as I drove, maybe the safest place to be was close to me, like inside the calm eye of a hurricane.

Who was I kidding? I was Typhoid Mary, and that was almost more distressing than the memory of probably-Maurice's wide eyes and final frozen scream. I shuddered. It was like he had a secret he needed to tell me, something that only the person who'd killed him and the fishes who'd swum with him would ever know.

I pulled into the library parking lot out of habit, realizing that I'd assumed Maurice had been murdered. I surveyed the mental image of his body under the ice. Except for the missing shoe and the fact that he was dead, there were no signs of violence. For all I knew, he could have been out walking on the ice, fallen into the precut Darwin's Dunk hole, and been too disoriented to save himself. I liked that story a whole lot better than the alternative.

I exited my car and walked toward the library. Since I didn't have a computer at home, this was as good a place as any for me to be. I still owed Ron an article on the Winter Wonderland and this week's recipe column. Maybe writing would help to organize my thoughts.

I locked the library's front door behind me and left the lights off, relying on the window-filtered light of the setting sun. How had the day gone so quickly? And horribly? Seated at my desk, though, I felt incrementally more comfortable. This was a spot where I had some control.

I fired up the computer, sucking on the end of a pen as I wondered what spin I could possibly put on the Winter Wonderland article: Plenty of Room on the Skating Rink at This Year's Winter Festival? Darwin's Dunk Sets the Bar Too High?

I swallowed past the oily lump in my throat. Sarcasm was my defense against any extreme emotion, but I couldn't move past the sensation that I'd played a part in Maurice's death. It was guilt that I was trying to bury. What if letting me and Mrs. Berns go had turned the two goons against him? They could have strangled him and stuck his body in the dunk hole, assuming it wouldn't be found until spring. Or they could have forced him into the hole while he was still conscious, slammed a chunk of wood over it, and sat on the edges until his desperate cries for help and finger-scratching stopped.

I slammed my fist on the desktop. I needed to corral my slippery mind. It was sliding toward ugly worst-case scenarios. Time to focus on something else.

But I knew better than that. My mind was a hungry, busy thing, and it wouldn't rest without answers. Who was Maurice? Who were Ray and Hammer? I had little to go on. Well, that is, if "little" actually meant "nothing."

I typed "Ray and Maurice" into Google. I searched ten screens in and found nothing. I added the word "ogre" and found a couple bizarre baseball stories, but nothing else. Gary had given me blessedly little to go on, except for—

My fingers flew across the keyboard. I typed "hammerhead sting-ray tattoo gangs" and hit the Enter key. The first four screens were consumed with tattoo parlor links and ads, as were the fifth, sixth, and seventh, but on the eighth, I found it—an article published the previous year:

> CHICAGO, Ill.—Chicago police's Fugitive Task Force arrested Scott Lenzo Monday morning. He was the sixth arrest in a seven-month investigation into the Sea Monsters, a criminal group whose members are required to get sea-creature tattoos. The Sea Monsters are believed to be involved in human, gun, and drug trafficking.
>
> Police still have arrest warrants for three other gang members, including one purported to have a hammerhead tattoo.
>
> Chief John Lart said the suspects are some of the highest-ranking leaders in the Sea Monsters, one of Chicago's most notorious gangs.

I printed out the article and searched for anything else that fit. Dead ends, all of them. That's when I realized I hadn't even toured the Prospect House, the central feature of the article I was to write. My head fell into my palm. What a waste of a day.

I felt hysterical laughter burbling in my throat. I would have released it if I hadn't just then caught sight of a neon-green child's Super Ball near my chair. Somebody must have lost it during the previous Monday's reading hour. I stooped to retrieve it and remembered the child I'd seen in the Prospect House's attic window, the little girl with the plump cheeks and wide, haunting eyes.

I'd glanced back at the window a couple times after I'd first spotted her, but no other faces had appeared. She must have gotten separated from her tour group. Or maybe I'd imagined her. Given how little sleep and how much stress I'd had, hallucinations would not be unexpected.

Well, I'd have to work with what I had. I opened my email and shot off a brief note to Carter Stone, the museum's director, requesting a private tour of the Prospect House at his earliest convenience. I didn't know him personally but had heard he was a nice guy, if a little eccentric. Surely he'd understand why I hadn't made today's tour.

Next, I conducted deeper research on the Prospect House. I should have probably done this before today's scheduled tour, but I'd figured I already had the basics from paging through the library's copy of *After the Battle*, a thorough softcover history book of Battle Lake.

In my preliminary research, I'd discovered that the Prospect House was a Battle Lake original, an eighteen-room Georgian mansion built in 1860 by Barnaby Offerdahl, a man whose family had come by money via the railroads. Barnaby, who'd never earned a blister a day in his life, lost his wife to childbirth in 1862 and decided to join the North's fight in the Civil War, enlisting with the First Minnesota Light Artillery Battery and leaving behind a newborn daughter. He didn't return, and she died under mysterious circumstances at age eight.

After that, the Prospect House and its surrounding acreage passed through various hands, falling into disrepair, until recently. Carter Stone, a local historian, had bought the mansion and its carriage house, minus most of the land, at auction the previous year. He and his wife, Libby, had moved into the carriage house and spent countless hours restoring the magnificent estate next door. In doing so, they'd uncovered many of the original furnishings, along with an extensive collection of Civil War artifacts. Carter had applied for nonprofit status, and today he and Libby had hosted the grand opening of the Prospect House and Civil War Museum.

That might be all there was to know, but I believed in due diligence. I clicked into the database I'd subscribed to after I'd decided to pursue my PI licensure last October. Once I'd discovered that a private investigator license in Minnesota required six *thousand* hours of work under a licensed PI, with a police department, or for a law firm, I'd almost quit the dream. But with a firm nudge from Ron at the newspaper, I'd taken my certification class last month in Willmar, near my hometown of Paynesville. I'd since lined up a handful of tiny jobs through a local law firm. Investigative work, surprisingly, was not much different from running a library. You looked up stuff online and listened to people.

My current Prospect House search was dead-ending, which was the way the day was going in general. I discovered that Carter Stone didn't actually own the Prospect House but rather had bought it through a nonprofit organization he'd created called Preserving History. I also found out that more than half of the lots skirting the Prospect House and a big, tear-shaped tract of undeveloped land behind it belonged to Gregory Offerdahl, presumably a descendant of Barnaby's.

I didn't see how either of those two pieces of information would flesh out my article, though. People wanted to know about the Civil War Museum hours and the cache of 1920s jewelry and flapper dresses Stone had reportedly discovered in the attic, not who owned what land parcels when.

I sighed. I wasn't going to uncover anything more today. I decided to think about it tomorrow, which seemed like a really good attitude to take when things weren't going as planned, which was most of my life. *I'll worry about it tomorrow.*

Still not ready to go home but mentally exhausted, I decided to do something I knew I'd be successful at: track down a recipe for my Battle Lake Bites column. In the past, I'd used the search term "weird Minnesota food" when looking for recipe inspiration. You'd be unsurprised at how many hits that turned up.

Since I'd started on my journey of personal growth, though, which included appreciating Battle Lake and its people, I'd been reluctant to toss Cool Whip on top of—or cream of mushroom soup into—something that was already gross and calling it an original Battle Lake recipe. In fact, despite today's gruesome discovery, or maybe because of it, I felt like serving up something truly delicious to the town. And what could be better than Nut Goodies?

Nut Goodies have been produced in Minnesota since 1912 by Pearson's, better known for their Salted Nut Roll. It would be generous to call the Nut Goodie a candy bar. It is more of a candy *pile*. Its base is a creamy maple center topped with unsalted Virginia peanuts, and the whole mass is covered in milk chocolate. It's so sweet it'll give your future children a toothache, but it's also heaven, particularly if consumed when frozen.

Sometimes I wondered if the Nut Goodie was jealous of the Salted Nut Roll's success, if it dreamed of finally fitting in and no longer being a Rorschach blob in a chocolate-log world, if it wondered what it'd be like to play all the major vending machines. But in the end, it was the hardest-working, humblest candy I'd ever met, and I loved it for that very reason. Why not share that joy with Battle Lake?

I searched for "homemade nut goodie" recipes and received more than 406,000 hits. Holy crap. I gravitated toward the ones with photos, of course, salivating as I read. In the end, I chose the simplest and most honest recipe, giving it a new name and a personal twist so I couldn't be sued for plagiarism.

Mmmm-Pies

Ingredients

Fondant:
3 cups powdered sugar
½ cup sweetened condensed milk
½ teaspoon maple extract
Topping:
1½ pounds milk chocolate, broken into 1-inch squares
¾ pound Spanish peanuts (not cocktail peanuts)

Mix the fondant ingredients together until well blended and stiff. Roll into ¾-inch balls. Place the balls 2 inches apart on a wax paper–covered cookie sheet. Flatten the balls with the palm of your hand, keeping them around ⅛ inch thick.

Melt the chocolate in a glass bowl in the microwave in 20-second increments, stirring between each, until the chocolate is smooth and melted. Be careful not to burn. Drop the peanuts in the melted chocolate. Stir. Pour the peanut-and-chocolate mixture over the fondant, allowing it to crawl lusciously just past the edges. Cool. Flip, spooning just enough of the chocolate-peanut mixture onto the bottom to cover the remaining fondant. When cool, turn over and store in the freezer. Remove and ingest as needed, particularly in moments of extreme stress.

I spell-checked the recipe and emailed it to Ron, feeling good about my work. I glanced at the clock on the lower right of my computer screen, wondering if I had time to shelve books before going home to prepare for my date with Johnny.

Despite my exhaustion, I got a warm, buzzy feeling thinking about a repeat performance of our previous night together. I didn't know if it was a result of the day I'd had, but for the first time in weeks, I was considering whether continuing to hold him at arm's length was good, or even necessary. When he was around, I was happy. I desperately needed that right now.

Johnny was honest and kind, and *man*, those hands of his. He'd slide them gently under the curve of my rear and pull me in for a long, deep kiss that left my knees trembling. He might be The One. Maybe it was time to let myself be vulnerable to him and try to see in him what he saw in me.

My eyes went misty from my hot daydream, and it took me a couple seconds and a few blinks to process the time. How could it be six o'clock already? My eyes darted to the windows. It was dark outside. Johnny would be at my house in half an hour! He'd said he would bring dinner and movies, but I'd hoped to at least have the house and myself picked up before he arrived.

Crap.

It'd been so long since I shaved that it looked like a possum had taken up residence in my underpants, and speaking of undergarments, it was laundry day tomorrow and I wasn't exactly wearing the starting lineup.

White bra with the puckered cups that was just too comfortable to throw away? Check.

Double crap!

I jabbed my finger at the computer's power button to force a shutdown, tugged on my coat, and hightailed it out the door, barely remembering to lock up behind me. My car had cooled down along with the night, but I didn't have time to let her preheat. I slammed the gear stick into reverse and tore out of my parking spot.

I hit rush-hour traffic on the way home, or at least Battle Lake's version of it. Pickup after pickup drove painfully slowly in front of me. Even though the skating rink had been closed for the day, I imagined the Prospect House had stayed open, probably drawing even more visitors as news of the nearby tragedy spread.

I pounded on the steering wheel. I didn't ask for a lot out of life, but after the last twenty-four hours, I was worried about my mental state if this night with Johnny crashed and burned.

My brain scrambled to make the best of my current circumstances. If I could make it home in ten minutes and Johnny wasn't early, that would give me exactly thirteen minutes to retrieve my machete and have a go at my legs before switching into the peach-colored, lacy push-up bra I'd bought in Alexandria last week. It made me look as though I had B cups, which was arguably a bait and switch if tonight went how

I hoped it would, but nobody expected the real thing to drive like the display model, right?

I finally passed the clogged traffic and careened a sharp right onto the gravel. This was a shortcut in terms of miles, but since I usually drove half speed on the back roads, it took longer. Not today. I squealed around corners, sliding across the ice and staying shy of the ditch with the help of spit and luck.

As I turned into my nearly mile-long driveway, I saw I had carved two minutes off my best drive-home time. *Excellent work!* I might even be able to apply lip gloss and empty the bathroom garbage so as to hide that I had bodily functions.

I was beginning to smile as I turned the final corner and pulled into the circle loop in front of Sunny's double-wide.

That smile lasted right up until I spotted Johnny's truck.

He was early.

Triple crap with a side of bacon.

Chapter 10

Sunny's place was gorgeous—a double-wide trailer plopped near a pristine little lake nestled in the middle of just over a hundred acres of untouched hardwood forest. Her sweet red barn and three matching sheds stood like comfortable sentries, and her cozy trailer, with its gray siding and maroon shutters, faced the frozen water.

Normally, living here made me feel both connected and independent, carving out my existence on some of the prettiest land in the Midwest. At the moment, however, it was the last place on earth I wanted to be. I considered doing a one-eighty and driving back into town, buying a pack of disposable razors at Larry's, and shaving myself in their bathroom.

That still left the granny bra.

Curse words!

When I'd decided that it was time to make myself more open to Johnny, I hadn't meant open to *revulsion*. Of course he'd be too kind to say anything, but when he pulled off my shirt or slid his hand down my pants, it'd be written all over his face. Horror. Doubt. Curiosity as to when things had gone so undeniably south in his life.

I pulled alongside his 1971 Chevy truck, rebuilt from a junker to a beauty. It was solid and stable, just like Johnny. I sighed. No way could I leave him alone in my house—I'd made the mistake of telling him where I hid the spare key—and worrying about me as the hour grew later, even if the alternative meant exposing him to baseline me.

I turned off the car, got out, and dragged my feet up the path to my front door. Normally, I loved this short walk. Right now, it felt like the green mile.

I opened the door, in the back of my mind still hoping for some way out of this. That's when it came to me. I could just dart into the bathroom, right? Tell Johnny that I wanted to slip into something more comfortable, and once the bedroom door was closed, I could sneak into the bathroom to shave my legs, switch out my bra, and hide the brush cleanings and Q-tips in the garbage under some clean but strategically crumpled tissues. It'd be perfect! I opened the door with a smile on my face.

I was greeted by Johnny, with an equally large smile on his.

Unfortunately—given my present circumstances—a smile was all he wore.

Chapter 11

Johnny was standing in the kitchen, the center island the only thing separating us. The smile fell off my face and landed with a thud at my feet (which, by the way, would have benefited from a run-over with a shaver, too).

Luna hurried up to sniff my hand, but I was in too much shock to pet her. Tiger Pop, my calico kitty, was draped across the back of the couch so as better to witness my humiliation, I imagine.

"Too presumptuous?" he asked, coming around the kitchen island.

I was immensely relieved to see that he was, in fact, wearing low-slung Levi's. The denim hugged his lean hips perfectly, showcasing his sculpted abdomen dusted with a light trail of hair. His chest was perfection, broad and muscled, and his rippled arms made me want to drop my own clothes. He held a bottle of champagne and two glasses in his beautiful, strong hands. And oh dear god, had he said "presumptuous"? I was used to dating men who didn't use a hand towel, let alone four-syllable words.

"You look delicious," I said.

He kept walking toward me, his lip quirking. "What?"

Had I said that out loud? "*It* smells delicious! *It*. What are you making?" I glanced at the chopped vegetables and herbs gracing my counter, a swirl of reds, greens, and oranges. It really did smell amazing. "And how long have you been here?"

He glanced at his wristwatch, and I swear my pants melted a little. Something about a naked-chested man wearing a watch drove me crazy. "About an hour. I knew you had a double shift today, the library and then the paper. I wanted to surprise you with dinner. I picked up the kitchen and living room, too. I hope you don't mind."

I glanced around the plant-filled living room, searching for the camera crew. While I could somehow get my head around having a hot, shirtless man offer me champagne and a home-cooked dinner, the picking up was too much. Johnny was clearly a robot planted in my life to study the *Dorkus allthetimeus* in her natural habitat.

"For real?"

His smile grew wider, and now he was near enough to smell. I didn't know if he actually wore cologne or if his natural scent was clean and spicy, like fresh-ground cinnamon. He locked eyes with mine, his so blue I swear I could see fish swimming in them. His smile changed into something a little more animal, and his eyes dropped to my mouth.

My heartbeat picked up. He leaned forward and placed his mouth on mine, warm and confident. My back arched and I leaned into him, feeling the impossible heat of his hard body against mine.

He held the two champagne glasses in one hand and the unopened bottle in the other. My hands, however, were free to roam. I unzipped my jacket and let it drop to the floor. Then I touched his chest lightly, trailing my fingertips down, around his waist, up his strong spine, and then back down to hook into his jeans and pull his hips tight against mine. I was trying to remember why I'd ever thought it'd be a good idea to hold him at arm's length. It felt so much better to have him close.

Really close.

His kisses grew deeper, and I sent one hand to his thick hair and the other to his tight butt. He made a low sound in his throat, like a growl. I ground my hips ever so slightly, and he almost dropped the champagne glasses.

"I need my hands," he said huskily.

I couldn't agree more. He set the bottle and glasses on the living room table. His body was gone from mine for only a second, but the loss of heat felt like an ache. I was back in his arms in a moment. He wound one hand into my hair and the other at the base of my back and kissed me like his life depended on it.

I was completely wrapped in his strength and his scent and his heat. I would have taken him right there by the front door if I hadn't realized we were being watched. Nothing like glancing up to see a cat and a dog watching like they're taking notes to kill the moment. I felt his hips swivel, followed by a gentle push as he steered us toward the bedroom, not pausing in his passion.

He closed the bedroom door behind us. The room was dark, a pair of dirty workout shorts on the floor. I suppose I could have excused myself to quickly shave my legs, but it'd be like cleaning your house when it was on fire, and who did that?

He pulled back, and even in the moonlit room, I saw the intensity of his gaze. "I want you."

I nodded, though it seemed like an understatement. I wanted oxygen. In that moment, I *needed* Johnny. We fell toward the bed in a tangle of undressing, kissing, stroking passion. He ended up on top, which was just the way I liked it.

"I've missed you," he whispered into my ear, unlatching my bra with one deft move. Thank god. The white cloth reflecting the glow of the moon was bright enough to read by.

"I've missed you, too," I said, grabbing him by the ears and pulling his mouth to mine.

"We should do this more," he said. At least that's what I think he said. I couldn't stop kissing him long enough to let him speak.

The taut length of his body melted into mine, his weight making me feel deliciously protected. My fingers dipped with the curve of his muscles when I ran them down his back and arms. We were both still wearing jeans, and suddenly, nothing seemed more urgent than being completely naked.

Immediately.

Johnny must have been reading my mind, because he pulled back to undo the top snap of my button-fly jeans. His eyes were the color of storm clouds in the dim room, his gaze penetrating as he ran it along the length of me, lingering on my mouth, then landing on my eyes.

"You're so beautiful."

The breath caught in my throat. I could feel my blood-hot pulse in every inch of my body. He leaned over to kiss my neck, undoing the second snap on my jeans.

"There's no place I'd rather be right now," he whispered. The kiss moved to the sweet spot under my ear, and I shivered.

The third snap came undone.

"I can't stop thinking about you." His mouth traveled to my collarbone, his tongue teasing me as it ran along the edges.

The fourth snap popped open.

His mouth moved to my breasts, warm and wet.

There was only one snap left.

A growing heat tickled the edges of my senses. I thought I was going to lose my mind if he didn't rip off my pants and take me right now. I was about to tell him that exact thing when the phone rang in the kitchen.

"Forget it," I said. Passion made my voice deeper than usual.

He didn't even slow to respond, his hot mouth driving me closer to ecstasy. My chin shot up as the growing heat began to vibrate inside me.

The phone rang again.

"The machine will get it," I whispered, tossing my head to the side.

It rang a third time.

Johnny undid the last snap. His eyes met mine, and it was electric.

He looked more animal than man, completely consumed, gorgeous.

The machine clicked over.

"Mira? It's Kennie." Her voice trembled.

The moment hung suspended in the air like a glass globe. Her next words shattered it.

"Gary Wohnt has been shot."

Chapter 12

Johnny and I were out of the house and in his truck in under five minutes. On the seventeen-mile drive to the Fergus Falls hospital, I copped to the dead body I'd discovered in the ice. I expected him to be horrified, but his predominant emotion was concern. I accepted his free hand in mine as he drove.

"Do you think the body is connected to Gary being shot?" he asked, after I assured him that I was fine.

The words felt far away when I spoke them. "I don't see how they could be, but I guess I don't even know what shape we're going to find him in."

It was a foggy night, a sure sign that a thaw was coming our way. Johnny pushed down on the gas pedal despite the dangerous conditions, and we picked up speed. And why not? We knew where the chief of police was right now, and I had to assume both officers were investigating the shooting. We reached the hospital in record time. Johnny parked his truck while I charged into the ER waiting room.

Kennie was perched on the edge of a plastic chair looking like she'd just lost the title of Mrs. Minnesota. Mascara ran down her chin, and a stream of snot snaked out of her nose. I speed-walked to her.

"How is he?"

Kennie gave me the first honest glance we'd ever exchanged. "You came."

"Of course I did. As soon as you called." Three chairs over, a man threw up into a plastic bag. Across the room, a teenage boy held a bloody towel over his hand. This was a dismal place to spend a Saturday night. "What are you doing here alone?"

Her shoulders moved the tiniest bit. "Who else would come with me?"

Her comment shoved me back like a gust of wind. Surely Kennie had friends, didn't she? But I couldn't think of one. Heck, I usually went out of my way to avoid her. The thought humbled. "Where'd it happen?"

Kennie shrugged and blew her nose into a Hello Kitty handkerchief. I felt bad for it. I imagined it had signed up for glitter and lip gloss, not copious boogers. "Just north of town. It was a routine pullover. Speeder. Gary got him on the side of the road and called in the license plate number. Ginny was working the call station. She heard the shots over the radio. When she couldn't get Gary to respond, she sent an ambulance to his location." Kennie hiccuped.

"Is it bad?"

"I haven't seen him. They won't let me. The doctor said Gary will make it, but that's all he could tell me because I'm not family. I'm not *anyone's* family!" She blew her nose again. It came out as a sobbing honk. I reached over to the admissions desk and yanked a handful of tissues out of the communal box.

"Here." I watched her wipe at the smudged mascara. I grabbed another fistful of clean tissues and waited until her breathing grew regular.

"They wouldn't tell you he was going to be OK if he wasn't," I said. I started to pat her back, but it felt odd, so I stopped. "It's probably just a flesh wound. And I'm sure you have family. Don't you?" I realized how very little I knew about the mayor of Battle Lake.

"Aunts and uncles sprinkled around the country, cousins . . ." She trailed off.

"Parents?"

The pause made me expect the worst. "They live in Florida," she finally said.

I exhaled. "Well, that's family."

"We don't get along. And besides, I meant my own family. A husband and kids. A dog. A garden."

The man three chairs over retched into his bag. Seemed like an appropriate reaction. Still, the smell was wafting toward us, so I pulled Kennie to her feet and steered us to the other side of the waiting room. "You don't even like to garden, and you hate kids. And where did all this come from?"

She patted her platinum hair. "I don't know. Gary going into the hospital has brought me closer to my mortality, I guess. What is my legacy on this earth, Mira? What am I leaving behind so people can remember me?"

I couldn't assure her that she was going to live for a good long time, because I bet that's what the man I'd stumbled over yesterday had woken up thinking, too, right before he got iced. I scoured my brain for an answer. "I know! Last night, you told me you're a plant and pet psychologist. You're helping two of the most important things in the world. That's a wonderful legacy!"

"I suppose," she said glumly.

"Oh, I'm sure you're very good at it. I bet people will talk about it long after you're gone." *Like a truly obnoxious party crasher*, I thought, *or a particularly rotten smell.*

"Do you really mean it?"

The hope in her eyes squeezed at my heart. "Of course."

She sat up straight, her expression immediately cleared. "Wonderful. When do you want me to come over for your plant and pet consultation?"

My mouth dropped. Had she just played me?

"Close that piehole, Mira. You don't know what sort of germs are flying around this place." She yanked a calendar out of her mammoth fringed purse. "Tuesday evening might work for me, but my schedule is filling up quickly, so let's keep that appointment floating, shall we? In the meanwhile, what say I officially deputize you so you can go find out how Gary is. I truly am worried about him."

Many questions battled in my head. What came out was, "You can deputize someone?"

She lifted her shoulders. "Why not? I'm mayor."

"You're mayor of Battle Lake. We're in Fergus."

"Then just be a good little detective and go ask that doctor. He was the one I spoke with earlier."

She pushed me out of my seat and toward a white-haired man wearing scrubs. At the same moment, Johnny entered through the sliding front door, his face drawn. I motioned him toward Kennie and strode to the doctor. "Excuse me? I'm wondering how Gary Wohnt is doing."

The doctor glanced up from a chart. "Are you family?"

"I'm his sister." I firmly believed that you shouldn't over-plan a lie. Rather, it's better to always be ready to hop on the lie boat if it drifts your way. "Mira Wohnt."

Shoot. I'd taken it too far by adding details.

It seemed to work, though. The doctor nodded and scratched behind an ear with his pen. "He's in surgery now. The bullet went in his upper left thigh and out the back. Missed the artery. Once he's sewn up, he should be fine, though he might not agree. It'll be a while until he's able to move as he'd like."

"Thank you." I swiveled to walk away. The doctor made a small coughing sound in his throat. I turned back.

"Would you like to know what room he'll be in after recovery?" He raised an eyebrow. "So you can tell the rest of your family?"

"Yes!"

He consulted his clipboard. "He's scheduled to be moved into 227, barring any unforeseen circumstances."

"Thanks again," I said, smiling. Then it occurred to me that a grin might be unnatural for a woman whose brother has recently been shot, so I frowned.

The doctor's eyes narrowed, but he walked away without comment. I raced over to Kennie and Johnny to share the little I knew.

Kennie, for all her denial of her feelings for Gary and her scamming me in the waiting room, seemed incredibly relieved by the news. "Did he say what time Gary would be out of surgery?"

"No, but he'll be in room 227."

She patted my cheek. "Thank you, doll."

I nodded. Johnny slipped his hand into mine. I looked down at it, surprised. I'd had to deal with a lot since I'd moved to Battle Lake, and while I had wonderful friends, I'd been forced to handle most of it alone. I looked over at Johnny and recognized strength in his eyes. I squeezed his hand.

Kennie honked her nose again. "Say, did you hear? They ID'd the man in the ice. They think he's a drifter. The only identification they found on him was a Chicago Public Library card. His name was Maurice Jackson."

Chapter 13

I spent a chaste, troubled night curled in Johnny's arms, both of us too tired to clean up the kitchen before we tumbled into bed. It sounded like Gary was going to be OK, but Maurice most certainly was not. Mrs. Berns and I were likely two of the last people to see him alive, besides his killer.

Something Kennie had said was bothering me, too. She'd said Maurice was a drifter, but I knew better—he'd been a regular for a whole week. I made a mental note to call the Chicago Public Library system to see if they could tell me anything about him, up to and including whether he'd recently checked out any books.

I must have fallen asleep near sunrise because the next thing I knew, I was alone in my bed and the clock was telling me it was 7:14 a.m. I sat up, trying to rub the sleep out of my eyes. I was disoriented, and at first I thought it was because Johnny was gone. Then I realized that the problem was I was sleeping on the mattress for the first time in weeks.

I fought the anxiety, leaning over to sniff Johnny's empty pillow. The faint scent of his spicy shampoo was comforting. I sighed and ran my fingers through my hair. At least I meant to, but it felt like the booglies had set up camp in it for the night. After dragging myself out of bed, I made my way to the kitchen, patting Luna's happy head on the trek. Tiger Pop stretched when she saw me.

"What time did Johnny leave?"

Luna tried to beat the answer in Morse code using her tail, but alas, I was too dumb to understand. Thankfully, Johnny had left a note on the kitchen counter, which he must have very quietly cleaned while I slept:

Sorry I had to leave before you woke up. Early day at work. You looked beautiful sleeping.

I smiled and pushed a lock of my brown hair out of my eyes. The whole tangled mass moved as one. I ignored it and kept reading:

I baked these cookies last night for dessert, but we didn't have time to try them. I hope they're good. I have evening commitments all week. Can you make it to our show on Friday? Call me.

—J

I was sorely tempted to scribble little hearts on that note and hide it under my pillow. That feeling doubled when I lifted the cover next to his note and uncovered a plate mounded with peanut butter cookies, my favorite. I was trying to lose a couple pounds in my belly, so I ate three of them fast, following the time-honored maxim that a cookie eaten quickly has no calories.

My next duty was to scrub out Luna's and Tiger Pop's water bowls, fill them with fresh water, and pour their daily ration of food. Somehow, Luna turned her portion into a lean German shepherd machine. Tiger Pop managed to put on weight, even though the ratio of her food to her body size was the same as Luna's. I suspected she'd figured out how to break into the cat food cupboard while I slept, or better yet open the fridge for snacks and then kick back on the couch and click on the TV to watch Animal Planet's blooper reels.

She was a cat. If she didn't want me to know, I wasn't going to know.

I scratched them both behind the ears as they ate. We weren't terribly active in the winter, which I occasionally felt bad about. Luna had her run of the acreage whenever she wanted, but I knew they both missed me when I was gone for long days.

"Maybe we could hit the sledding hill sometime this week," I suggested. Tiger Pop arched her spine when I scratched the sweet spot where her back met her tail.

Once I was satisfied both animals knew they were loved, I hopped in the shower, applying extra conditioner so I stood a chance of forcing a comb through my shoulder-blade-length brown hair afterward. I also shaved, though I had to change razors halfway through. I lotioned up afterward, rolled on some honey-flavored lip balm, and tossed myself into a clean pair of blue jeans, my comfy white bra (which I had to dig out from behind the nightstand), and a rainbow T-shirt that read Freedom to Love.

Today's plans were informal. The library was technically closed on Sundays, though I'd agreed to open the space to host a birthday party for Matthew, one of my favorite story-hour regulars. He turned five this week. Before the party, I had a meeting scheduled with an attorney at the Litchfield Law Firm. He said he had a small investigative job that he'd like to talk about over a cup of coffee.

I also needed to interview Gilbert Hullson about Jiffy, the ice-diving dog, and I wanted to stop by the nursing home to visit my friend and amateur historian Curtis Poling to ask him some questions.

Dangit, I should probably stop by the hospital in Fergus and check on Gary as well.

Phew. I was tired just thinking about my supposed day off. I gave the animals some more love, tugged a cap over my wet hair and my down jacket over my T-shirt, and headed into the cold world.

Chapter 14

Samuel Litchfield was in his seventies, white-haired but sharp. His son had hired me back in November to investigate an apparent hunting accident. Another corpse later, I'd solved the crime, but not before uncovering an ancillary drug operation very close to home on top of nearly losing my own life. The fact that Samuel was willing to hire me told me that his law office had very low standards.

Fine by me.

"Ms. James! So glad you could make it."

He motioned me to sit across the booth from him at the Shoreline Restaurant. The Shoreline was the Winchester House of Battle Lake, perpetually being added onto. It'd started with a cute dining room and kitchen. Then a cavernous seating area had been added in the back, beyond the restrooms. Next a bar and ice cream parlor were attached, and a bowling alley came next. The layout felt a little jigsaw puzzled, but it was easy to forget once you dug into their fluffy omelets or, better yet, their heavenly eggs Benedict.

Samuel had chosen a booth at the bay window facing West Battle Lake, the perfect location to see who was coming and going. In the distance, I spotted the ice castle spires peeking over the trees.

"Have you been waiting long?" I asked.

He pointed at a small white plate dusted with crumbs. "Long enough to polish off a piece of homemade cherry pie. My wife would kill me if she knew I was having that for breakfast."

The three cookies in my stomach nodded in sympathy. "It's Sunday," I said. "A day of rest and desserts."

He leaned forward conspiratorially. "Don't suppose I could talk you into your own piece of pie? I'd feel better if I wasn't the only one who slipped."

I took the seat across from him. My jeans were already feeling a little tourniquet-y around the waist, but they'd surely loosen as the day wore on and the fabric had a chance to stretch. (It felt good to have a plan.) "Sure. Caramel apple for me."

He ordered that and another piece of cherry for himself, because "a gentleman never lets a lady eat alone." I added on a cup of coffee with real cream.

While we waited, he slipped into the reason he'd brought me here, Lutheran-style—which was to say, inefficiently and roundabout.

"Heard about the hoo-ha at the lake yesterday," he began. "Damn shame. Do they know who the young man you found in the ice was?"

The waitress set my coffee mug down and poured me a steaming cup. The rich smell comforted me instantly. I studied Samuel covertly as I mixed in the cream and two sugars. I'd met him only in passing when dealing with his son at the law firm. I knew he came from a farm background and had been the first in his family to attend college. By all accounts, he'd worked hard for everything he had, and he was well liked around town. Even so, there was something crafty in his eyes that put me on guard.

"They think he wasn't from around here."

Samuel rubbed his chin. "Been a lot of fly-by-nighters around Battle Lake lately, it seems. It used to be that I recognized everyone in town in the winter. Now I can't go to Larry's without running into at least five strangers, some of whom look like they're from the rough side of the tracks. Do they think that drugs were involved?"

I sipped the coffee. The creamy, sweet liquid poured down my throat, sending shivers of satisfaction to my fingertips. "No idea."

I took another sip and watched him. Would he be disappointed that I couldn't tell him more? If so, tough noogies. I wasn't on the clock. Yet.

He shrugged, glancing back toward the dessert cooler. The waitress was pulling out two pies that had been baked fresh that morning, no doubt. The apple pie was unbroken, the latticework crust on top drizzled with thick ropes of homemade caramel. A little bit of drool ran out of my mouth, and I wiped at it, hoping Samuel hadn't noticed.

"Well," he said, pulling his attention back to me. "It's a sad business, but not why I asked you here. What can you tell me about Aaron Offerdahl?"

"Never heard of him, though I know the Offerdahl name is tied to the Prospect House."

Samuel nodded. He'd expected that. I was starting to think nothing I could say would surprise him. He'd known exactly how this interview would go before I walked in the door, and truly, it felt like a job interview. "Aaron is about your age, maybe a little younger. He was a troubled kid, might still be. Troubled, that is, obviously not a kid anymore. I was hoping you could track him down."

Some stubborn streak in me refused to ask him why. "Do you have an address?"

"We think he's living within fifteen miles of Battle Lake."

My brain snagged on the "we." "Any idea of who his friends might be?"

"He graduated high school here, but all his friends, if he had any, have moved on."

"How long do you think he's been back?"

"A month, maybe two."

A lovely wedge of warm caramel apple pie with a scoop of melting vanilla ice cream was slid in front of me. I smiled. Yesterday might have been a crap sandwich, but today was going pretty well so far. I ate my pie and pretended to contemplate everything Samuel had told me. I hoped my face somehow radiated thoughtful intelligence, because my brain was cycling over two words, again and again: *pie . . . good.*

I finished the whole slice, barely coming up for air, wondering if the speed-calorie conversion applied to pies as well as cookies.

"You must have been hungry," Samuel said.

I looked up to see he was only on his second bite. Second bite of his second piece, though, which did not exactly give him carte blanche when it came to the judgment chair.

"Thank you," I said. "For the pie. It was delicious. If I take the case, how much time do I have to find Offerdahl?"

"Two weeks from today."

I did the math in my head. "I could give you twenty billable hours in the next two weeks, at forty dollars an hour. I'll log all the sites I visit and leads I follow. If I don't find him, you still pay."

I had made all this up on the spot, but he nodded as if what I'd said were reasonable.

"Deal." He held out his hand.

I shook it, trying not to notice the thick cherry ooze smeared across his teeth like blood.

Chapter 15

My meeting with Gilbert Hullson had far fewer layers. In fact, I'm not sure it had even one layer. I tracked him down at the hardware store, where he worked part-time. He was in the screw aisle, on his knees, sorting through a bin.

"Mr. Hullson?"

"None other."

He kept sorting, not bothering to glance my way. He wore flannel and, except for a spectacularly bulbous nose, looked like your average middle-aged Midwesterner.

"I'm Mira James. From the *Battle Lake Recall*? I'm here to interview you about Jiffy."

That got his attention. He immediately stood, his eyes alight. "You shoulda seen it! One minute I'm planning her funeral, and the next, she's shooting out of a fish hole like popcorn. Poor thing was wet and shivering to beat the band, but she was alive. Ooh, if she could talk, she'd have a story to tell, wouldn't she?"

Huh. "So she really went into one hole and came out the other?"

"As sure as these two hands." He held his gnarled palms toward me. He was missing the ring finger on his left hand, which confused the analogy somewhat.

"Do you have witnesses?"

He flashed a sly smile. "I'm a fisherman. I can always come up with witnesses."

I felt a mirror smile tugging at my lips. The guy was an absolute weirdo, and he was beginning to grow on me. "Good enough. Don't suppose I could come by your house later tonight and snap a photo of Jiffy? To run with the article?"

He returned his attention to the screws. "She'd be pleased to meet you."

Chapter 16

In eighth grade, our health class took a half-day trip to Paynesville Manor, the local nursing home. We were each assigned an honorary grandparent, and our job was to listen to their history and write a mini-biography from it.

That was one of those exercises that must look great on paper, a bunch of teachers chuffing at each other around a table, talking about active and experiential learning. In reality, we were already struggling with acne and the unshakable belief that all human interaction was merely a setup for humiliation à la face-plants, sneeze-farts, spontaneously inappropriate confessions, and/or getting the answer wrong. To expect us to navigate an unfamiliar elderly population was pure cruelty.

Because of that experience, and because in my teens and twenties I'd been confident I'd never grow old and so why bother hanging out with those who were, I'd never entered another nursing home.

Until I'd moved to Battle Lake.

A series of circumstances had led me to the Senior Sunset to seek out Curtis Poling. Those who didn't know Curtis believed he was in the middle stages of dementia, an incorrect assumption that he cultivated by casting off the roof of the Sunset into the dry lawn in the back whenever it was sunny and "the fish were likely to be biting."

In truth, Curtis was as wily as they came, with sharp, clear blue eyes that didn't miss a thing. He'd gone from being my informant to my friend, the man I visited weekly to play cards with, laugh with, and, in the summer, get gardening tips from.

Today, as I strolled into the Senior Sunset's foyer, I was struck by how comfortable I'd become with the predominant scents of a nursing home—antiseptics, Bengay, and dusty-floral old-lady perfume. I signed in at the front desk and made my way to Curtis's room. I knocked at his door.

"Who is it?" he called out. "Is it Satan? Because I'm not ready to go just yet."

"Hey, Curtis," I said through the door. "It's me. Mira."

"Timothy Leary?" he responded, his voice still raised. "I'm too old for that psychedelic crap."

"Mira," I repeated, keeping my voice level. I smiled as a short nursing assistant walked past in the hallway, wearing burgundy scrubs and a suspicious expression. "Mira James."

"Etta James?" There was still a door between us. "What are you doing this far north?"

I sighed. He liked to bust my balls. "I brought doughnuts."

"Door's unlocked."

I let myself in. Curtis lived in a standard suite, set up much like a hospital room except for the extra dresser and the plants in the window. He had a bed and a nightstand, a TV mounted to the ceiling, an easy chair by the window and a plastic chair for guests, a closet, and a private bath. He was sitting by the window, reading H. G. Wells's *The Time Machine*. Upside down.

When he was sure it was me, he flipped it right side up.

"Why do you pretend?" I asked. "All the smart nurses must realize you're sane."

He shrugged. "I make it easy on 'em by being consistent. And the odder I act, the more they leave me alone." He was wearing a dark-blue terry cloth robe. His thin calves poked out like chopsticks. Thankfully, his bony feet were stuffed into the toasty knit mukluks I'd bought him for Christmas after I'd accidentally caught him barefoot.

Old farmers' feet were the stuff of nightmares.

"Where are they?" he asked.

"What?"

"The doughnuts."

"I lied about those." I could bust my own balls. I pulled up the plastic chair so I was sitting across from him. "What was the deal with giving me the runaround in the hall?"

"New nursing assistant. Comes up about to your shoulders, shaped more like a square than a circle?"

I nodded. "She passed by while I was trying to get in. She looked fine, maybe a little curious."

"Shows what you know. She's convinced I'm mentally stable and has made it her mission to prove it."

"Smart, too." I crossed my legs. "I think I like her."

He scrunched up his lips in a pout, and for a moment, he resembled a baby more than an old man.

"Fine," I said. "I'll bring doughnuts next time. Promise. Do you have a few minutes right now?"

"That might be all I have. Never know when the ticker is going to punch out." He winked. "So what do you want to know?"

First I asked him about Gary's shooting. He'd heard that it'd happened, of course. You might not think someone in a nursing home would have their finger on the town's pulse, but you'd be wrong. He still had friends on the outside, and stories were currency at the Sunset. The elderly traded news like gold and pearls, and it all, somehow, rolled downhill to Curtis.

Unfortunately, he didn't have any more information on Gary than I did and was in fact happy to learn that Gary's wound wasn't serious.

The next topic of conversation was Maurice Jackson. Curtis didn't ask me if I was OK after finding another body, and I loved him for that. He treated me like I was normal. He did say that he'd heard there were new drugs in town and a gang on the fringes, and that he assumed they were connected.

"What do you mean, 'on the fringes'?" I asked.

"They don't live in Battle Lake, near as I can tell. In fact, I don't know why they'd even bother coming here, with our small population. But they've been showing up often enough."

"Do you think Gary's shooting is connected to the gang?"

He rubbed his chin. "I'd be surprised if it wasn't. I've lived here for ninety-three years, and never has a Battle Lake police officer been shot. It'd be quite a coincidence if a gang comes to town at the same time Gary's attacked, and there's no thread between the two. What'd you think of the Prospect House?"

"I never made the press tour," I said, noting his abrupt shift in topic but not commenting. "I'm hoping for an email back scheduling a private showing."

He stared out the window. I was struck by how ocean blue his eyes were, and how similar they were to Johnny's. "She's a gorgeous old building, that Prospect House. I'm happy other people are going to get to experience her. I stole my first kiss there, did you know that? She was a girl from Saint Louis, visiting for the week with her parents. They owned a mercantile back home, I believe. I courted her all seven days she was in town, and the night before she left, I snuck into the Prospect House and met her at the base of the grand staircase. I pecked her cheek. She giggled and ran upstairs. Never saw her again." His eyes grew misty and faraway.

I couldn't help smiling. "That's beautiful. What was her name?"

"Amelia. Prettiest girl you ever saw, except for my wife, God rest her soul."

His use of the word "girl" reminded me of the face I'd seen in the window when I'd been skating. I didn't see any reason to bring it up. In fact, the further I got from the event, the more certain I was I'd imagined it. I'd need a full night's sleep soon or I'd be completely loopy. "Sorry to bring you back to earth, but I have one more question. What can you tell me about Aaron Offerdahl?"

His eyes immediately focused. He began chuckling. "How much research did you do on the Prospect House?"

"I know it was built by Barnaby Offerdahl. I imagine Aaron is related to him."

"Good. I was worried you were getting soft. Aaron must be the . . . let me see now . . . the great-great-grandnephew of Barnaby. There might be even one more 'great' on there. Aaron can trace his lineage straight from Barnaby's brother. He has blood from the bad side of the family."

I sat forward with interest. "Meaning?"

"He's been nothing but trouble since he was born. That's true of that whole remaining Offerdahl branch. Aaron's parents still own a lot of the land surrounding the Prospect House, but they had to sell off the house to pay gambling debts. I'm surprised they haven't sold the land as well, given how much it'd be worth."

"Are his parents still alive?"

"His mom, no. She died a decade or so back, heart attack, I think I heard. His dad is older, in his seventies, I believe, but as far as I know, still alive. They had Aaron late in life. He's an only child. After he graduated high school, they moved to Phoenix or Texas. Somewhere warm."

"Any idea where Aaron is now?"

"How many doughnuts are you planning on bringing me next visit?"

"How many do you want?"

He considered. "This is worth at least a half dozen Long Johns, but not with that fake chocolate in the middle. I want jelly."

"You got it."

He nodded. "Last I heard Aaron blew back into town about the same time the gang did." He raised his eyebrows to make sure I understood what he was implying. "He's living somewhere around Swederland."

Swederland was a two-bars-and-a-post-office town a five-minute drive from Battle Lake. "That's where the new brewery is, isn't it?"

"O'Callaghan's. But *that* is a whole other story, and you'd have to bring me a dozen doughnuts for that."

I wanted to hear more, but Curtis's eyes were drooping, and his hands had grown minutely shaky on his lap. He was tired, and he was trying to tell me gently. I stood and kissed the top of his head. He still had thick white hair, which was a point of pride with him. It smelled like Brylcreem. "That's a deal. I have to be running, though. Have an appointment and all that."

He took my hand. His was as dry as paper, but strong despite the tremor running through it. I glanced at his face, surprised by the affection.

"You're going to be OK, kid." He smiled and released my hand. "You're like a cat, curious as the day is long, and always landing on her feet."

The bloom of warmth in my chest caught me off guard. "See you soon," I said. I glanced over my shoulder on the way out. His eyes were closed.

Chapter 17

I arrived at the library with a full hour to go until the birthday party. I decorated with a roll of lavender crepe paper and flicked on the twinkle lights, then went to my computer.

Navigating into my paid database, I first ran a search on Aaron Offerdahl. There was only one hit, his current address listed as north Minneapolis. I also uncovered a list of misdemeanors he'd committed, including vandalism, petty theft, and public intoxication. Most of his crimes had taken place in Minnesota, with the exception of a case of trespassing in Chicago.

He'd done jail time, a month here or there, but on paper, he appeared to be more of a directionless punk than a serial criminal.

I tracked down a single photo of him, a fuzzy shot where he had his arm wrapped around a woman's neck in a possessive hug. He had brown hair. I couldn't tell what color his eyes were, but he wore a spike through his right eyebrow. The rest of his features were bland. The woman had a beautiful, heart-shaped face accented by a lip ring and thick black liner rimming her eyes.

I clicked on the photo and was brought to the woman's SixDegrees page. I knew of Degrees, of course. Who didn't? I didn't have an account I posted to, though, just a skeleton page to allow me to log in and research others. What had our culture come to that people needed to advertise that they had a cold and were going to shop for cheese later that day? Made my job easier, but still.

The woman's name, according to the page, was Lil Angie, and she lived in Minneapolis. I couldn't find any other photos of Aaron on her page or any more mention of him. I wrote down the URL and logged off, glancing at the clock. The birthday party guests would arrive in five minutes.

Just enough time for a curiosity-driven search on Maurice Jackson, so I returned to my subscription database. I received twenty hits on the name in the greater Chicago area, with phone numbers and addresses for all of them. Whether they were current—and whether any of them were the iced Maurice—would remain to be seen because, at that moment, the first knock came at the glass front door. It was Matthew and his mom. I waved them in with one hand and clicked the "Print" button with the other.

Matthew's friends weren't far behind, and soon I had the library filled with giggling, Duck, Duck, Gray Duck–playing kids. They were extra banana pants, hiding in plain sight under chairs and telling jokes with no punch lines. It must have been the weather, which one parent told me was going to reach the low thirties today.

"Above freezing?" I asked.

"I know!" she said, seeming as surprised as I was.

Mrs. Berns, who'd promised to help me with today's party, showed up as the worst was over and we were about to cut into the cake and ice cream.

"Nice timing," I whispered, as she laid her coat over the front counter.

"Thank you!" she said brightly. "Is it marble cake? That's my favorite."

I glanced over at the sheet cake Matthew's mom was cutting, slicing right into the green frosting tail of a brontosaurus. Marble cake was my favorite, too. Could I have cookies for breakfast, pie for a snack, and cake for lunch? I was excited to find out.

"I don't know yet. Where were you?"

"Late night," she said. "I was playing bridge with some friends, and then I went to the Rusty Nail to sing karaoke."

I asked, despite myself. "What'd you sing?"

"'Like a Virgin,'" she said, straight-faced. "Let me help!" She ran over to where Matthew's mom was sliding the first slice of cake onto a plate. "I can be your distributor."

Matthew's mom smiled gratefully and handed the plate to Mrs. Berns, who added a big scoop of vanilla ice cream on the top and then returned to my side.

"Aren't you going to pass it out to the kids first?"

"Charity starts at home." She dug into the treat.

I threw my hands in the air. I scurried over to help with the cake, making sure all the kids and parents had what they needed, all the while wishing I'd laid plastic on the floor. It looked like I was going to have to bring in a professional to shampoo the carpet after this shindig. The thought killed my desire for cake, so I made my way back to Mrs. Berns. She was talking to a woman who'd brought her grandson to the party. The lady was showing Mrs. Berns a photo book. I assumed the pictures were of her grandson and was surprised to make my way out to the side and see they were instead of a golden retriever.

"It's my Sandy," she said in answer to my expression. "She's lived with me for two years. I don't know what I'd do without her. Dogs are the only creature that love another person more than themselves."

"You've obviously never been to an Al-Anon meeting," Mrs. Berns muttered under her breath.

"Wait, you have?" I asked her.

The grandma took that moment to snap her book closed and return to the party, an annoyed expression on her face.

Mrs. Berns wiggled her eyebrows. "There's a lot you don't know about me, missy."

I was taken aback. She was absolutely right. She was so honest and forthright—and I was so comfortable with her—that I hadn't bothered to plumb her past. Her husband had died ten years ago, that much I knew, and her kids had tried to confine her in a high-security nursing home last October. I also knew that she got laid more in a bad week than I did in a good month. She'd lived in or near Battle Lake her whole ninety years, she never let life get her down, and she preferred to wear replica six-guns holstered at her sides, though she'd given up the accessory for the winter.

But did she dream of traveling the world? What had her life with her husband been like? What was her favorite drink?

"Quit looking at me like that," she said.

"Like what?"

"Like I'm a commercial for an animal shelter and your brain is running some pitiful commentary along the bottom of my screen. I just made that crack to get rid of Melinda. If she'd referred to her dog as her 'child,' I woulda had to kick her, and the Al-Anon comment seemed kinder."

I cocked my head. She was sounding more like her old self. Still, something was a little off. "You sure you don't want to talk?"

"You sure you want me to tell this roomful of children that when you're alone, you dream of Chief Wenonga walking his fiberglass legs over to your house and showing you his totem pole?"

"OK," I said, turning to the children and clapping loudly, my voice dripping with false cheer. "Time to get cleaning!"

The kids groaned and fell to the ground as if their bones had turned to rubber, but we were already fifteen minutes over the scheduled time. Even if I didn't have Mrs. Berns's threat burning the tips of my ears, I wanted to make visiting hours at the hospital so I could check in with Gary.

The moms began cleaning up the party area with the precision of worker ants. If the United States could only harness mother power, we'd break our dependence on oil once and for all.

The library was empty in less than twenty minutes, and I could have sworn it was cleaner than it had been pre-party. No thanks to Mrs. Berns, of course. She'd sneaked out as soon as the picking up began. I made a note to myself to track her down soon so I could dig into her past more. At this moment, though, my priority was visiting one Gary Wohnt so I could question him about the shooting.

Chapter 18

Entering the hospital empty-handed seemed in poor taste, but I didn't want to buy Gary flowers and I didn't know what kind of food he liked. Operating on the belief that if you brought something *you* liked, you knew at least one person would be happy, I purchased four Nut Goodies at a gas station on my way.

I polished off one before I hit the parking lot, leaving three, which seemed like a better number anyhow, and here's my reasoning: If there was someone else already there, we'd each have one. If I brought in four Nut Goodies, though, it'd devolve into one of those embarrassing social situations where everyone had to pretend like they didn't want the extra one.

Gary's room was on the second floor. I made my way to the elevator, trying not to stare at the people wearing robes and pushing IVs as they shuffled down the hallway. It seemed to me that if you were admitted to the hospital, you should stay in your room or go home, but what did I know?

No matter how many times I'd visited a hospital, I still couldn't get used to the sense that germs were settling on every inch of me in a light mist. I hit the button in the elevator with my elbow, smiling apologetically at the man I was sharing it with.

"Germs," I said, showing him my jazz hands.

He pretended not to hear me, and so I pretended the elevator came to a screeching stop on the second floor, forcing me to rub my germy elbow against him to keep my balance.

"Sorry," I said.

I'd been hanging out with Mrs. Berns far too long.

I followed the signs to room 227 and stood outside the cracked door. It struck me—probably much later than it should have—that I was about to see Gary Wohnt vulnerable. In bed. Possibly wearing little more than a gown.

I took a deep breath, steeling myself, and slipped through the crack in the door.

No part of my imagination could have prepared me for what happened next.

Chapter 19

"Miranda Rayn James!"

Gary knew my middle name. And he was alone. The top half of his bed was raised so he could sit comfortably. One leg lay relaxed over the comforter, and the other was bandaged and suspended from the ceiling in some sort of sling.

Both appendages were naked, but that wasn't what shocked me. It was his expression. He looked as joyful as a child who'd gotten a pony for Christmas, and he was directing all this happiness at me.

I glanced behind. Had someone else entered, a woman with the same name as me but whom Gary actually liked?

"Come in! I was hoping you'd visit." His words were slurred and his dark hair tousled, a thick lock of it dangling over an eye. He wore a blue hospital gown, and I was thankful to see boxers peeking out from the bottom of it.

"Gary?"

"Have a seat!" He patted the small open spot on the single bed he occupied. There was no way I could sit there without our hips touching. This from the man who regularly treated me like I was something he'd accidentally stepped in.

My forehead crinkled in confusion. "Have you found God?"

He visibly pondered the question. While he did that, I checked the tag on his IV drip. Cephalosporin and morphine. Mystery solved.

"I have looked for God, I truly have," he said, his serious expression almost charming.

The corner of my mouth tipped. It had been a crappy couple days. Hell, it'd been a crappy decade. You could let that get you down, or you could find joy in the small moments, like this one. I actually had the upper hand over Gary.

"You're not wearing pants," I said, both to test his awareness and to divert a possible sermon.

"Pants." He pronounced the word as if he were tasting it. "Pants."

"When do you get out?"

"Groundhog's Day?" he asked, chuckling. It was a deep, cheerful sound, but he covered his mouth like a schoolgirl while he did it. "But only if we have six more weeks of winter."

I pulled up a chair. Gary Wohnt, high and pantsless. This was going to be more fun than a roomful of drunk nuns, to borrow one of Mrs. Berns's favorite sayings. "What happened to you, anyhow? Who shot you?"

He glanced at his leg, surprised. He fought for focus, and for a moment, he looked like Police Chief Wohnt. "White male, twenty-five to thirty, wearing a cap yanked down low. I pulled him over for speeding and driving without a license plate. I approached; he shot."

My heart clutched. I realized how lucky Gary was that it hadn't been worse. "What kind of car?"

He scowled. "Is that your business?"

Dangit! Had the morphine just worn off? I flicked the IV tube with my finger in case there was a blockage. "I want to help."

"You can help by getting me some water." He pointed at the table just out of his reach.

I stood and poured him a glass. When I turned, I caught him staring at my butt as though it held the secret of the Sphinx. I cleared my throat.

"Miranda Rayn James! You came to visit." He accepted the water, the glassy look back in his eyes. "So many dead bodies you could be finding, and instead you're here with me." He giggled again.

There was something infectious about it.

"Well, I gotta keep it lively," I said, grinning.

"Yes, you do." He knit his brows together. "Say, can you help me?"

"You want me to reach something else for you?"

"I want you to gather information on the guys who're bringing the drugs. The gangbangers. Can you do that for me without getting into trouble?"

"Was Maurice a gangbanger?" I asked, pulling my chair up close.

"Dunno." He looked around. "Do you know where the remote is?"

"Gary." I put my hand on his arm. He studied it. "Was Maurice part of a gang from Chicago that is bringing drugs into this area?"

"Dunno." He wrinkled his nose. "But I do know the gang showed up the same time as the OxyContin patches. Don't know where their home base is. We just know it's near town."

"Battle Lake?"

He smiled dreamily. "Battle Lake."

I needed him to focus. "What did Maurice die of?"

"Death." His smile widened. "Have I ever told you how beautiful you are?"

My skin flushed from head to toe. I definitely had *not* foreseen this conversational turn.

"Kiss me," he said, his voice gruff. "Kiss me now."

I stood so fast that I knocked over my chair. This couldn't be only the morphine talking. He must also be having an allergic reaction to the antibiotics.

"Um, I should be going."

"Pretty, pretty, pretty. I think you're as pretty as a peach." He held his finger to his mouth in a comically exaggerated "sssh." "Don't tell Kennie," he said in a drunk man's whisper.

The fun was definitely over. This was not at all what I had planned. "How about we don't tell *anyone*? In fact, how about we forget that I even stopped by?"

I was in such a hurry to escape that I dropped a Nut Goodie. I would have gone back for it, except Gary had started singing "Unforgettable."

I stress-ate the remaining two Goodies before I reached my car.

Chapter 20

I'd forgotten the Maurice Jackson printout at the library, so I had to stop by there on my way home. Once inside the toasty building, the encounter with Gary fading to an unpleasant memory, I decided I might as well finish my research. I flicked on the track of lights over the front desk, turned on the computer so I could cross-reference as needed, sharpened one of the stubby library pencils, and grabbed two manila folders.

I labeled one Operation Offerdahl in honor of the case I'd been hired to research. I tossed around a couple names for the second folder before settling on Cold Case. It was dark humor, to be sure, but the name had less to do with the way Maurice had died than the fact that I had few leads and no reason to look for more. I had no tangible stake in finding out who Maurice really was or what'd happened to him, no incentive other than curiosity and a feeling like I owed him something for saving Mrs. Berns and me in the alley.

Once my meager paperwork was organized, I made my first call, to a Maurice Aames Jackson at 1355 West Greenleaf Avenue in Chicago, Illinois. There was no answer. I put a chicken scratch next to his name, shorthand for "tried once." The next name on my list was Maurice Carver Jackson, living at 1640 North Orchard Street. He picked up on the second ring. He sounded old, and I hadn't rehearsed what I was going to say.

"Hello, sir! I'm calling from the Chicago Public Library, and some-one has returned a library card with the name of Maurice Jackson. Have you by chance lost your library card?"

"Chicago Public Library?"

"Yessir."

"Then why does my caller ID say 'Battle Lake Public Library'?"

Shit. He was going to make detective before me. "All our library calls are routed through one central location."

"Izzat so? I suppose you have a bridge you want me to buy, one that just so happens to span the Dumbass River?"

I was torn between the urge to hang up and the desire to ask if he was single so I could set him up with Mrs. Berns. "I'm sorry. I *am* calling from the Battle Lake Public Library. It's in Minnesota. I really did find a Chicago Public Library card with the name of Maurice Jackson on it, and I'm trying to track him down."

"It ain't mine, but can I offer you some advice?"

That's a question that rarely deserves a yes. "Sure."

"Tell the truth."

Click.

He had a point. Then again, I had so few natural skills—lying being toward the top of the list—that it seemed counterintuitive to limit myself.

I tried three more numbers. Two were home, both dead ends. It was a bit demoralizing, particularly since I didn't even know how old the library card was. Maurice Jackson could have moved out of Chicago months ago. I decided to take a break from calling numbers to do the work I was actually being paid for. Going on Curtis's tip that Aaron Offerdahl had been seen around Swederland, and specifically in the vicinity of the new brewery, I dialed their number.

"O'Callaghan's." The voice was female and perky.

"Hi. Is the brewery open for tours?"

"Of course! We have tours at the top of every hour Tuesdays and Saturdays from noon to eight."

"Do I need a reservation?"

"Not this time of year."

"Sounds good. Hey," I said, hoping I sounded like I just thought of it, "is Aaron Offerdahl working this Tuesday?"

"I'm sorry. We can't give out employee information."

Was it my imagination, or had her voice gone frosty? "I don't need any personal info. I'm just wondering if he's working. I haven't seen him in a while. It'd be great to catch up."

"I'm afraid I can't help you with that. Is there anything else you need?"

I recognized a brush-off when I heard it. "No, thank you. I appreciate your time."

"O'Callaghan's thanks you for your interest! We hope to see you soon."

That they will, I thought, as I hung up the phone. *Probably this Tuesday, in fact.* I was about to shut down the computer when the front door opened. Hadn't I locked it?

"Sorry," I said. "We're not open on Sundays."

The track lighting above me was illuminated, but I hadn't bothered to turn on the overheads by the front door. The person was definitely a male, his head leaning so far down that the top of his cap faced me.

"Sir? We're not open. You can come back tomorrow at ten."

He stepped into the light at the same time he lifted his head.

It was Ray, the mewling, tweaking freak Maurice had saved me from.

My throat locked up.

Chapter 21

Every cell in my body lifted its skirts and ran for high ground. I stepped back involuntarily, one hand fumbling for the phone and the other scrabbling inside my desk for something substantial to whack Ray with. Why had I left the stun gun in my car?

He kept moving toward me, and the closer he came, the clearer the tattoo on his neck grew. A stingray's barbed tail licked at his ear, leading to a widening of the body, most of which was tucked into the collar of his thick winter jacket. Sting*ray*. I wondered if the tattoo had given him his name, or vice versa. I also wondered where he'd gotten the warm winter coat and how the helicopter I'd been stupid enough not to lock the door.

"Stop. I have a gun. And I've pushed the alarm."

"Shit, this is a library. What you got that anyone wants to steal?" He stopped, though, and glanced behind him, his hands shoved deep into his pockets.

"That's close enough. Now, you have exactly two minutes to get out of here before the cops arrive."

"Two minutes?" He nodded. "All I need."

Why couldn't I have said thirty seconds? Our eyes were locked. His pupils were far less jittery than the night we'd met. He also wasn't making that trapped-baby-animal noise. In fact, he appeared entirely calm. Still, when he began to draw one hand slowly out of his pocket, I instinctively raised my stapler.

He saw it and started laughing wheezily. "Stop! Don't collate me." He held up his empty hands in mock horror.

"That's a pretty odd verb choice," I said, still gripping the stapler.

He dropped his hands and shrugged. "I used to work in a copy shop. I got, what, a buck thirty seconds now? Here's the deal. I heard there was a chick detective in town and that I could find her at the library. I got a letter I was supposed to hand over to the police if anything happened to Mo."

"Mo?"

"Maurice." His face darkened. "My friend who was ganked. They found his body in the lake yesterday."

"Wait," I said, dropping the stapler by my side, "you didn't kill him?"

Ray drew his head back. "What's wrong with you, woman? We don't kill our own. So you want the damn letter or not?"

"I thought you were supposed to give it to the police."

He exhaled through his nose. "I look like I get along with the police?"

Point taken. "Say, speaking of police, I don't suppose you happened to shoot an officer of the law last night?"

His eyes narrowed dangerously. "I ask you one more time: You want the letter or not?"

I leaned over the desk and held out my hand. He pulled a crumpled sheet of paper from his coat pocket and stepped forward as if he were going to drop it into my hand. At the last second, our hands so close I could feel his body heat, he balled up the paper and tossed it over my head.

"Sorry." His eyes had gone as flat as a doll's. "It must've slipped."

He raised an eyebrow and started backing toward the door. My heart thudded a sick beat against my ribs. I'd made the dangerous mistake of thinking he might be human since he'd done a favor for a friend. He was reminding me what he really was and who held the power in this room.

I let him walk out, neither of us blinking or dropping our gazes. When the door closed behind him, I snapped off the track lights and simultaneously flipped on the lights outside the door. The contrast made me feel a tiny bit safer.

I watched him slip into a rusty white sedan. When he was out of sight, I darted out from behind the desk and locked the door, leaving on the outside lights. Then I scurried back to my desk and fumbled in the drawers until I located a penlight I'd received for free when I opened a checking account at First National Bank.

I flicked it on and was pleased to see that the light was narrow but bright. I quickly located the crumpled paper and then tucked myself behind the tall counter, where I could read without anyone seeing me.

Chapter 22

I smoothed the paper on the carpeted floor and shined the flashlight beam into its center. I discovered it was a grainy photocopy of a hand-written letter:

> *18 January 1865*
>
> *Dear Octavia:*
> *I wish I could write with better news. In Minnesota, they do not believe the messages I bring. I do not think I can stay here. I pack my bags to return home to you, my dearest wife, tomorrow. Should anything happen to me, look to the tunnel of justice.*
>
> *With a heart that beats only for you,*
> *Orpheus Jackson*

I flipped the letter over. It was blank. I flipped it back and reread it.

The letter raised more questions than it answered. Was the date accurate, and was Maurice Jackson a descendant of Orpheus? If so, who was the "they" and what were the "messages" referred to in the letter? And more importantly, what in the world did a 135-year-old letter have to do with Maurice's murder?

I sighed and rubbed my temples. For all I knew, Ray had killed Maurice and dreamed up this letter based on something he'd seen at the copy shop and was using it in a ridiculous attempt to throw the police off his scent.

I wished I'd had time to read the letter before Ray left so I could question him. Then again, I was happy that he was gone. I peeked over the top of the desk and pulled the phone toward me, bringing it down to ground level. I dialed Jed's number from memory.

One ring.

Two rings.

Three rings.

Click.

"Hey, you! Thanks for calling me. You know it's Jed, right? Well, I'm not here right now, so leave a message with the phone, and I'll call you back when I get home."

Beep.

"Hey, it's Mira. Hope you're well. I'm calling to find out what you know about any recent drug or gang activity in the area." To anyone else, that message might sound a little offensive; Jed didn't operate on that level. "Give me a call back."

I hung up and considered calling Johnny to ask him to walk me to my car. If I did that, though, where would it stop? I'd never be able to go anywhere on my own again. Besides, if Ray had wanted to hurt me, he would have. No way had he bought that I had a gun or an alarm. I just had to be alert from this moment forward.

But not stupid.

I called Gilbert Hullson and told him I'd be over in ten minutes to meet Jiffy and asked him to call the police if I wasn't. I placed my skimpy research into the appropriate manila folders. Then I set the library door to lock automatically behind me and dashed to the car so fast that my feet barely kissed the icy ground.

Chapter 23

Funny.

Running to my car, I'd wished for ol' Z-Force, the stun gun, more than anything in the world.

Now that I'd spent thirty minutes sitting across from Gilbert, who had Jiffy perched on one meaty thigh and a fishing scrapbook on the other, I was glad I didn't have Z. I would have zapped either Gilbert to shut him up or myself to keep awake.

The tiny bungalow two miles north of town hadn't been hard to find, and the neat yard with a shoveled path leading to the house gave no indication that Gilbert was a hoarder. When he opened the door, though, I saw the truth. The sheer mountainous concentration of stuff crowding the house's interior was overwhelming. He'd carved a path inside the house that mirrored the one outside, and it wove through shoulder-high piles of food wrappers, fishing magazines, tackle, old life jackets, decoys, and more. It was as if someone had emptied a gigantic fishing boat into his house at the end of a trip, and it smelled like that trip had ended a decade or two ago.

". . . and that was 1984. My 1985 to '90 albums are more walleye-oriented. Let me grab—"

I sat up so quickly that Jiffy erped, which was how dogs that size must bark: *Erp.* "I really appreciate your time, Mr. Hullson, but I'm afraid I can't stay. I just need a photo of Jiffy." She wagged her stumpy little tail at the mention of her name. She was a darling chihuahua, though her eyes looked perennially about to pop out.

She'd been staring at me desperately since I'd arrived, almost begging for me to take her out of this hoarder's castle.

"Well," Gilbert said, sensing, I imagined, that he was about to lose a 135-pound white girl off his line, "you should at least see a picture of the hole she fell into before you go."

"Really? You're going to show me a picture of a hole?" Resignation, not surprise, colored my voice.

Jiffy erped again: *You have to save me, lady from the outside! This isn't my life!*

"Sher thing," Gilbert said, pulling out a thick photo album labeled MIRACLE JIFFY. He paged through it until he found what he wanted. He flipped the album so it was facing me and thrust a sausage finger at a blurry square. "See?"

I leaned forward to look at the photograph. The Naugahyde ottoman I sat on—the only accessible piece of furniture besides Gilbert's easy chair—squeaked as I did so. Gilbert flashed me a look, but I didn't bother making excuses. He owed me that much.

In the photo, Gilbert had placed a paperback next to the ice hole to lend perspective.

"She must have just fit in there," I said.

"Yup. If it wasn't for those gangsters shooting up the ice, I never would have let her out of my sight. I think she was going after a fish. I almost lost her." He bundled Jiffy into his arms and hugged her. She closed her eyes and ducked her head into his arm.

My ears pricked up. "Gangsters?"

"Two of them. Couldn't get a good look because they were too far away, but I could tell by their clothes that they're not from around here. Hoodies, baseball caps. No fisherman wears that. They were shooting into the air, hollering. I turned around to ask Jiffy if she thought I should call the police, but she wasn't there. I panicked. By the time she popped back out of the ice a few houses over, the kids were gone."

"When was this?"

"Thursday night. Right before they started setting up for the festival on West Battle."

My pulse was racing. "Is that where you were? On West Battle?"

"Yup. Not far off from the ice castle."

So, two men who were "not from around here" had been near where Maurice's body was found shortly before he died, and wearing clothes very similar to those Ray and Hammer had worn the night they attacked Mrs. Berns and me.

The letter supposedly written by Orpheus Jackson was looking fishier and fishier.

Chapter 24

Monday morning dawned before I did. I lay under my bed, eyes closed, wondering if I'd left the bathroom faucet on.

Drip. Drip.

Willing myself not to care, I snuggled deeper into my patchwork quilt in the dark safety. The alarm hadn't yet gone off, which meant that I had more time to sleep, though I could tell by the light filtering underneath the bed that I didn't have long.

Drip.

I sighed. The water wasn't going to let me sleep. I rolled to the edge of my bed and cracked one eye. A knurdled pair of socks and yesterday's jeans lay on the floor, inches from my face. I crawled over the fallen clothes, then like a puppet master, hauled my upper body into a sitting position. I ran my fingers through the front half of my hair, stopping when I met resistance.

I'd slept terribly last night, fitful murmurs of rest pockmarked by nightmares of skating over a frozen lake, hundreds of corpses suspended in the ice, and just below those, undulating, predatory sea creatures waiting for the ice to melt enough to drop their prey.

As if that weren't bad enough, the same nightmare had featured a symphony of tiny dogs popping out of holes that erupted like geysers. I'd tried to skate to safety, but the more I scrambled, the farther away the shore moved.

Ugh. I stumbled into the bathroom and tightened both of the sink faucets. Still, I heard the drip. Next I checked the shower faucets, even though the showerhead was dry. The kitchen faucet was good, too. Luna followed me to the center of the house, wagging her tail but also whining.

"What's dripping, sweetie?"

She wagged and padded to the door.

"You want to go outside?" I yanked the front door wide open, hoping the fresh air would clear my mental cobwebs.

There it was—the dripping, louder than ever. It was coming from the side of the house, where all the icicles were in a mad race to see who could thaw first. The snow had the ice-sheen of water melting on itself, and the air smelled like the color green.

I laughed out loud. "Luna! A real January thaw! I guess those farmers knew what they were talking about."

To have a smell other than ion and snow was a gift. I knew it wouldn't last—it couldn't—but in this moment, I was filled with the hope of spring. It pushed away my stress like only nice weather could do. "Woo-hoo!"

Luna dashed outside and ran wild circles over the snowdrifts in the yard, picking up on my energy. I glanced over my shoulder at the living room wall clock. It was 7:12 a.m. I had time to shower, drive to the Fergus hospital to show Gary the letter, and still open the library on time.

I'd arrived empty-handed. I couldn't afford to bring any more treats to people. I barely fit in my jeans as it was. All I carried with me was a fervent wish that Gary's morphine dosage had been lowered.

"Gary?" I said, ducking my head into his hospital room. "It's me, Mira."

He was in the same position as he had been the day before, except his leg was no longer in the air, and he wore a crisp navy-blue Battle Lake Police T-shirt and matching sweatpants. He also wore reading glasses halfway down his nose and held a newspaper. He did not glance my direction.

"Gary?"

He still didn't stir. I stepped into the room. "I have something to show—"

"Halt," he commanded, still not looking at me.

I stopped. I counted to thirty. He didn't say anything. "Did they switch your meds?" I asked.

"I don't know what you're talking about."

"When I came yesterday—" This time I stopped myself with his help. Was that a blush creeping up his neck? "You remember I was here yesterday, right?"

"I was on heavy painkillers. They shouldn't have allowed anyone in." His voice was sharp.

"You were pretty fun," I said, beginning to enjoy myself. "A real laugh riot."

The blush made a full migration to his scalp. He must have had just enough memory of yesterday to be embarrassed. I tamped down a smile and pitched my voice serious. "You made me deputy, Gary. You promised we could start a task force as soon as you were released from the hospital, and that we'd go on stakeouts together. You don't remember any of that?"

He turned the page on the newspaper with such force that it sounded like a slap.

"Gary," I said, making my voice soft and falsely injured. "You told me you loved me."

He glanced at me, stricken. Then he caught my expression, and a fiery rage lit up his eyes. I swear I could have roasted marshmallows over it, which I normally would find funny except for the flash of unguarded emotion I'd just witnessed.

It had been only an instant, but it was enough to unsettle me. Did he have feelings for me? I immediately discarded the idea as impossible. He was drawn to me like a cat to water. I must have seen something else in his expression. Indigestion?

He returned his attention to his newspaper. "Get out."

"My pleasure," I said, adopting a bravado I certainly didn't feel. Whatever emotional roller coaster he was riding made me infinitely uncomfortable. I stepped out of the room, the letter tucked safely inside my jacket.

No way was I going to show it to Gary now.

Chapter 25

The book-return bin was overflowing when I arrived at work. How it could fill up when the library was closed always amazed me. There must have been some sort of traveling virus that compelled mobs of people to bring back all their books at once. Either that, or it was connected to the phases of the moon.

It didn't matter because reshelving books was one of my favorite parts of the gig. It provided for me the same satisfaction as weeding my garden in the summer, letting me sink into the meditation of putting things where they belonged, removing stuff that didn't, and generally restoring order to the universe.

My opening duties took all of twenty minutes. I unlocked the front door three minutes early and stopped by my computer to check email before the first patrons arrived. My inbox was littered with spam offering me big boobs, sexy love mustachioed partners, and access to Jessica Simpson's beauty secrets. If I possessed any one of those, I was sure I wouldn't need the others. I deleted the spam and was left with one legitimate message, from Carter Stone at the Prospect House:

> Mira,
> Sorry you missed your visit in all the commotion, but of course we understand. Drop by anytime for a private tour.
> Carter

I hit "Reply" and wrote that I'd like to visit after work today between five and six o'clock. Might as well get to it lickety-split. Email responded to, and since I didn't yet have clientele or any pressing work, I figured I might as well open up the Cold Case file and call the rest of the Maurice Jacksons in Chicago so I could cross another item off my to-do list. Finding someone who could tell me more about him might shed light on what he had been doing in Battle Lake, and specifically what had gotten him killed.

I made thirteen successful calls—"successful" in that I reached either a Maurice Jackson or the wife or child of a Maurice Jackson— but all thirteen were dead ends, with the Maurices either not owning a library card or never having been to Minnesota. I left a message with the two others, one that had a male voice on the answering machine and the other with a female voice. I left my name, my home number, and said I was calling from Minnesota and looking for Maurice, and then I made a note next to both numbers so I'd know who I had left to talk to. The library was starting to pick up, so I organized my notes before going to work helping people find books, shelving returns, and generally picking up the library.

Mrs. Berns showed up around lunchtime, still seeming a bit off. She didn't want to talk about it, though, so we both kept about our business. I was trying to clean a dusty, musty corner of the textured ceiling, all the little boinkies dropping on my upturned face and shoulders, when I heard a familiar throat clearing.

"Hi, Brad," I said, not glancing down.

Brad—Bad Brad, as I referred to him in my head—had been my boyfriend in Minneapolis when Sunny first asked me to house-sit. We had broken up right before she called, and ending our dating life was one of my smartest moves ever. It was a comical irony that he now lived in Battle Lake. *Good one, Fate. Maybe you could reintroduce into my life every bad choice I've ever made on some sort of rotating schedule, starting with my seventh-grade Ogilvie home perm.*

"Hey, Mira."

I recognized the particular voice he saved for rare moments of sadness. I chose to concentrate instead on delicately wiping the ceiling, imagining the boinkies to be ancient stalagmites and my dustcloth a huge bat weaving in and out.

He sighed, a long, tortured, drawn-out sound.

I did the same. "What is it?" I finally asked, dropping my arms. My hands instantly began to tingle as the blood returned to them.

"What do you mean?"

I rolled my eyes. Bad Brad was a handsome guy, it was true, with a sort of blond Jim Morrison thing going on. Plus, he was in a band, and I'm sorry, but that counted for something. He was also as smart as mud and as deep as a wading pool. And right now, his mascara was smudged, makeup being his new hallmark since he'd formed his latest group, Iron Steel, tagline "twice the metal."

"You look like you've been crying," I said.

His shoulders slumped even farther, and he made a pitiful swipe at his eye. "I think my girlfriend is cheating on me."

I snorted, but at his wounded expression turned it into a cough, which ultimately came together as some sort of donkey honk. Cuz here's the deal: Did I mention that I'd actually *caught* Bad Brad cheating on me? I'd witnessed him giving skin flute lessons after a hunch had me staring down a skylight into a borrowed bedroom, but I never confronted him because I sincerely doubted he could juggle an erection and a confrontation without burning through his wiring. So I'd simply moved without telling him why.

"The vomit returns to the dog," Mrs. Berns said, walking by with a stack of books in her arms. I didn't know if she was referring to me or Bad Brad. I glared at her in case it was me.

"I'm sorry to hear that," I told Brad, mostly truthfully. It was easy to forgive an ex after you realized you never should have dated him in the first place.

"I was going to marry that woman," he said, his face hanging so low that he resembled a bloodhound. Opening for KISS. He was wearing a leather jacket, a beaded scarf, and a full face of makeup, after all.

"What's her name?" I asked, unsurprised at his confession. He'd proposed to me twice while we were dating, once because he felt bad for showing up late and another time because he really liked my dress.

"Catriona. She's an insurance salesman in Alexandria."

"I think you mean 'agent.'"

"No," he said. "She sells insurance. For sure. I've been to her office."

My head hurt. A home perm would actually have been preferable to this conversation. Heck, I'd even wear jelly shoes and acid-washed jeans while Fate put the curlers in. "That sounds really crappy, Brad. I'm sorry for you. But I've got a lot of work to do."

"That's what I'm here about," he said, his face brightening marginally. "I want to hire you to find out what Catriona is up to."

Mrs. Berns cackled from the other side of a bookshelf. I stepped off the ladder I'd been using and stood in front of Bad Brad. I had to crane my neck to look him in the eye. Up close, he smelled like the Calvin Klein Obsession cologne I used to buy him.

"I can't help you," I said. "It'd be a conflict of interest since we used to date."

And you're always broke, and I'd rather roller-skate naked through town than dig around your personal life.

All hope drained out of his face. My heart tugged for a moment, but I held firm. It really was the best thing for him. Plus, Mrs. Berns was now laughing so hard that I couldn't hear myself think.

Bad Brad nodded dejectedly and shambled out without another word. Mrs. Berns walked over to me, and together, we watched him go.

"I'm not saying the boy's dumb," she said, "but I'd be real surprised if he could fart and chew gum at the same time."

I nodded. Truer words. "Do you think his girlfriend's cheating on him?"

"I sure would," she said. "He's got the cute, but that doesn't fill up a woman for long. Anyways, why would you care? He's getting what's coming to him."

"I suppose." I turned my full attention on her. "Hey, why do you have your coat on?"

"I'm punching out early today. I got errands."

"Like what?"

"Like none of your business," she said.

And then she left.

Chapter 26

The driveway leading to the Prospect House had been recently salted, which was good, as the unusual warm-up had slickened the roads. I'd also noticed it was making people overly jumpy, like hibernators who've been awoken prematurely.

I'd caught two separate library patrons—regulars, both of them—leaving without checking out their books first, and one couple making out behind the encyclopedias. When I dropped a heavy book to get their attention, they both jumped up and scurried away, their expressions dazed. The weather was doing something to us. I could feel it in my own blood, which seemed to be flowing a little faster and hotter than usual. Too bad Johnny was out of town tonight, performing in the Cities with the Thumbs.

As I parked my car and climbed out, I realized it was the only one in the Prospect House lot, which gave me the opportunity to pretend like everything I laid eyes on was mine. The rear of the stately, shabby-chic mansion had ornate woodwork with a matching servants' building next door. Maybe I was just returning from a quick jaunt to Italy to check on my vineyard, or a short flight to New York to visit with my stockbroker? Possibly my housekeeper was waiting inside with dinner.

Or maybe I'd slipped on yesterday's jeans this morning, the only pair that hadn't shrunk overnight, and was about to get a tour of a cool old mansion so I could write a story about it. Yeah, that version fit best.

The front door was regal, ornate oak trimmed in hand-carved designs with a huge metal knocker hung in its center. That door, Carter had informed me, was unused because it needed too much work, which was why the path wasn't shoveled. He'd instead requested I enter through the rear, a very plain wooden door that opened just as I reached for its knob.

"Mira James, I presume? Welcome!"

Carter Stone and I had never crossed paths, which in a town the size of Battle Lake was a small miracle. I'd seen photos of him on the *After the Battle* contributors' page, but those had been black-and-white and fuzzy.

In real life, he was a handsome man in his sixties with an aging Peter Fonda circa *Easy Rider* air about him. His face was defined by a bushy gray-brown mustache and smile crinkles at the edges of his brown eyes. He wore a Civil War–style cap, a flannel shirt tucked in dark-blue jeans, and work boots.

"Thank you. And thanks for making time to see me."

"Glad to have you. Any press we can get for the Prospect House is good press."

He led me into the kitchen, which looked and smelled like any farmhouse kitchen, though larger, with a mix of antique vases and modern appliances crowding the cupboards. A movable butcher's block stood in the center of the room, loaded with memorabilia. The far wall displayed reproduction postcards of the Prospect House from the early 1900s.

"These are so pretty," I said, stepping over for a closer look. "Do you have the originals?"

"Thousands," he said. "When I bought the house, every square inch was packed with antiques."

I thought of Gilbert Hullson. "Were the owners hoarders?"

He pushed his hat back and scratched the top of his head before pulling the cap back into place. "I don't think so, at least not in the traditional sense. Everything was neat and organized. It's just that the house had become so expensive to heat that they ended up using it more as a storage space than anything."

"That's terrible."

He shook his head. "Best thing that could have happened, really. I don't have all the rooms cleaned out yet, but the ones that are have given up treasures you wouldn't believe. That's why I turned this into a museum. We've got Battle Lake's history here, and a good piece of the Civil War to boot. Unfortunately," he said, chuckling, "I'm a bit house poor at the moment. I'm hoping to get the place on the historical registry so I can save it, but until then, I've got to keep people coming through so I can afford to heat and update it. That's why I'm offering tours before all the rooms are done."

"How much are you charging?"

"I ask for goodwill donations."

"What?" I shook my head. "How're you going to make money that way?"

He shrugged and led me into the next room, the dining room. "Anyone who wants to should be able to check out what we have here. Like this—see this rug?"

I glanced down at the gorgeous ruby-red Persian nearly as large as the room and patterned with exquisite golds and greens. I nodded.

"I cleared off boxes and found it underneath, good as new. I had an appraiser here who said it's a hundred years old."

Every room he brought me into had a similar story of some treasure discovered. My favorite was the master bedroom, where he'd discovered pearl and jade jewelry from the 1920s that now lay out on a dresser.

"Can I touch them?" I asked. I was drawn to a carnelian necklace, the stone the size of an apricot pit and set in gold. The chain was cleverly crafted into an interlocking leaf pattern.

"Be my guest."

I picked up the necklace. It was surprisingly heavy, the gold so bright yellow that I questioned its authenticity. I flipped it over.

Tiffany & Co. was stamped on the back of the carnelian's setting. My breath caught. "You just leave this jewelry lying out?"

"Yup."

"What if someone steals it?"

"We don't have the money for locked viewing cases yet. If I don't set them out, people won't be able to see them."

"Can I take photographs?"

With his permission, I began snapping pictures of the jewelry, handcrafted furniture (some of it original), and delicately hand-painted wallpaper. The building and collections were amazing, stunning, and right in my backyard. I couldn't believe he let people walk through here unsupervised and for free if they couldn't afford better. Even if everyone were as honest as Carter seemed to believe, what would stop a child from slipping a shiny bauble into her pocket? That thought spurred a memory. "Can I see the attic?"

He stopped, his hand on the third-floor stairway newel. "Afraid not. It's sealed off. I just recently cleared out space in the landing that would take you there."

I called up a picture of the little girl's face as it had appeared in the attic window on Saturday while I'd been skating. I now knew definitively that it had been a sleep-deprived illusion. Yet . . .

"Any rumors of this place being haunted?" I asked. Suddenly, the stairway felt like a threat, the shadows malicious rather than quaint.

He kept walking and I followed, tamping down my fear. It wasn't easy, as I had the feeling he was deliberately avoiding answering me. We'd reached the third floor, which had an Alice in Wonderland feel due to the close walls and six-foot ceilings. He pushed a black button in the wall, and a string of yellow lights lit up. He pointed toward a far corner, past desks and tables and boxes and garbage bags. "That leads to the attic. As for haunted, it's an old house. There's always been rumors. Most of them center on the hanging."

I swallowed hard. "What hanging?"

"A man hung himself on the grounds near the end of the Civil War. Didn't know if he was from the North or the South, didn't know where to send his effects. It was the landowner's daughter, an Offerdahl, who stumbled across the body. She was found staring up at it, if the stories are true, and she was mute from that day forward. She died a year later."

I felt the devil walk up my spine. "I think I've seen enough up here," I said.

"Then let's go to the basement!" His eyes danced. "That's where all the Civil War memorabilia is."

◆ ◆ ◆

Two hours later, my head was full of Civil War facts, dreams of vintage jewelry, and a nagging sense that I was missing an obvious connection. Maybe food would help. I stopped at Mrs. Berns's downtown apartment on my way home to see if she wanted to join me, but no one answered her door. I popped into the Turtle Stew to purchase Tater Tot hotdish with a side of green beans to go. My stomach growled as I waited. Had I eaten lunch? Could I drive and eat hotdish at the same time?

When the waitress handed me the Styrofoam square, it had a satisfying weight. I took a big sniff, enjoying the smell of crispy, salty tots layered over a creamy blend of mushroom soup and ground turkey. I may have moaned a little. I wanted to race home to eat it but decided to stop by the library to pick up a copy of *After the Battle*, so I could further research the Prospect House from the comfort of my couch, my animals near, my belly protruding as it happily digested two pounds of hotdish like a snake with a rabbit.

Unusual for me, my strategy unfolded exactly as planned. An hour later, I'd licked the inside of the Styrofoam clean, settled onto the sofa with Luna at my feet and Tiger Pop on my lap, and was paging through *After the Battle*, an open notepad at my side. I turned the pages slowly, sucked into the town's history against my will.

The book contained photographs of downtown Battle Lake in the 1800s looking exactly like a *Little House on the Prairie* set, and copies of newspaper articles a hundred years old with titles like America's Answer to Humanity's Challenge. There was even a photo of Richard Nixon visiting Glendalough State Park in 1956.

I eventually made it to the page devoted to the Prospect House, which I'd read before, though not with the same perspective as I had now. Unfortunately, it didn't offer any new information, so I perused the newspaper articles looking for anything related to the house. The first I found was a near-identical recounting of the story Carter had told me:

Young Offerdahl Girl Finds Negro Hanging in Woods

Poor Mabel Offerdahl, who lost her mother the day she was born and whose father died a hero in the war, has been dealt another blow. In a gruesome discovery, she found the body of an unidentified man, believed to be a recently freed slave, hanging from an oak tree in the woods behind the Prospect House. The body was in a serious state of decay, leading authorities to believe he had been hanging there for at least two months.

He was dressed in a black jersey sweater, a collared shirt, gray or brown trousers, and new black shoes. The rope he hung himself with was new and much better preserved than his clothes or flesh. He was dangling nearly three feet off the ground, and it is surprising his body was not found earlier, as it was in a well-traversed area, though it is winter.

Unless identifying information is found in the effects or someone comes forward, the hanged man's identity will probably never be known. Mabel is currently under the care of her uncle, Hugh Offerdahl, and his wife, Adelaide Offerdahl. She is being treated by Dr. Olson for debility.

The article was dated March 7, 1865. I read it twice and could still not process the focus on Mabel Offerdahl over the poor man whose life had been lost. I realized it was a different time, but the reminder of just *how* different left me unsettled.

I continued to page through the newspaper section of the book, hoping for a follow-up article. My search seemed fruitless, I thought, as I flipped one page after another and scanned the headlines. Then I turned to the final page, and there it was: Scarlet Fever Epidemic Claims Its First Victim: Mabel Offerdahl. Below that was a photo of an eight-year-old girl with haunted eyes and the exact same heart-shaped face I'd seen in the Prospect House's attic window.

It wasn't a hallucination. She's haunting the house.

A greasy chill crawled down my spine. I suddenly had a strong urge to lock my door, even though that would offer little protection against a ghost. Still. It couldn't hurt. I gently lifted Tiger Pop off my lap and stood, glancing over my shoulder and all around.

"Hey, Luna, come to the door with me." It was all of seven feet away from where I'd been sitting, but that suddenly seemed a great distance.

She was game, though, and stood, tail wagging. I smiled. "Thanks—"

Before I got out her name, her ears flattened to her head, and she growled, a low, primal sound that scared my last wit, the one that'd been holding strong. She was staring at the front door. Her scruff stood in the air, and she crouched.

The room was suddenly charged with a buzzing energy. I was soul-terrified, prickles of heat and cold alternating across my skin.

Just when I thought I'd lose my mind in that humming, horrifying waiting space, a knock struck the front door like Death's knell.

Chapter 27

I squeaked and dropped to the ground. Where that instinct came from, I didn't know. Maybe a fainting goat as a distant ancestor?

I considered my situation from where I crouched. I'd been standing in front of the sofa when the rap on the door came, facing the bay windows, which were jungle-thick with green plants, the closest I could get to gardening in the winter. The plants and my attention on the book explained why I hadn't noticed someone walking to the door, right? For sure it wasn't because my guest was actually an invisible ghost who could reconstitute herself enough to knock when she returned to feed on living souls.

I listened to my shallow breath, the nub of the carpet digging into my sore knee. I was sure there was a perfectly safe, normal, live human on the other side of the door.

Still, all instincts said a dark closet was the best place to be right now.

I was in midscurry, aiming for the bedroom, when the front door opened. Kennie popped her head in, her glance immediately catching me on all fours scuttling across the room.

"Yoo-hoo! You said to come in, didn't you? What're you doing down there? Did you drop something?"

Only my heart and about five pounds of chicken fat. "What are you doing here?"

Kennie cocked her head like a curious bird, an effect enhanced by the feathered Mardi Gras mask she'd pushed to the crown of her platinum hair. She was otherwise sedately dressed, for her—at least the parts of her I could see peeking inside the door. She wore a brown fur stole around her neck, matching gloves, and a black cloth coat. "I told you I was going to stop by, silly. To counsel your pets and your plants?"

Luna amped up her growl, but at a blinding smile from Kennie, she switched to a whine and hunkered down on the ground alongside me. I felt bad for her. She was a smart dog, but like most canines, she didn't know she could prevent many things from happening to her. For example, me putting sunglasses over her tail and taking giggling pictures of her "Gonzo face," or turning her ears inside out and telling her I could see her brains. Tiger Pop, on the other hand, took advantage of the open door to slip outside without Kennie seeing her.

I stood and brushed off my knees. That was when I noticed that her fur stole was wiggling. Luna observed it, too, and her growl returned, low in her throat. I put my hand out to comfort her.

"Are you *wearing* Peter?"

Kennie's face brightened, and she stepped fully into the house, closing the door behind her. She reached around her neck to pull the alert wiener dog off and into her arms. "I sure am," she said, nuzzling his pointy nose. "It's easier than carrying him when he has one of his spells. So, where should I start?"

Resistance only made it stronger. "I don't have many plants, just these in the window," I lied. "And Luna."

Tiger Pop would surely not return while Kennie was still around.

"Perfect." Kennie set Peter on the floor. He wiggled over to Luna, and they sniffed noses. Luna placed her big German shepherd paw on Peter's side and pushed him gently to the ground. Peter stayed there, feet in the air, tongue lolling out. Luna smiled back at him, then went into the kitchen to drink some water.

Kennie ignored both animals, instead focusing on my aloes, jade tree, ferns, ivy, African violets, and ficus. She introduced herself to each one and gave them a chance to say a little something about themselves. At first I was sure it was one of the loopiest things I'd ever seen, but then I started to feel a bit jealous. What if they liked her more than they liked me? Or worse, what if they revealed some of my secrets?

Ohmygod. The loopiness was contagious.

"Will this take long?" I asked Kennie.

She slipped off her coat, revealing a dress constructed of green, purple, and yellow Mardi Gras beads. "Not too long, love. I have a party to go to."

"Mardi Gras isn't until February."

"Mm-hmm," she murmured, staring at a jade tree I'd grown from a clipping. She leaned in close, leading with her ear, as if it were telling her its life story. "It's not a Mardi Gras party."

Under the dress, she wore fishnet stockings and four-inch black heels. I had to admit, she had killer legs. I was positive I didn't want to know any more about the party, however. I knew for a fact that Kennie did things behind closed doors that should never see the light. I'd stumbled upon a houseful of such activities last May.

"Are you almost done?"

She ignored me, staring fixedly at the plants as if her eyes were the sun. I began to clean my kitchen, slamming cupboards a little louder and running water a little longer than necessary. It made me itchy having Kennie in my house, and particularly watching her bestow attention upon something besides herself.

"Know anything about Gary Wohnt?" I asked when I couldn't bear her silence any longer.

"He gets out of the hospital tomorrow," she said. "He'll be behind the desk for a while, but he should be fine. As far as I know, they still have no idea who shot him."

"How about the body in the ice? Do they know any more about him?"

She turned to face me. The lamplight reflected off the lip of her perched mask, giving her eyes a deep-set, glittering cast.

"Maurice Jackson had two gunshot wounds to his chest, but they don't think that's what killed him. He had water in his lungs. You know what that means, right?" She blinked slowly. "Somebody shot him and then shoved him in the lake to drown."

Chapter 28

My restless, fretful, under-bed sleep was fraught with nightmares of pink piñata pigs dressed in Mardi Gras streamers and strung from the ceiling, getting whacked with sticks shaped like wiener dogs. I'd ejected Kennie from the house in less than an hour, but the damage to my psyche was likely permanent.

I rolled out from under the bed and padded straight to the shower, not even bothering to brush my hair. Standing under the hot water, I focused on sending all my stress to the skin level so it could wash off like dirt.

Maurice, the man who'd saved Mrs. Berns and me, had been murdered, and I hadn't been able to locate any information about him beyond the Chicago Public Library card. The next day, police chief Gary Wohnt had been shot in what appeared to be a routine pull-over. In his drug-induced haze, he'd called me beautiful, which was about as desirable as finding a bug crawling in your underwear. That was followed by one of the men who'd threatened me tossing me a copy of an obscure, cryptic letter that I didn't know what to do with.

On the Operation Offerdahl side, I needed to locate Aaron, who was somehow tied to the Prospect House. In addition, I still owed Ron Sims an article on the house, something was up with Mrs. Berns, and Kennie Rogers had spent the better part of an hour cooing to my plants and sending "healing chi waves" into poor Luna's brain.

Did that just about cover it? Wait—almost forgot. I now slept under my bed, and I liked it.

The only normal thing in my life was Johnny, and I hadn't seen him in two days. It was too much. My head was ringing.

And ringing.

It wasn't until the answering machine clicked over that I realized it was actually the phone I'd been hearing. *Let the machine get it.* I stretched my arms under the steaming stream of water. I had a stress knot the size of a tangerine between my shoulder blades.

I listened for the sound of a voice through the bathroom door, but none came.

Must not have been important.

The ringing began again almost immediately. I didn't want to abandon the hot shower for the brisk morning air. Didn't want to dribble all over the floor. Didn't want to face the day. My internal whining kept me through the next cycle of ringing, which ended again as soon as the machine clicked on and started up the second my voice recording stopped. Whoever was calling was not going to be deterred.

Reluctantly, I turned off the water, wrapped a towel around my hair and another under my arms, and trod softly to the kitchen, trying not to slip in my own footprints. I snatched the phone just before the machine got it. "Hello."

Silence.

"Hello?" I strained my ears. Was that crying I heard in the background? "Hello, this is Mira James. Do you need help?"

"Naw, hold on." The female voice had a distinct twang, an authentic southern lilt that Kennie could never manage. "Timothy, you get your sister a bottle, you hear? I'm on the phone."

I stood, water dripping off me and pooling at my feet. I held the towel closed over my chest and balanced the phone in the nook of my shoulder so I had a free hand to crank up the thermostat. Sixty-two degrees was great when you were saving energy but brutal when you were wet and there was snow outside.

"Yeah, is this Mira James?"

"Yup." I refrained from adding "still" on the end of my sentence. The baby's wail grew louder in the background.

"This is Taunita House. You called me yesterday? Left a message looking for my boyfriend, Maurice Jackson?"

My heart picked up, and I looked around the kitchen for a pen and paper. "You're in Chicago?"

"That's where I live, but I'm actually in Minnesota now. I'm trying to track Maurice down. His kids want to see him. So do I."

I paused with my hand halfway to the notepad magnetized to the side of the fridge. I gulped, feeling like I'd just swallowed a cold rock. I'd made the connection, but at what cost? Maurice had kids, at least two. And a partner, who apparently had no idea he was dead. "Can you describe your Maurice Jackson?"

I heard the shrug over the phone line. "About five ten, hundred forty-five pounds. Skinny sucker, skinnier than me. Turns twenty-four in February. Kept his hair trimmed short, earring in his left ear. Was wearing a green Land's End parka I bought him for Christmas when he left. He took off three weeks ago to look up some old relatives in Minnesota, he said. He hasn't picked up in over three days, though, and his work leave has about dried up. It's time for him to stop this nonsense and come home, but since he clearly doesn't have the sense for that, I'm coming to get him."

The rock dropped into my stomach. That described the Maurice I'd helped at the library—and whose corpse I'd stumbled over—to a T. "Have you tried all his friends?"

"I have. And now I'm trying you. In your message you said you were looking for him, too. Why?"

The crying in the background had stopped. Now I heard a giggle. "How many kids do you and Maurice have?"

"Two," she said impatiently. "Timothy is three years. Alessa was born a year ago last Christmas. Maurice said it was his present for me. I told him he better get me something that makes less noise next holiday."

She laughed ruefully, but then her voice grew serious. "I miss him. Have you seen him?"

I couldn't do it. I couldn't ram the truth into her ear with her kids laughing in the background. I told her the version that I could bear. "I live in Battle Lake, northwest of the Cities? Maurice came into the library where I work last week. He left his Chicago library card, and I was hoping to track him down."

"Well, that's some service," she said wryly. "If he stops by again, tell him Taunita and the babies want him to call, OK?"

"Will do," I said, feeling like a monster for not coming clean.

I kept that feeling with me as I finished getting ready that morning, and it was hung so thickly over me that I almost walked out of the house without noticing my plants. Something was off with them.

It took a lot of squinting before I realized what it was: they looked healthier than they ever had.

Chapter 29

The parking spot immediately in front of the Fortune Café was open, which was the first good thing that'd happened since I'd woken up. I steered my Toyota snugly between a Ford and a Chevy pickup, one rusty and the other spanking new but road-splattered and sporting a Ducks Unlimited sticker in the rear window.

A handful of people on the street took mincing steps as they went about their day, trying their hardest to stay upright, as the two previous days' brief thaw—warmer during the day, freezing at night—had turned the sidewalks into treacherous frozen sheets. I chose to not lift my feet off the ground, instead skating over the top of the greenish-black ice.

When I yanked open the café door, I was immediately awash in the warm scent of freshly ground dark roast and cinnamon scones, and the happy burble of gathering people. Buddy Holly crooned softly in the background.

I yanked off my mittens, tapped the winter from my boots, and got in line. I didn't recognize any of the half dozen or so people sprinkled around the main room, though I spotted Farah Nordman, co-owner of the bead store, making her way into the computer / library / board game back room with a steaming mug in one hand and what appeared to be a cherry Danish in the other. My stomach growled so loud that the woman in front of me turned and flashed a smile.

I grinned back, embarrassed. When my turn came, I knew exactly what I wanted. "Everything bagel, toasted, with Greek olive cream cheese and a slice of fresh tomato, a large green tea with honey and soy milk, and maybe a cherry Danish for later?"

"Hi to you, too," Sid said, grinning. She owned the café along with her partner, Nancy. Nancy was not a people person by nature but was a brilliant pastry chef and kept mainly to the kitchen. Sid was friendly and never seemed to become stressed, no matter how many people were in line. She'd helped me through a tough patch in August, and we'd been fast friends ever since. "You must be hungry."

I blushed for the second time in under four minutes. "Sorry. You seem so busy. I didn't want to waste your time with chitchat."

"Like talk about a police chief who was shot, or a mayor with a strange new business, for example?"

I pointed my chin at the gorgeous row of plants lining her front window. "You obviously don't need Kennie's help. I've never seen your plants look better."

"Kennie *was* here," Sid said, sounding as incredulous as I felt. "I think that's why they look so good." She turned her hands palm up. "Maybe she finally found her thing."

I was surprised to feel another pang of jealousy. Gardening had been *my* thing. I loved digging my hands into the dirt in the summer, dropping seeds into the thick black earth, watering them, mulching them, petting the soft shoots when they first popped up. Come winter, I'd started a mini greenhouse herb garden in the back bedroom, which I'd intentionally hidden from Kennie. I felt the envy sprout and took a deep, deliberate breath. Really, what was there to be jealous about? The more love the plants received, the better.

"Maybe," I said agreeably. Well, almost agreeably. OK, I was still pissy.

Sid continued to talk as she poured the hot water into the travel mug I'd brought and popped the two halves of my bagel into the toaster. "Know anything about Gary?"

"Kennie said he's getting out of the hospital today, but she didn't know anything about who might have shot him."

"As uptight as he can be, it'll be nice to have him back, what with all the robberies." She ducked her head into the counter fridge and came out with a tub of cream cheese.

"Robberies?" My stomach growled again. The Fortune's cream cheese was amazing, the perfect blend of creaminess accented with salty slices of green and black olives.

Sid nodded. "Empty cabins around the lake. Whoever is doing it is taking TVs and computers, some kitchen appliances if they look valuable, I guess. They're not damaging the cabins, except for the new one that went up on the north side of Silver Lake. Over in your neck of the woods. They trashed that one."

I knew the area well. I'd had a run-in with a scalped corpse there a few months back. The memory made me shudder.

Sid glanced at me sympathetically, as if she were reading my mind. She slid the wax paper–wrapped bagel into a small brown bag, and stacked a cherry Danish and a lemon Danish on top of that, another thin sheet of wax paper separating the two. She winked. "For lunch."

"Thanks," I said, taking the bag and sliding her a five. The food was ridiculously inexpensive. "Wait! I almost forgot. I owe Curtis some treats. Can you make up a bag for me to take to the Sunset?"

Another five dollars later, I headed for the exit with two bags in one hand and my travel mug filled with steaming tea in the other. I was in the process of trying to open the Fortune's door when it swung open. In walked Mrs. Berns.

"I have had just about the most terrible day of my life," she said to me, as if she'd expected me to be standing exactly where I was.

"What happened?" I looked her up and down, checking for an injury or torn clothing.

She scowled. "Is that any of your business?"

"What? You just . . . forget it." I would have thrown my hands in the air if they weren't so full. Something was clearly still amiss with Mrs. Berns, and she was going to tell me in her own sweet time. "Are you coming to work today?"

She stretched her arms. "Doesn't sound too exciting. What else can you offer?"

I sighed. "I'm touring the new microbrewery in Swederland as soon as I close the library. It's part of a small case I got from the law firm."

"Now you're cooking with Crisco! Pick me up at five o'clock."

She held the door open for me as I eased out and slid-walked to my car. I balanced the bags and the tea on the Toyota's roof and brought them in with me as soon as I had the door open.

I let my car reheat while I devoured half my bagel, loving the chewiness of the fresh-baked roll, the cream cheese oozing out the sides, the sharp earthiness of the tomato the perfect foil for it all. I polished off the second half before I reached the nursing home. I ran the treats in to a grateful Curtis, then pulled into the library parking lot fifteen minutes early.

All in all, I'd had worse mornings. At least, I had until I saw Bad Brad standing outside the library door, hands in pockets, head hung like a dog on the way to the vet.

Chapter 30

Rather than speak to Bad Brad, I acted as if he weren't there at all. He followed me into the library like a droopy shadow and stuck close to my side as I went about my duties. It got so I almost forgot he was there, until he chose to speak.

"Have you looked at her SixDegrees page?"

"Whose?" Of course I knew who he was talking about.

"My girlfriend's."

"Why would I look at your girlfriend's SixDegrees page?"

"I thought you'd change your mind about the conflict of interest and help me out."

"Nope."

I flicked on the front desk computer and stepped from behind the counter to switch on the public ones. When I returned to the front, I saw Brad was standing at my desktop, clicking away.

"What are you doing? You can't be on that."

His shoulders dropped lower, if that was possible. He pointed at the screen. "See for yourself."

I sighed. "If I look at your girlfriend's page, will you leave?"

"Yes."

I dragged my feet around the counter and stood beside him. He'd pulled up a purple-rimmed page on the computer. It featured a head-shot of a pretty blonde. A lake panorama was spread out behind her head. Her name, according to the page, was Catriona Lehmkuhl. "I don't see anything."

"That's the problem." He pointed to a white box under her photo that declared her birthday and that she was female. "Why doesn't it say she's in a relationship?"

I squinted at the screen. "It's supposed to say that?"

"It can, if the person chooses to make that part of their status."

Wow. I did not like this new world, where there were so many more ways to be embarrassed. My brain flitted through some possibilities. A person could break up with you on SixDegrees, and the whole world would know before you did. And after the breakup, you could return to your ex's page and check out what they were up to, maybe see if they'd moved on before you had. It was enough to make a person crack.

Thank goodness I had dependable, sane, loyal Johnny. The thought of him sent a delicious sparkle across my nerve ends. Man, that boy was good-looking. And an amazing kisser, who also smelled clean, laughed at my jokes, cooked amazing meals, and picked up after himself. Why hadn't I immediately rescheduled our interrupted Saturday night date? I added him to my mental to-do list.

"Are you having a hot flash?" Brad asked, studying me. "Your face is all red."

I flushed deeper. Last spring, it had taken him two weeks to notice I'd moved to Battle Lake, but here he was being all Amazing Kreskin with my arousal state. "I think I'm allergic to SixDegrees."

He minimized the window. "Will you take the case? Please, Mira. For me. I love this woman."

I had a million retorts to that, but none I could summon in the face of his obvious heartbreak. "Fine," I muttered.

"Thank you!" He bundled me into his arms and kissed the top of my head. "I owe you one. Whatever you need, you just tell me."

"I need you to leave so I can get some work done."

"Great! All these books make me nervous, anyhow." He wrinkled his nose. "What if my Iron Steel fans see me in a *library*?"

"That will surely set their tongues a-wagging," I said dryly. "Now, be off. I'll get in touch if I find anything."

"You're a good person, Mira," he said, before the door closed pneumatically behind him.

I watched him disappear around a corner. I had zero romantic feelings for the guy, but maybe we could be friends. His case would have to wait, though. I pulled out my Cold Case file and retrieved the letter supposedly written by Orpheus Jackson and smoothed it on my desk.

18 January 1865

Dear Octavia:
I wish I could write with better news. In Minnesota, they do not believe the messages I bring. I do not think I can stay here. I pack my bags to return home to you, my dearest wife, tomorrow. Should anything happen to me, look to the tunnel of justice.

With a heart that beats only for you,
Orpheus Jackson

If the letter was, in fact, real, I had a hunch that Maurice had believed he was related to Orpheus. Was this somehow connected to the relatives Maurice had told Taunita he was coming to Minnesota to find? I strode back to the local shelf, where Maurice had spent many hours the week before his death. I paged through all the references, looking for notes or dog-ears, and tipped them all sideways, hoping something would fall out.

Nothing.

But my Cold Case file was thin, and I sensed there was a connection—real or imagined—between Maurice and Orpheus. Using the search terms "Orpheus Jackson" and "1800s," I didn't come up with a thing. When, on instinct, I threw "Barnaby Offerdahl" into the mix, though, I was brought to a full article on the Battle of Honey Hill, a Civil War clash that took place in South Carolina on November 30, 1864.

O. Jackson was listed as a freeman from the North serving in the Fifty-Fourth Massachusetts, and B. Offerdahl as a landowner in the First Minnesota Artillery Battery. The battle was a failed expedition under Major General John P. Hatch. The Confederates were too well entrenched to rout, and the Union lost 89 men, with 629 wounded and 28 missing.

The date on Orpheus's letter suggested he'd been one of the Union survivors, but was this the battle that'd killed Barnaby, and if so, what did that have to do with Orpheus? And why had Orpheus traveled to Minnesota in 1865? Was he bearing a message from Barnaby? If so, what could the message possibly have to do with Maurice, nearly 150 years later?

I had more questions than answers. To save myself the head-ache of carrying them spinning in my head, I wrote them down and shoved them into my Cold Case folder before moving on to Operation Offerdahl and the search for a present-day member of the family.

I returned to my database and set a wider search, looking for anyone who shared the surname. There were tens of thousands of Offerdahls, but when I narrowed it to Minnesota, there were far fewer. When I tightened it even further, adding a search for criminal history, I found a Gregory and Patrice Offerdahl. A quick call to Curtis verified these had been the names of Aaron's parents. They were both mostly crime-free except for a line of bounced checks following them all the way to Phoenix, Arizona.

My records showed Patrice had died a decade earlier, and that Gregory still owned seven prime lakefront acres abutting or near the Prospect House, but little else. Gregory was seventy-eight and currently resided at 1923 Orangetree Lane, Phoenix, Arizona.

I printed out the records and got to work running the library.

My morning passed in a blink. I finished four special orders, including tracking down and ordering a nonfiction book on abominable snowmen and another on tapping into your psychic ability. I watered the plants and dusted their leaves, wondering if I should have Kennie visit as a favor to a snake plant that was looking yellow and tragic around the edges. I showed an elderly man how to access the internet and watched happily as he began researching classic car restoration. For lunch, I slammed both Danishes and promised myself I'd start working out just as soon as nature joined my team and melted the rest of the snow.

I spent the afternoon preparing the library's February budget, helping patrons check out books, planning activities for next week's children's hour, answering emails requesting use of the library's public meeting room, and updating the library website.

By the time closing rolled around, I felt like I'd run a marathon. I did a last walk-through of the stacks to make sure I'd shooed everyone out and no surprises had been left behind before running across town to pick up Mrs. Berns. I was hoping we could make it to O'Callaghan's for the six o'clock tour.

My car idled outside her apartment building. I honked, hoping to save myself a trip into the cold air. I fumbled with the radio knob while I waited, wishing, as I always did, for something more than country or Journey. I settled on "Saturday in the Park." My car was too old for a CD player, and I didn't have the heart to carry mixed tapes with me. I took what I could get.

A flash of color caught my eye. I looked over to see Mrs. Berns leaving the building wearing a full German getup. She carried her own massive beer stein. When she slipped into the car, she smelled like face powder and dish soap.

"Lederhosen?"

She held the stein in the air, a broad smile on her face. *"Prost!"*

I smiled back. I couldn't help it. She was lovely, with newly apricot-tinged white hair curling around her ears, penciled-in eyebrows, and watery blue eyes rimmed by uneven green eye shadow. Her mouth was a perfect heart of coral lipstick. The deep lines of her face were highlighted by the wide grin.

"I think the brewery supplies cups with their samples," I offered, indicating her stein.

"Pah. Probably little Dixie cups. I need a woman-size taste to know if I'll like it or not."

We drove in companionable silence for three or four miles. At least, I thought it was companionable, until Mrs. Berns punched me in the arm.

"What was that for?"

"You didn't ask me what's wrong."

"I asked you a couple days ago, and then the day after that! You nearly bit my head off."

She nodded agreeably. "That's how you know I care."

I tapped my signal to turn right and rubbed my arm. "Your love kinda hurts."

"Hmph." She shook her head.

"All right, I'll bite. What's wrong?"

"What makes you think something's wrong?"

I groaned in frustration. "Besides you asking me to ask you just now? Well, you've been a Crabby Appleton since you made that Al-Anon crack at Matthew's birthday party, and it seems like you're avoiding me."

She didn't respond. I tossed her a tentative sideways glance and was horrified to see fat tears rolling down the canvas of her face. I pulled over immediately and pushed the button for my emergency lights. I gathered her into my arms, amazed at how fragile she felt, like a grounded sparrow.

She pushed me away almost immediately. Almost. "I'm not a big baby. You can let me go. I just had something in my eye. An onion, I think."

I crossed my arms. "I'm not going anywhere until you tell me what's up."

"Fine." She pulled a handkerchief out of her chest freezer–size purse and blew her nose. "My husband was a drinker. He was a good man who paid the bills and never raised his hand to me or the children, but once his work was done, he'd drink whiskey until he passed out."

Sounded familiar. I wondered why Mrs. Berns hadn't told me any of this before. She knew all about my dad.

"When he finally died ten years ago," she continued, "I didn't know what to do with myself. I loved him, of course, but between taking care of him and raising my kids, I'd never had my own life. I started going to Al-Anon and moved willingly into the nursing home because that's what my kids wanted. Then one day, about when you came to town, I realized it isn't what *I* wanted. I wanted to finally be my own person. So I rented an apartment and started living my life in the open. Turns out I like to dance, and sing, and kiss men half my age. Hell, I *love* it. I love everything about my life."

"Then what's wrong?"

She tried to set the beer stein on the dash, but it was too tall. She sighed. "It's my grandkids. They're coming to visit this week."

I had met five of Mrs. Berns's kids, most of whom lived within an hour or two drive and another who lived in Arizona, but never her grandkids. "Isn't that good news?"

"They haven't met the real me. They remember me from when their grandpa was still alive, or from me visiting them. They haven't seen me in my natural habitat."

I rubbed her arm encouragingly. "But you don't care what anyone thinks of you!"

"I guess I do." She laid her hands in her lap. "I've decided it's easier to pretend I'm someone else for a couple days, but that decision isn't sitting well."

It took me a minute to digest this. Mrs. Berns was pure confidence, or so I'd thought. She was everything I wanted to be when I grew up. "How old are your grandkids?"

"Trevor is a year or two older than you. Michelle is twenty-seven. They live in Arizona. The last time they visited, I was in the Sunset and plenty happy to act a role for them. It's what grandparents do, so all you kids don't know we have better sex and take better drugs than you could ever dream of."

Her words carried the ring of truth. "Are they brother and sister?"

"Yup. Only one of my kids had kids, which should tell you something. They're coming because Michelle is being transferred to Fargo, and Trevor wants to help her move and visit family."

I thought back to July, when Mrs. Berns had faux-kidnapped the adult male mascot from the Chief Wenonga Days parade. She'd had her cap guns slung low at her side and he'd been dressed like a stereotypical Indian when they'd last been spotted. A friend had been about to file a missing person's report on the mascot's behalf when I'd discovered the two of them in a very compromising position. How'd she ever kept a personality like that under wraps?

I exhaled loudly and patted her arm. "They'll love you exactly as you are, hun. In fact, I'd be pretty surprised if they didn't know more about the real you than you think."

She studied my face thoughtfully. A quiet moment stretched out between us. "You are a wise, dear friend, Mira. I don't know what I'd do without you."

I felt a tear warm my eye. "Really?"

"No." She fluffed her hair. "That was pure horseshit. You know what I'd do without you? I'd see fewer dead bodies, that's what. What I was doing there was a little thing called acting, and I happen to be very good at it. Now drive." She smacked the dashboard. "I've done enough whining. It's time to soldier up and accept the inevitable."

I put the car into first gear. "You gonna show them the real Mrs. Berns?"

"I'll let you know when I decide. And if you tell anyone about my moment of weakness, I swear to God I'll tattoo a mustache on your face in your sleep."

"I love you, too," I said, smiling inside.

Chapter 31

There were plenty of signs pointing the way to O'Callaghan's, all of them featuring a green shamrock and the promise of "the best beer brewed in Minnesota." I believed that title was about as significant as being the "tallest leprechaun," but that might have been an unfounded stereotype.

We took what was promised to be the "final turn before O'Callaghan's" and found ourselves in a farm's circular driveway. The grounds consisted of a cute, slanted-roof farmhouse, a red barn and two matching outbuildings, and a tow truck with the words TYRANNOSAURUS WRECKS painted on the side.

"T. Wrecks? This can't be right," I said. I drove up to the house, intending to turn around when I noticed the man leaning on the porch rail wearing lined Carhartt coveralls. He appeared to be staring at a lone cow in a pasture about three hundred yards away.

"Is he cute?" Mrs. Berns said, squinting in his direction.

"Hard to tell from here. I'm going to ask him where the brewery is."

"I'm coming with," she said. "It's time to diversify my dating menu. Besides, remember that you're on the job. You might need backup."

I doubted it. The guy was maybe five eight, a little paunchy. In his sixties, judging by the way he hunched and the bits of gray I spotted sneaking out of his John Deere cap. Mrs. Berns got jazzed about "working cases" with me when she had a chance, though, so I didn't stop her.

"Hello?" I said as we approached the porch.

He must have heard the car pull up and the doors slam, and he most certainly heard my greeting. He didn't turn. What was he concentrating on so intently?

"Sir? We're looking for O'Callaghan's. Are we close?"

By way of answer, he pointed at the cow. She was your standard black and white, standing in a barren snowscape broken only by a metal pole and a heated water barrel. "You see that?"

"Yes," I said, exchanging a woo-woo look with Mrs. Berns. "The cow?"

"Not just any cow," he said, shaking his head. "She is my nemesis. Kicks me when I try to milk her, breaks free of the fence every day and out of the barn every night no matter how often I mend both, and moos so much I want to cut my own ears off. I want to catch her to sell her, but she's too smart. See that metal pole? I coated it with salt. Figured she'd lick it and I'd get her good. But she won't lick it. She just stares at it."

Mrs. Berns walked around to the farmer's front and flicked him on the head. "That's about the batshittiest plan I've ever heard. Why don't you just corral her in the barn?"

He stepped back, surprised. "I can't. She slips away."

"You're getting what you deserve, then," Mrs. Berns said, hands on hips. "Now where's the brewery?"

The front door of the farmhouse slammed open, and a woman dressed in head-to-toe winter camo and holding a speargun-looking weapon tromped onto the porch. "You folks lost?"

"Yep," I said, taking an involuntary step back.

Mrs. Berns did the opposite. She leaned forward and touched the gun. "That a paintball gun?"

"Vortex barrel Autococker," the woman said proudly.

"What're you hunting?" Mrs. Berns asked, scratching her head.

"Hunters."

A crafty smile crossed Mrs. Berns's face. "Only thing legal to hunt right now is wolves."

"Exactly," the woman said. "I have no problem if someone wants to hunt for meat. If you're going to hunt for sport, though, prepare to have the tables turned." She held her weapon in the air.

"I'm in!" Mrs. Berns said.

The woman's face lit up. "The more the merrier. I've got an extra gun inside. Name's Vienna, by the way."

I stared in disbelief. "You can't hunt hunters! They've got real guns."

"I wear orange when I go out," the woman said, "and I'm in a deer blind."

"That is the worst idea *ever*," I said, "and I've heard some pretty bad ideas." I looked to the farmer for support, but he'd returned his full attention to the cow in the field, who was in turn staring at the salty metal pole as if it were a Gordian knot.

"I took a wrong turn and ended up in Cuckoo City, Iowa," I said, shaking my head in disbelief. "And I thought Battle Lake could get weird."

"You said you were looking for O'Callaghan's," Vienna said. "Turn's a hundred feet past our driveway. Their land abuts ours. You can't miss it, once you know where to look. Hopefully when they get the new sign up yonder, people'll stop pulling in here."

"Are you coming, Mrs. Berns?"

"Pick me up on your way back," she said, tugging on the orange vest the woman handed her. "I'm going to seize this moment."

I felt the distinct stress knot between my shoulder blades expanding to the size of a grapefruit as I drove away. It was grappling toward my arms, head, and lower back like an octopus after prey. Deep breathing didn't touch it.

Maybe beer would.

I'd gone on the wagon in August and slid off a couple times since. I didn't want to go down the same path as my dad. Unfortunately, I'd pinballed between exactly reliving his drinking habits and being completely dry. Neither seemed to work for me, and so last month I'd decided to try drinking like a normal person. It was a hard thing to gauge in a county where consuming alcohol qualified as a winter sport, but my goal was to only imbibe socially and never have more than two at a sitting. I had no interest in ever being drunk again. I'd made too many bad choices in that state.

The second road past the T. Wrecks driveway led me directly to O'Callaghan's, a sprawling log lodge planted next to a factory building. Both were tucked behind a hill, making them invisible from the road. A dozen or so vehicles peppered the parking lot in front of the lodge, and a large banner with white letters was strung over the door, WELCOMING ALL TO O'CALLAGHAN'S MICROBREWERY!

Just inside the door, a woman in her early twenties with a wide smile handed me a kelly-green sticker in the shape of a shamrock. "Are you here for our six o'clock tour?"

"I am." I gaped at the enormous interior. It was one big room, with tills lining the wall directly inside the door, a shopping area in the middle, a full bar in the back left, and tables in the back right. The ambience was half–box store, half–Irish pub.

"Wonderful! Stick the shamrock on your coat, and you can wait over by the rear door with the rest of the folks."

I followed her finger to the other side of the lodge, where I counted eight people—two couples, two kids, and two college-age men—wearing green shamrocks and standing by a metal door marked TOUR.

"That's quite a few people for a Tuesday," I said.

"We've been very popular," she said, her smile widening.

Her name tag read Aednat. I pointed at it. "Is that Irish?"

"Yup. It's pronounced 'ey-nit.'"

"Do your parents own the brewery?"

She laughed. "I wish. We have the option of taking Irish names for our shifts."

I thought back to the woman I'd spoken with on the phone when I initially called O'Callaghan's. "Does everyone do it?"

"That's up to us," she said, "but you'll find out all about it on the tour. It looks like they're leaving, so you better skedaddle!"

She was right. A man in his late thirties dressed all in green and wearing a leprechaun's hat had appeared at the rear door. He must have said something funny, because the tour group started laughing. I threaded my way through the racks of O'Callaghan's sweatshirts, mugs, bottle openers, and knickknacks, tossed a glance at the carved-wood bar on the far side of the lodge backlit by the crackling fireplace, and tried to blend into the tour.

"Welcome!" the guide said when I reached the group. "What's your name and where are you from?"

Judging by the expectant looks I was getting, I assumed everyone had already introduced themselves. "Mira, from Battle Lake."

That was the first time I'd uttered those words all in the same sentence—I was born and had grown up in Paynesville and spent most of my twenties in Minneapolis before relocating to Battle Lake. I was pleased with how comfortable it had sounded rolling off my tongue.

I indicated his name tag, too far away for me to read. "And yours?"

He looked down. "Niall," he said. "Pronounced like the river in Egypt."

I wondered if he also went by Aaron Offerdahl. The single photo I'd seen had been fuzzy. Niall's hair was brown, at least what I could see of it peeking out from under his hat, but he did not have a spike through his right eyebrow and appeared about fifteen years too old. The spike could have easily been removed, however, and if he was heavy into drugs, that could have added years to his face. I vowed to get to the front of the group at some point during the tour so I could inspect him up close.

Niall led us outside. It was growing dark, but the path was lit by white twinkle lights that sparkled beautifully off the iced snow. The drifts were so perfectly formed that the grounds behind the lodge looked like the top of a lemon meringue pie.

It was cold, the brief thaw over, but above zero with no wind, so the short walk to the factory was pleasant. Niall was lecturing about how the O'Callaghan family—originally from Ireland but based out of

Chicago in the past eighty years—had been searching the Midwest for the perfect location for their microbrewery. They'd made their money in the carpet business but wanted to build something more creative as well as return to their family roots.

When their Realtor found the hundred acres just south of Swederland a little over a year ago, they realized it would be perfect. The lakes area brought in thousands of tourists every month, taxes were low, and labor would be cheap. They bought the land, started building immediately, and had begun distributing their beers and offering tours a month earlier.

The company grounds, he said, were made up of the lodge we'd just left and the brewery we were about to enter, plus the dorms and the O'Callaghan family home on the other side of the far hill.

"Dorms?" I said, interrupting his speech.

"Yes," he said, smiling. "Room and board are part of our employment package. The dorms are like our own little village. Plus, we get health care and money for college."

I narrowed my eyes. "That sounds too good to be true."

He chuckled. "That's what I thought, too. The O'Callaghans figure if they are good to their employees, we'll stay on and work hard. And they're right. They treat us like family."

He fell back into his spiel. Right now, O'Callaghan's was bottling four different beers: a seasonal ale, their signature dark, and two lagers. The recipes had been passed down from generation to generation. Apparently, the original O'Callaghans of County Galway had been whiskey distillers and brewers. Though it was too early to tell how the current iteration of the beers would be received, early buzz was good, no pun intended.

Niall held open the factory door. The warm scent of yeast and something sour washed over us. I was the last to pass the guide and stared right into his face. I was disappointed to see no visible hole in his right eyebrow.

"Say," I said, before slipping inside, "can you tell me what time my friend Aaron Offerdahl's shift starts? I was really hoping to run into him."

Niall didn't skip a beat. "Aaron Offerdahl? That doesn't sound very Irish." He tipped his hat and moved to the front of the crowd.

"This is the main factory." He spread his arms to indicate the Wonka-esque room filled with enormous copper vats and tubes that ran to and fro and all the way to the top of the three-story room. He walked us through the malting, milling, and mashing, passing around a test tube of hops for us to inspect. Then he explained the lautering, boiling, fermenting (which accounted for the faintly sour bread smell), conditioning, filtering, and finally, packaging.

The packaging area was a separate part of the factory set up exactly like I assumed Laverne and Shirley's workplace had been arranged. The label maker was the most fascinating part, turning an ordinary brown bottle into a tiny, perfect, utile piece of art.

"Who designs all your labels?" I asked over the din of the operating factory.

"I do," he said, his face lit with pride. "I used to do graphics work for the carpeting company in Chicago, and now I design the labels, the marketing materials, everything." He bowed. "And lead tours, of course. At least until we expand our line. Many of the employees here multitask."

"Cool," I said, accepting the sample label Niall handed me. It was for O'Callaghan's seasonal beer, called Castle. The image on the front looked familiar. It took me a few beats to recognize that it was a cartoon version of the O'Callaghan's-sponsored ice castle on West Battle. I wondered how the bad publicity was affecting business, but it seemed rude to ask.

Niall finished up the tour, fielding questions about beer flavors (they'd add more in the summer if the current stock sold well), whether they were hiring (not at this time, but applications were always welcome), and how long it took to brew a single bottle of beer from the malting stage to the bottling (twenty-two to forty days on average, depending on what type of beer it was).

When all the questions had been answered, Niall asked who was ready to try some beer. Apparently, everyone but the two children had come for exactly that reason, and the group headed toward the exits en masse. I lagged behind so I could sing "Schlemiel! Schlimazel! Hasenpfeffer Incorporated" under my breath and snatch another label from the on-deck machine feed, this one far more interesting to me.

The colors had initially attracted me—deep blues and purples with a flash of silver—but it was the name that hitched my breath: Sutler's Civil War Ale. I thought immediately of the Prospect House, and Orpheus Jackson. The label's spidery font was old-fashioned, and the words were undercut by the sharp edge of a bayonet. The overall effect was a peculiar cross between edgy and quaint, but somehow it worked.

I stuffed the label into my coat pocket and caught up with the rest of the tour. I passed a door I hadn't noticed before and tried the handle on impulse. Locked. The room must have contained fragile materials or been where they hid the garbage.

The cold outside was bracing after the brew factory's steamy closeness. A soft winter breeze had picked up, sending tiny eddies of snow dust over the frosted drifts and making the twinkle lights glitter magically. The tour group was nearly inside when I caught up with them. Niall was holding the door. He tapped my shoulder lightly as I passed by him.

"Did you get lost?" His smile seemed genuine, but his eyes carried an emotion I couldn't read, more than a question but not quite a warning.

"Sorry," I said. It wasn't really an answer, but I'd discovered the word was a ticket out of most minor social infractions. I plucked my two beer coupons from his outstretched hand and made my way through the main lodge and into the bar in the rear.

Although the lodge itself was one open room, the bar had been cleverly designed with its own faux-cobblestone roof to make it seem like a separate, authentic Irish pub within the larger space. My tour group had already bellied up to the buttery wood counter and were enjoying their first drink. The kids were sucking down root beers.

I considered whether I should imbibe. I absolutely loved beer, but I didn't know if this counted as a social situation. Plus, I didn't want to get schlitzed before I drove. A couple sips couldn't hurt, though, right? In fact, I was almost obligated as part of my research. I slid the blue coupon to the bartender when he strolled to my end of the bar. He was in his forties, too old to be Aaron, and his name tag read Turlough.

"A sample of the Civil War Ale, please."

He shot me a quizzical glance. "Excuse me?"

I almost pulled out the label. "Sutler's Civil War Ale. I saw the labels in the factory."

He smiled and handed me a menu. "I'm afraid that one will never see the light of day. Something in the recipe was off. Here's a list of what we do offer."

Peculiar. You'd think they'd test the recipe before bothering to print out labels. I studied the menu. "I'll try the chocolate stout, please." Beer that tasted like chocolate? Hi, really good idea.

He opened the tap into a miniature mug that I assumed they used only for tastings. The beer pulled out deep and creamy with a gorgeous head. When he set it in front of me, the smell hit me first: bitter, dark, and rich. I closed my eyes and inhaled. When I opened them, he was still standing there with his hands on his hips, watching me like a proud parent.

"The chocolate stout is my favorite," he said.

I smiled and held the glass to my lips, smelling it through my open mouth before tipping back the glass and letting it wash in. The flavor was transcendent, dark-chocolate notes on my tongue, a light carbonation on the sides of my mouth, and a deeper, wiser flavor in the back of my throat. I swallowed and moaned.

"Amazing," I sighed.

He nodded in satisfaction. "You can see why we guard the recipes so carefully."

"Where can I buy some?" I swiveled in my stool. I hadn't noticed beer for sale amid all the other O'Callaghan's merchandise.

He began wiping mugs, keeping one eye on his other customers. "Minnesota law. Breweries can't sell their bottled beer on-site."

"What?" I drew the chocolate stout closer to me. This might be all I'd get for a while.

He shrugged. "Something about distribution lobbyists needing their cut, I think. You can buy it in the area liquor stores, but we can't sell you anything but growlers, and we don't have the space or license for that. Only samples."

A more ridiculous law I had yet to hear, but the delicious headiness of the beer might have been fueling my righteousness. Everyone should be able to drink this nectar wherever they wanted. It was filling my empty stomach with a nice bubbly bliss. Actually, I decided on the spot that it was dark and thick enough to count as a meal. I finished all four ounces and handed him the mug.

"What would you like to try next? Our pale ale is very popular."

I shook my head. "No more for me, thanks. I have to drive." I started to walk away and then turned back. "Oh, hey, I almost forgot. Can you give this to Aaron Offerdahl for me?" I held out the first item I pulled from my pocket, a Turtle Stew receipt for the hotdish I'd ordered the other night.

Turlough smiled amiably and reached for it. He almost had it before his face tightened. He withdrew his hand and shot a glance toward Niall, who was talking to Aednat at the front door. Niall wasn't looking, and Turlough turned his back to me to help another customer.

That was all right. I'd gotten what I'd come for.

Chapter 32

I sat in my idling car outside the T. Wrecks farmhouse and honked my horn. I wasn't sure if Mrs. Berns would be back from her expedition, but I hoped so. I was relieved when she popped her head out, waved at me to hang tight, disappeared back inside the house, then ran to the car five minutes later with her arms full of books.

"Holy moly," she said, hopping in next to me. "What a busy afternoon!"

"What's that smell?" I sniffed her hair. The odor reminded me of woodsmoke, but sweeter.

She shrugged. "I'm an old lady. It could be any number of things. Check this out." She held up the top book on a stack of seven. Its ragged cover proclaimed *Yoga Spirit!* in a 1970s psychedelic font. "I'm gonna be a hippie!"

"You're only a few decades late for that train." I took another whiff. "That's it! You smell like pot. Were you *smoking*?"

"I'm too old to start smoking anything." She patted her chest. "I have plans for these lungs. Bob and Vienna may have been partaking, though."

"What kind of name is Vienna for a person, anyhow?"

"I had the same question. Her dad's name was Vince and her mom's name was Alenna, so they named her Vienna."

"Does Austria know?"

She punched my arm. "Why are you so crabby? Aren't you happy that I have a new friend?"

I found myself pouting as I pulled out onto the icy blacktop. I performed a body scan and realized that I was tense all over. First it was Kennie with the greener thumb, and now it was Mrs. Berns making a new friend. But of course I wanted her to have as many people in her life as possible. I tried to turn my attitude around. "Sorry."

"You should be. That late husband of mine who was a drinker? He was a jealous one, too. Kept a tight rein on me, as if I went anywhere besides home and the grocery store. I vowed never to let anyone possess me again."

"You sound like the heroine of a romance novel."

"But you get my point."

I sighed. "I said I was sorry."

She patted my leg. "It's all right."

One of the many admirable things about Mrs. Berns was that if she accepted your apology, she meant it. I knew we wouldn't be speaking of this again.

"Now listen," she continued. "Vienna is amazing. She's sixty-nine and has the body of a fifty-year-old. Says it's because of yoga and how she eats. She teaches classes and everything, and does most of the cooking for the kids who stay on at the brewery. I'm going to turn back the clock!" She pumped a tiny bird fist into the air, her smile lighting up her face in the dark of the car.

"Too late," I said fondly.

I let her ramble on about all the ideas Vienna had given her and all the life changes she was going to make. While she talked, I realized I was missing Johnny terribly, and maybe that's why I was being so possessive of Mrs. Berns and my plants. It had been too long since I'd seen him. Rather than get grabby about things that weren't mine, I should appreciate what I had.

The owners of Bonnie & Clyde's in Clitherall let Johnny's band use the back half of their bar as practice space on Tuesdays. It was a slow night, so no one minded if the music was a little rough. I could drop Mrs. Berns off, go watch my guy practice, and maybe even see if Bonnie & Clyde's was carrying O'Callaghan's chocolate stout. Then, after Johnny was done practicing, he and I could slip back to his house and finish what we'd started the other night. The thought of it revved up my blood and sent it to all sorts of delicious places.

"What?" I asked, becoming aware that Mrs. Berns was quietly watching me.

"Have you heard a word I said?"

"Several."

"You know how some people have faces like statues?" she asked.

"Yes."

"You're not one of them. Say hi to Johnny for me. And drop me off at the Rusty Nail. They've added karaoke on Tuesdays, and I have a hankering to sing 'If I Could Turn Back Time.'"

She didn't wait to get out of the car to start practicing. I promised her I'd drop the borrowed books off at her apartment, and I did just that before heading east to Clitherall, another two-bars-and-a-church town four miles up the road from Battle Lake. When I parked out front of Bonnie & Clyde's, I heard the jukebox playing "Crazy Train."

Johnny's band must be taking a practice break.

I left my car and glanced up at the crossed rifles on the Bonnie & Clyde's sign, suddenly feeling self-conscious. I wasn't wearing any makeup, which wasn't unusual, but I also hadn't combed my hair since this morning and was wearing everyday clothes. Plus, a string of sleepless nights had left dark bags under my eyes. Johnny would be with his friends, and there would most certainly be a cadre of lady fans of all ages. He had his very own groupies, even on practice nights.

I jogged back to the car, dragged a brush through my hair, and coated my lips with honey-flavored lip balm. That was the best I could do, though I decided to enter through the back so everyone wouldn't stare as I came in.

I made my way to the rear, passing the white van used by the Thumbs. I heard some soft talk and giggling and almost turned around to enter through the front. Instead, I peeked around the corner to make sure I wouldn't be interrupting anything uncomfortable.

I blinked for several seconds and still couldn't make sense of what I saw: Johnny, his arms wrapped around a stunning blonde.

Chapter 33

No matter how much I stared, it just didn't make sense. When my eyes began to fog, I realized it was from tears and yanked myself back into the shadows. Luckily, Johnny hadn't spotted me. His attention was completely focused on the blonde.

I speed-walked back to my car, my head down, my legs numb. I started the engine automatically and pointed the Toyota toward anywhere but here, taking the sharp corner known as the Clitherall Car Wash so quickly that I started fishtailing.

Breathe, I told myself. I pulled my car back into a straight line and began rationalizing. It had been bound to happen: Johnny was gorgeous, smart, funny, kind, and in a band. How had I ever thought he'd want more than a fling?

When I'd finally slept with him in December, I knew I'd put it off for so long because I was afraid this was exactly what would happen. I slammed my palm into my steering wheel. How could I have been so stupid?

We hadn't said we were exclusive, though. Had we? I kept driving, but it was hard with the tears streaming down my face. I'd be OK. For sure I would. I'd survived worse. I should have known better than to get my hopes up in the first place. I was punching way above my weight class with Johnny.

I found myself standing outside the Battle Lake municipal liquor store. The mirror of the glass door reflected a runny nose and tears glistening off my puffy cheeks. I rubbed a mittened hand over my face and entered. I passed the display of O'Callaghan's and went straight for the vodka.

I kept my head down as I paid, not wanting to see the pity in the cashier's eyes.

I knew I wasn't bringing this bottle home. I didn't want to be alone tonight. For a crazy moment, I considered driving to Kennie's house, but then it hit me.

I knew exactly where I was going to sleep this evening.

Chapter 34

"Hey, baby, you want waffles?"

Whose voice was that? I opened my eyes and saw only blackness. I was blind! It was exactly what I deserved. I shifted my head slightly. My brain had a distinct lag behind my skull, and it hammered against its cage when it finally caught up. I groaned and realized that I'd been face down. With my head now to the side, at least I could see.

"Cuz if you do, you'll need to go out and grab some waffle mix. Oh, and syrup. Butter, too, if they have it. Man, waffles sound good. Can you get some bacon, too?"

Sweet Jesus, was that Bad Brad's voice?

I groaned again, this time sounding like a wounded whale. I could *not* begin to imagine the half-life on a mess-up like this. I slowly pulled myself into a sitting position and cracked my eyes wider. I was on Brad's couch. Daylight sliced through his dusty blinds like blades of fire. I rubbed at my face, feeling the imprint of his cheap, stinky couch from forehead to chin. Maybe we could just pour syrup on my face.

I sucked in a breath and let my hand fall lower, to where my clothes should be—*dear god, please let me still be wearing clothes.*

Shirt, check. Bra, check. Underwear, never wore 'em. Pants, check. I almost wept with relief.

"Hey, did you sleep in those clothes? Weirdo. Right before I crashed last night, I told you to make yourself comfortable, and you told me to make myself invisible. Ha!" He scratched his head. "I forgot how much fun you are when you've been drinking."

I focused on Brad, who was wearing only tighty-had-once-been-whities. I held up my hand to shield my sight, and he slapped a cup of coffee into it.

"Here you go. It's instant, but you have *got* to need this. Man, I didn't know you could sing."

Sing? My fifth-grade choir teacher had taken me aside after the first day of class and quietly asked if I would mind lip-synching. I hadn't warbled in public since. I took a tentative sniff of the coffee. It smelled like ashtrays and butt. Again, exactly what I deserved. I sipped it in penance.

"Good thing I had my recording equipment here. It's still OK if I use it as a backing track for Iron Steel's punk cover of 'The Gambler,' right? 'You gotta know when to hold 'em!'" he screeched like a cat while air guitaring.

"Brad." It came out as a whisper so as not to unbalance the delicate gyroscope of my spinning brain. "Brad." A little louder this time, but still not loud enough to break through. "Brad!"

He dropped his air guitar. "You don't need to yell, baby."

"Did we do . . . anything last night?"

"Yeah, totally. We recorded those tracks and talked philosophy of life. Oh, we played hide-and-seek, but you kept trying to, you know, conceal yourself under the kitchen sink, except you didn't fit."

That explained the egg-size lump on my head. I hoped. "No, I mean, did we . . . make out?" The sip of coffee I'd swallowed threatened to return to its cup.

"Naw, man, don't be stupid. I'm with Catriona and you're with Johnny. That's what you kept telling me, anyhow, though I'm still confused about the part where you're going to let him have multiple wives if that's what he needs?"

My pain dropped from my head and rose from my stomach, meeting squarely in my heart. Johnny was seeing another woman. *That* was why I'd come here in the first place. Scratch that—I'd come to Brad's because I was weak and scared.

Thank god the dumb monkey had been his best self last night. Maybe dating him wasn't the *worst* mistake I'd ever made. Top five, no question, but no longer dead first. "I have to go."

"Bathroom's right over there."

"I mean I have to leave for work." I tried standing and swayed only a bit. "What time is it?"

"Quarter to ten."

Crap! The library was supposed to open in fifteen minutes. I didn't have time to run home and shower, or even change. I wobbled to his bathroom and made do with scrubbing my face with Ivory soap and water, using my pointer finger with some toothpaste as a toothbrush, and slapping on a layer of Brad's industrial deodorant. It would have to suffice.

I yanked on my shoes and snatched my jacket, cursing the nausea that threatened with each movement. I paused on the way out. Brad was sitting on the couch, earphones in his ears and a distant smile on his face as he bopped along to a silent beat. I motioned for him to remove an earbud.

"Thanks," I said.

"What for?" he asked, his voice far too loud.

"For being a friend."

He waved and tucked the earbud back in his ear. I scurried out to my cold car and started it up, feeling somewhat refreshed by the frigid air. She turned over on the first try and was purring within seconds. I brushed a light snowfall off the windows with the wipers.

It was one of those blinding days where the sun had no barrier between itself and new snow, turning the landscape into a shimmering diamond mine. I was not in the proper state to appreciate the visual splendor and slipped the car into first gear, leaving before it warmed up.

Thankfully, Brad's apartment was in town, and so I arrived only seven minutes after the library's scheduled opening. My heart sank when I spotted Mrs. Berns waiting outside the door with two patrons.

I turned off the car and jogged to the door, key already out.

"Apologies," I said, deliberately avoiding eye contact with Mrs. Berns. "Car trouble."

"Sorry to hear it," Mrs. Berns said, leaning into me. "Say, is that a new perfume you're wearing? It smells like stupid and guilty."

I swallowed hard and hurried into the library, flicking on the lights and turning up the heat on my way to the front computer. To my chagrin, Mrs. Berns followed so closely that she tripped me near the main desk. I caught my balance but not without knocking my elbow on the corner of a table.

"Ouch," I said, rubbing it but still not looking at her.

"You look like a puppy that got caught peeing on the rug. Out with it."

I pulled my eyes to hers. Her arms were crossed and she was tapping a foot. The determined expression on her face told me there was no way through this but straight. My confession spilled out in one long, rushed sentence. "I surprised Johnny at practice last night but he was with another woman so he didn't see me but I saw him and I was so angry that I bought a bottle of vodka and went to Bad Brad's but nothing happened and I regret it so I don't need to feel any worse."

Getting it out felt a little bit better, right up until Mrs. Berns swatted me upside the head.

"Why in the world would you go to Brad?"

She'd hit me right on the goose egg I'd hatched trying to sneak into Brad's cupboards. I rubbed at the double-sore spot.

"Johnny's cheating on me."

"How do you know?"

"I told you. I saw him hugging another woman. And they were all whispery, like they knew each other naked."

"I give a grand total of zero shits about that," she said, fists on hips. "You don't know anything for a fact, and rather than find out the truth, you chose to spend the evening with a man who, if he were any more stupid, would need to be watered twice a week. Can you explain that?"

I felt tears pushing up. I was about to apologize when Mrs. Berns gathered me into her arms, just as I'd done for her yesterday. She was four inches shorter than me, but somehow, she made me feel safe.

"Look," she said while she patted my back, "you have to make yourself vulnerable in love. There's no other way to do it. Maybe Johnny stepped out, maybe he didn't. Either way, you're going to be OK. But you need to find out the truth, and you need to be able to stand by your choices, even the ones you make when you're down."

I nodded, my chin bobbing on her shoulder. "What will I do if Johnny doesn't want to be with me?"

"You'll feel like microwaved poop for a while, and then you'll get better. But don't borrow trouble. Focus on what you know, which is nothing."

I sniffled. "You're right."

"Of course I am, dummy," she said gently. "Now go blow your nose. My jacket is made out of polyester, not vinyl."

She let me go, and I looked straight at her for the first time that morning. "Did you get your hair done?"

"Yup. Me and Vienna met at the salon this a.m. and got perms. We're going to shop later and maybe catch a movie. She's the most fun I've had without liquor or a man for a long time."

I quelled the now-familiar surge of jealousy. *One problem at a time, thank you very much.*

"Oh, don't look at me like that. You're fun, too," she said. "You're just familiar. Vienna is new. Plus, she's got kids and grandkids, so she understands what I'm going through. It's exactly what I need to pull me out of my funk." She glanced at the wall clock. "I better get going. I have some grocery shopping to do before this afternoon. I just stopped by to tell you I can cover lunch if you have anything you need to do."

"Thank you." My head was throbbing, and I still felt like a hungover, cheated-on lump, but at least I had Mrs. Berns. She left me to get my face in order and run the library. I had to rush the opening duties as much as my battered brain allowed. I was almost on track when a man walked through the door in a gigantic jacket that reached his knees, the fur-lined hood of his parka up.

When the man slipped off his hood, he was half-wide smile, half-curly hair, and 100 percent Jed. "Mira Bo Beera! I'm returning your call."

I tried to smile back, but it hurt to move my face. "What call?"

"You rang me up Sunday," he said, pulling off his massive mittens on his way to the front desk. "You wanted to know about new drugs in the area."

Mrs. Craigmile, a retired second-grade teacher and library regular, was twirling the mystery rack near the front of the library but paused midrotation to shoot him and then me a shocked look.

"For the article I'm writing," I said in an exaggerated voice, staring directly at Mrs. Craigmile. She quickly withdrew her eyes, but I could tell by the way her head was cocked that she was still listening.

"Whatever," Jed said, shrugging amiably. "Sorry I didn't get back to you sooner. I've been doing a lot of work on the ice castle for O'Callaghan's."

"They're still opening it? I thought they were closing down all those lake attractions since the body was found."

He reached for the box of tissues I had on the front counter and blew his nose before arcing the crumpled ball into a nearby garbage can. "They shut it all down for the Winter Festival, sure, and had me dismantle the Darwin's Dunk. No one wants any part of that. They're still opening up the ice castle, though. Something to do with a new beer they're unveiling."

"Wasn't the ice castle already good to go?"

"For outside viewing, yeah, but they want to make it so people can go inside. I'm working with a crew. I don't know what it's going to look like when it's done, but it's going to be pretty cool. There are even ice sculptures around it now."

I wondered how this was the first I'd heard of it. "I'm glad you're finding work." I lowered my voice. "So have you heard of any new drug activity around here?"

Jed leaned in with a stage whisper loud enough to be heard in the rear of the library. "I have."

I waited. He waited.

"And?" I finally asked.

"They're new to town, some sort of gang out of Chicago. Guess it was getting too hot for them there. I got high with a couple of them at a party on New Year's. They started out nice, a little edgy. Cool tattoos, all of 'em. They didn't want to stop at pot, though, so I left. Haven't seen much of them since, but I know they're selling. OxyContin, mostly."

That fit with what Gary had told me, back in the moment when he'd been high enough to like me. "Do they show any signs of leaving?"

He held up his palms. "No idea."

"You know anything about Aaron Offerdahl?"

"The Dahlster." Jed nodded agreeably. "Yeah. He graduated about the same time I did. I heard he's been back in town a month plus but is laying low at the brewery."

"A month plus. Is that about how long the gang has been around?"

He put a finger to his chin. "About. Might be coincidence, though."

"Maybe," I said, pulling the Operation Offerdahl folder out from under the counter. My experience was that coincidences were rare. "I really appreciate your help."

"Anything for you," he said, the sweet smile back on his face. "How's Johnny?"

I cracked the lead of my pencil on the notebook. "Good. You seen him lately?"

"Nope. Seems like he's practicing all the time. The Thumbs are playing Friday. Are you going? We could catch it together."

"Maybe," I said, brushing the lead off the paper. "Can I get back to you on that?"

"Sure!" He grabbed his mittens off the counter. "Anything else you need to know?"

"I'm good for now." My head hurt too much to nod. I wanted to gnaw on a pie-size ibuprofen.

"Then I better get back to work." He shoved his hands in his mittens, yanked up his hood, and headed back into the cold morning.

Chapter 35

Samuel Litchfield's office assistant rang me through immediately. Samuel picked up on the second ring.

"Hello?"

"Hi, Mr. Litchfield." For some reason, his first name felt too uncomfortable. "It's Mira James. I'm calling about the Aaron Offerdahl investigation."

I needed some information before I'd proceed. The hangover was riding me like a troll, and sure, that was my fault, but I found myself unwilling to give up Aaron Offerdahl until I knew why Samuel Litchfield wanted to find him. Or maybe I just wanted to pick a fight.

"Mira! Did you find my boy?"

I paused. Had this descended to the realm of soap operas? "Aaron Offerdahl is your son?"

He laughed. "No. It was a figure of speech."

Hmm. An odd one for anyone but Thurston Howell III. "I haven't turned up anything yet," I lied, "but I'm following some leads. I'd like more insight before I go any further. Specifically, why do you want to locate Aaron?"

"I'm sorry." Did his voice suddenly sound strained? "My client has asked me not to reveal that, as I mentioned. You can locate him without that information, am I correct?"

This guy had a knack for rubbing me the wrong way. I ignored his question. "If you can't tell me that, can you tell me why you believe he's back in Battle Lake?"

"Rumors."

I wasn't in the mood. "You've got nothing?"

He laughed again, but it sounded forced. "Not anything that you couldn't find out on your own. That's why I hired you."

I decided right then and there that I'd investigate Samuel Litchfield—and specifically why he was after Aaron Offerdahl—before I told him that I'd likely located Aaron. I didn't have a solid reason for my evasiveness, just a sense that I didn't want to show my hand yet, even if Litchfield had bought the cards. I thanked him for his time and promised him a full report within seventy-two hours.

I hung up the phone and sketched a couple angry faces in my notebook. Nobody liked being in the dark, but I had a special intolerance to secrets, always had. Maybe it was due to growing up in a house full of them. In any case, I craved answers like a fish desired water.

I glanced at the clock. Noon. If Mrs. Berns showed up over my lunch hour as promised, I could jog to the police station and find out if there was any new information on the local gang activity, Gary's shooting, or Maurice's murder.

Noon became twelve thirty, though, which quickly turned into one o'clock. When my stomach's growl drew annoyed glances from patrons, I headed to the break room and rummaged through the miniature fridge. I found a tub of roasted red pepper hummus that was good for another two days and, in the cupboard, a bag of only slightly stale spelt pretzels. I carried them to the counter and snacked while emailing overdue-book notices. An automated system would be nice, but so would a lot of things that cost money.

It was two o'clock before Mrs. Berns finally sashayed in, looking relaxed and smelling like sweet smoke and delicious food.

"Where have you been?" I asked.

She held up her white bag. "I got takeout from the Turtle Stew so I could eat while I watched the place for you, just like I said."

"It's two oh five!"

She dropped the bag on the counter so her hands were free to slip out of her winter jacket. "Take it or leave it."

"You smell like pot again," I said suspiciously.

"Vienna showed up early to take me to a meditation class. Very relaxing. We listened to a Deepak Oprah tape and quieted our minds."

"Chopra?"

She glanced at my tub of hummus and shrugged. "Sure, I'll try anything once."

"No, his name is . . . forget it." I lifted the lid and slid it over to her, along with what was left of the pretzels.

"Is there any meat in this?" she said, sniffing the hummus.

"Why do you care?"

"I'm a vegetarian now. Vienna says avoiding animal flesh is an important component of being healthy and whole."

I raised my eyebrows but didn't comment, even though it was killing me. Mrs. Berns was the most carnivorous person I'd ever met. She swore it was what fed her sex drive. "The hummus is vegetarian."

"Great." She grabbed a pretzel, scooped a mound of hummus, and popped the whole works into her mouth. I watched her chew, a faint smile on her face. The smile turned into a grimace and she snatched the pretzel bag, spitting the mouthful into it with all the subtlety of a hand grenade.

"What the hell was that?" She scraped her tongue with her nails.

"It's *hummus*. Garbanzo beans and tahini."

"Speak English," she said, dipping into her own white bag and coming out with a wax paper–wrapped sandwich. "Good thing I brought my own food."

I watched her unwrap it. "Is that a BLT?"

She took a big bite. "Mm-hmm," she said, wiping at the mayonnaise on the corners of her mouth.

"Isn't there meat in that?"

She swallowed. "Nope, just lettuce, tomato, and bacon. Did I tell you that the meditation class was held at a cool new workout center near Vienna's house? They have a pool, a gym, dorms. There's even a grope room."

I thought of the distinct marijuana smell that accompanied her after her visits with Vienna. "You mean 'grow' room?" I'd had a recent experience with one last November, when I'd uncovered a healthy pot industry in the area.

"If you say so."

That would seem incongruent with a fitness center. "Did you actually *see* the room?"

"No, Vienna only mentioned it in passing while she was toking on a spliff. Said it's hidden, and I better not tell anyone."

Interesting, yes. Related to Aaron Offerdahl? No idea. "How long can you stay?"

"I got an hour, then Vienna is coming back."

"You don't let her drive when she's smoking, do you?"

"Don't be ridiculous. I do the driving."

That would be less ridiculous if Mrs. Berns possessed a valid driver's license, but that was a point I'd never been able to make with her. "All right. I'll be back in an hour."

I retrieved my coat from the rack and left the library, trying not to jostle my tender head and hoping that Gary Wohnt wouldn't be at the police station when I arrived.

Chapter 36

If luck were pennies, I couldn't afford a gumball. Gary glanced up as I walked in before immediately returning his attention to an open file on his desk.

"You're out of the hospital," I said, surprisappointed.

It didn't even garner me an eyebrow raise.

"Those crutches yours?" They were leaning against the edge of his metal desk. I reached out to touch one, but he snatched them away, stacking them against the wall behind him.

I took the seat across from him and watched him work, or at least pretend to work. It must have been hard to concentrate with me staring. With his face pointed down, I had front row seats to the top of his head. He wasn't going to go bald anytime soon. I kept up the staring silence for all of four minutes before cracking. "I know about cabins in the area being robbed, and I think I know who's doing it."

He sighed but did not speak.

"I also know about Aaron Offerdahl."

This earned a glance. He lifted his head slowly and appraised me with his black eyes. "*What* do you know about Aaron Offerdahl?"

Good question, one I didn't yet have an answer to. "Stuff," I said cleverly. "I also know Maurice was not a drifter. He has a job, a home, and family in Chicago. A girlfriend and two kids."

"Interesting." Gary leaned back. I could tell he did it too fast, given his recent injury, because his face paled before he regained his composure. I was sure he wasn't supposed to be back at work this soon after the shooting.

"Yes," I agreed. "Interesting. Now why don't you tell me what you know?"

His eyebrows met over his nose. "Not how this works."

I thought of the letter Ray had given me. "I might have more to tell you, if you trade information of your own."

"Might, or do?"

Officer Diego walked in, bringing a gust of cold air and the smell of drugstore cologne with him. We nodded at each other, and then he disappeared into the station's back room.

I ran my finger along the edge of Gary's desk. "Depends."

When I pulled my eyes back to Gary's, he was staring at me with such intensity that it felt like an X-ray. I held his gaze, though it was one of the more difficult things I'd done that week. I could feel the flush creeping up my neck.

"Do you know anything about OxyContin?" he asked.

"Prescription pain reliever, widely abused. Is that what the gang is dealing in?"

"How about fentanyl patches?" he asked, ignoring my question.

"Never heard of 'em."

"It's a hundred times more potent than morphine." Was that a blush at the mention of the drug that had made him over-reveal? "It's highly addictive, dangerous, and popular. Doctors prescribe it in pill, sucker, or patch, but the patch is the most popular back-alley form."

"Sucker? Like, candy that kills pain?" And I'd thought frozen Nut Goodies were awesome. Neither of my reactions—admiration and envy—seemed appropriate, so I continued. "And you're seeing OxyContin and fentanyl patches around here?"

"Look it up. You're the reporter."

I noticed he didn't call me a detective. "Why would you only tell me part of the story?"

He ran his fingers through his hair. He wore a fat silver ring on his right hand, and it caught the light. "The question is, why would I tell you any of it? The answer: because this is dangerous. It's not kids snitching their parents' liquor or selling pot. This is big-city drug running, and I want you out of my way."

The words weren't new—he'd warned me away from cases many times before—but the growl in his voice was.

"I have no interest in infiltrating gangs or uncovering drug operations," I said truthfully.

He scowled. I could tell he didn't believe me.

"Look, I just want to know what happened to Maurice. I found him, you know? I want to put that to rest. Also, Litchfield hired me to locate Aaron Offerdahl. The sooner you help me with those two, the sooner I get out of your way."

"You've told me everything?"

"Yes." I really had. Except for the letter. I shoved my hand into my pocket, and my fingers curled around the edges of the paper. I hadn't come in expecting to show it to him, but maybe he could help with that, too. Or maybe it would help him. Sharing was unlike me, but it felt good to not have to do this one alone.

His voice cut into my thoughts. "Good. Thank you. I don't want to see you again. *Ever*, if you can swing it, but if not, certainly not before this case is over. If we cross paths, consider yourself arrested."

"For what?" I sputtered, my hand shooting out of my pocket, empty.

"Don't give me a reason to decide." He held me in his stare, his eyes sharp.

"Screw you," I said, suddenly so angry that I wished I could start fires with my brain.

He quirked an eyebrow, which was the last view I had of him before I spun on my heel and stormed out.

Chapter 37

The soft shuffle of the library faded into the background as I typed an article in hopes of distracting myself from the boiling anger at Gary's harsh words.

Battle Lake's Prospect House and Civil War Museum Opens to the Public

The grand old Prospect House has opened her doors for the first time in years. The House is a Battle Lake original, an 18-room Georgian mansion built in 1860 by Barnaby Offerdahl, a railroad man and Battle Lake transplant. When Offerdahl didn't return from the Civil War, the house was willed to his daughter and then his brother. It left Offerdahl hands in an 1882 sale, when James Allison "Cap" Colehour purchased it, turning it into a seasonal resort in 1886. The Prospect Inn was the first and largest resort operating in the area for the 38 years it was open. With a prime location near the railroad, it became a popular travel destination for people from all over the Midwest, famous for its clean rooms and excellent meals.

The inn reverted to a private home in the early 1920s and was completely remodeled in 1929. In a rare stroke of luck, the house's furnishings have not been changed since. Carter Stone, a local historian, bought the mansion, minus most of the land, at auction last March. With the help of a dedicated group of volunteers, Stone has spent hundreds of hours searching through piles of treasure inside the house. They've uncovered most of the original furnishings, intact clothing and jewelry collections dating as far back as Barnaby Offerdahl's time and an extensive collection of Civil War artifacts.

"I found a chest filled with nearly 200 Civil War letters," Stone said. "I found the sleeves to Barnaby Offerdahl's original uniform with a bullet hole in each one from the first and second time he'd been shot during the Civil War. I discovered a fife, buttons from a uniform, a cartridge box, a tent, a cap box, a powder flask, a bullet mold, two diaries, typhoid serum, a Lincoln-Johnson campaign poster, belts and buckles, a flag and battlefield souvenirs. There are many pieces of this large historical puzzle still yet to be found."

Eager to share their historically exciting finds with the world, Stone and his helpers have opened the house and museum to the public even though only approximately half of its treasure has been cataloged. The Prospect House and Civil War Museum is truly a jewel in Battle Lake's crown. You can tour during their open hours and find out more at www.prospecthousemuseum.org.

I hit "Send." Ron would proofread the article and make any necessary changes. I glanced at the wall clock. Twenty minutes to close. I spent that time searching for any online records pertaining to Charles or Samuel Litchfield. I discovered where he'd been born, how much money he made in an average year (significantly more than a part-time librarian/reporter/detective), his home and cabin addresses, two speeding tickets, both paid, and that's it. I shooed out the last two library visitors and headed home.

◆ ◆ ◆

My answering machine was blinking when I walked into my living room, shaking off the cold. I hit "Play."

"Hey, it's Johnny."

My heart soared, then plummeted. He didn't know I'd witnessed him embracing the blonde last night. He also didn't know I'd spent the evening at Brad's.

"I have a surprise for you. Call me back. Miss you."

I felt like I was gargling my heart. It was a vile cocktail of sadness and guilt. I could address part of that by putting distance between Brad and me. Maybe I really should find out what was up with his girlfriend so I could file him away as "in a committed relationship."

The sadness I didn't know what to do with.

Luna nuzzled my hand, and I dropped so our eyes were level. She licked my nose. Jed had installed a pet door while I was away over Christmas—his holiday gift to me, he'd said—and so I knew the animals had been able to come and go as they pleased, but I felt bad that I hadn't gotten them any fresh water this morning. One more chit to add to the guilt pile.

"How've you been, girl? Me, I've been pretty crappy, and that's at least half my own fault." She licked my ear this time. I strolled over to check her and Tiger Pop's food and water. I was rinsing out their stainless steel bowls when a knock came at the door. Luna didn't growl, which meant it was either someone she recognized or someone who was safe. For a moment, I hoped it was Johnny. It was unlikely given his message, but in that weak moment, I yearned to make up with him.

I went to the door and tugged it open.

It for sure wasn't Johnny.

Chapter 38

"Can we come in? It's cold out here."

"Taunita?" I guessed.

The woman was African American, early twenties, balancing a baby on one hip and holding the hand of another child, both kids so thoroughly wrapped in snowsuits, scarves, hats, and mittens that they had to tip back the top half of their body to see me in the yellow glare of the yard light. Their names were Timothy and Alessa, if I remembered correctly.

"Yeah. Your dog friendly?"

I glanced at Luna. She was trying to play it cool, sitting next to me on her haunches, but her tail was slapping against my ankle. She loved kids.

"Yep," I said, stepping aside to let them in.

"Puppy!" the little boy said when his mom led him into the house. I loved the way kids said that word. It was all wrapped in love, like they hadn't known until that moment how awesome the world could be.

"Puppy!" he repeated.

Taunita set the baby on the couch. The little child's snowsuit was so thick that she could only lie immobile like an insulated taco. Taunita talked while she unzipped and unraveled both children.

"I know about Maurice," she said, "so you can stop looking so worried. I don't expect you to tell me anything new."

She'd just met me, and she already knew my worried look? *Mrs. Berns must be right about my poker face.* "I'm sorry. How'd you find out?"

"Hammer." She laid the snowsuits on top of each other, then stacked the mittens, hats, and scarves next to them. Free of his bindings, Timothy ran over to Luna and hugged her like a champion. He was wearing one of those little matching button-down flannel shirt and elastic-waisted corduroy sets that squeezed my heart. With his curly brown hair and wide eyes, he was a perfect three-year-old doll. Alessa sat on the couch where Taunita had propped her, watching me with serious owl eyes. Her nose was exactly as big as a button, and her curls stood up around her head, recovering from the static shock of her hat being pulled off. I remember Taunita mentioning on the phone that Alessa had recently turned a year old.

"He's not good for a lot, but Hammer at least had the decency to tell me the truth about Maurice," she continued. "He also said you're a detective. That right?"

Timothy was trying to crawl on Luna and ride her like a pony. She kept wriggling away and then finally rolled on her back. He trailed his fingers through her tummy hair and giggled. Tiger Pop still hadn't shown her face. Historically, she liked kids only a little more than she liked baths.

"No," I said truthfully. "I'm in training, but I've got another five thousand or so hours until I'm official in Minnesota. Is that why you came here? To see if I could find out who—" I glanced at Timothy. I didn't know if he was old enough to understand that his dad was dead. "Who's responsible for what happened?"

"Oh, I *know* who's responsible. Somebody who was buying, or somebody who was selling. That's how that works. Maurice tried to get out of that life and was almost there. That's why he came to Minnesota, you know? He was gonna look into an inheritance. He must've been offered some side work while he was here, big enough to call Hammer and Ray out with him, and he was stupid enough to take it. Last mistake he'll ever make." Her words were fierce, but tears sparkled in her eyes. Her face was swollen, as if she'd spent a lot of time crying.

"How long were you two together?" I asked.

"Five years. We met in community college. I was going for computer programming and he was gonna be a mechanic, and then I got pregnant."

I nodded. I was frankly at a loss. Timothy had moved on from Luna and was pulling my CDs off the rack and stacking them like blocks. Alessa hadn't taken her solemn eyes off me. "Can I get you anything to drink?"

"You can heat this bottle up," Taunita said, digging through a diaper bag. "And you can find Orpheus Jackson for me."

Chapter 39

The letter. "If it's the same Orpheus I'm thinking of, he's pretty dead."

The hint of a smile touched her cheeks. "He is. He was Maurice's great-great-great-grandpa. When Mo's mom passed two months ago, he discovered the letters from Orpheus. He read them over and over again, like they were a real page-turner. Maurice ended up believing he had some land due him around here, land that was stolen from Orpheus. I don't have much else right now, and I'm asking you to help me find out if my kids at least got this."

I made my way to the microwave, unscrewed the nipple, and popped in the bottle, my brain working furiously, adding up what I knew. The letter Ray had tossed at me was real, or at least a copy of an authentic letter, written by Maurice's great-great-great-grandfather to his wife. In the letter in my possession, Orpheus had written, *They do not believe the messages I bring.* I didn't know where the letter had been mailed to or from, but I did know that Orpheus had served in the Civil War with Barnaby Offerdahl.

"Twenty seconds should be good," she said.

I nodded and jabbed the buttons. Timothy had followed me and was eyeing the bag of dill pickle potato chips on the counter. I'd eaten half of it a few nights ago, and if I finished the rest, I might need to ask Timothy if his elastic-waisted cords came in larger sizes. "Can he have potato chips?"

"Sure," Taunita said, not looking up from her diaper changing.

I handed Timothy the bag.

"Thank you," he said, only it sounded like *tank-oo* because he was tiny and precious.

"You're welcome." I retrieved the bottle from the microwave, wound the top back on, shook it holding my finger over the hole in the nipple, tested it on my wrist, then handed it to Taunita.

"You have kids?" she asked.

"God no. Did a lot of babysitting growing up, though. Did Maurice mention where he thought this land was?"

"Battle Lake." She pointed out the window and made an encompassing gesture. "Here. He thought it might be around where his grandma used to own a cabin, but he found out she just rented it. Guess *her* grandparents took her there when she was little, too."

"Anything more specific than that?"

She shrugged, cradling Alessa as she fed her. "He said the letters didn't say much, almost like Orpheus was afraid someone else was going to read them."

"Don't suppose you brought the letters with?"

"Don't suppose I did." Her eyes narrowed. "It wouldn't make any difference, anyways. I read 'em all myself. They don't say anything."

"Except that Orpheus was owed land in Battle Lake."

"Didn't even mention that. That's just the return address that was on the letters, and then there was some family legend that they were all supposed to be rich once they got their hands on this land."

"That's not a lot to go on."

"I know."

Alessa's eyes were growing droopy as she drank, and Timothy sat cross-legged near my feet, trying to feed Luna potato chips.

"His funeral is gonna be here," Taunita said softly. A tear coasted down her cheek and dropped onto Alessa's forehead. The girl's eyes popped open, then grew heavy-lidded again.

"In Battle Lake?"

"He doesn't have any family left, except us. Might as well be here."

I had a thought. *After the Battle* lay open on the coffee table in front of her. "Grab me that?"

She reached over, expertly balancing Alessa, and handed me the book. I walked to my coat and pulled out Orpheus's letter, smoothing it on the counter. Then I paged through the book until I located the article on the man found hung in the woods. Orpheus had written his letter January 18, 1865. The unidentified body had been discovered March 7 of the same year, with the note that it had been hanging for at least two months. Was the hanged man Orpheus? I had some more questions to ask Carter Stone, it appeared.

"I'll see what information I can uncover," I said, "but this is a long shot."

"Thank you," she said simply.

"Where will you be staying so I can tell you if I find anything?"

She kept her eyes on Alessa. Timothy took that moment to wipe his greasy fingers on my pants leg. An awareness began to dawn on me. "You don't have anywhere to stay."

"We're quiet," she said. "And clean. I can help you out around here. Your plants look good, but you've got some cobwebs in the corners that might need a jackhammer to get them down."

I looked where she was pointing. How long had those been there? More importantly, how could I possibly live with a stranger and her two little kids? Luna whined, drawing my attention. She waited until our eyes were locked and then licked salty, giggly, boogery Timothy.

I want to keep him, the gesture said.

I sighed so deeply that I swear the cobwebs that had just been pointed out moved. "Fine. You can have the guest room. But I'm not used to living with people. Especially little people."

Taunita smiled at me, the first unguarded expression I'd seen on her since she arrived. It was gorgeous, happy, grateful. Luna and I lugged in her suitcases and a box of toys out of the back of her Honda Civic and set them up in the spare bedroom. I inflated an air mattress for her and Timothy to share, and she and I put together the travel playpen for Alessa. By the time we had the room comfortable, both kids were asleep, their faces vulnerable and perfect.

◆ ◆ ◆

For the second time in four days, I was awoken by the sharp trill of the phone, this time in the middle of the night. My immediate reaction was chilly fear. When I answered it, I realized the response was appropriate.

"Mira?"

"Gary?" Even in my dream-fuzzed state, I recognized the police chief's deep, measured tone. My next words came out like a plea. "It's one in the morning." *Please don't tell me anyone I love is hurt.*

"I'm sorry." He hesitated before continuing. *Gary never hesitates.*

My brain separated from my body. "Who is it?"

"Curtis Poling has been attacked. He's in the Fergus Falls hospital. He's in rough shape."

I gripped the phone, my heart pounding a sick beat. "What? What happened?"

"You should get there soon. Do you need me to drive you?"

"No," I said reflexively. I rested the phone in its cradle and looked around my bedroom like it was the first time I'd seen it.

"You OK?"

I started. I'd forgotten that Taunita and her kids were here. She stood in the doorway, appearing ghostly in a white nightgown.

"No," I said.

She nodded. She was used to things not being OK. "You need to go somewhere?"

I stood and began pulling on clothes. "Yeah. The hospital."

She disappeared and returned with my coat and boots. "I'll watch your animals. You call back here if you need anything."

Chapter 40

Curtis Poling had been out for a midnight walk, a habit of his that he had refused to give up when he entered the nursing home. I'd caught him at it late one August night, when I was one of the last customers to leave the Rusty Nail. I'd at first thought real dementia had kicked in.

He'd convinced me he was out for pleasure and that he did it every night. He said he never walked far, but that he had to get out because the only time he could think was when the world was quiet. He'd managed to sneak out all those evenings without alerting the nursing home attendants, so who was I to deny him his simple pleasure?

Last night, however, he'd been attacked behind the apothecary. It was only good luck that Theadora had found him when she came to check on the alarm that'd gone off.

"I thought he was a pile of rags." She kept twisting the tissue in her hands. "When I saw it was a person, I couldn't remember the phone number for the ambulance at first. Is that the stupidest thing you ever heard? I couldn't think of three simple numbers."

I kept my arm around her. "But you *did* remember them."

She nodded. "I was afraid to touch him. He looked so fragile, as if he'd been dropped from the sky. I didn't even recognize it was Curtis right away, there was so much blood. And someone had stolen his coat. Who does that?"

I had a good idea exactly who had done that. I felt as if my insides had been scoured by metal, like somehow I should have done more to stop Ray and Hammer. Maybe then Curtis wouldn't be in surgery, which was all the doctor could tell us.

And when I said "us," I meant me and a significant portion of Battle Lake. Familiar, tired faces had begun shuffling in, people who'd been reached by the phone tree and told that one of their own was hurting. We milled around in the waiting room like zombies, our numbers growing, everyone careful not to speak too loudly, possibly afraid of waking one another and realizing this wasn't just a terrible nightmare.

Theadora had stood by Curtis until the ambulance arrived, covering him with her own coat despite the plummeting temperatures, telling him it was going to be OK, crying. She told me she hadn't seen anyone else in the alley, just all that blood in the snow, like someone had spilled a pitcher of cherry Kool-Aid.

"Weren't you concerned whoever did this to him would come back?"

Theadora blinked. I could tell it hadn't occurred to her to worry about anything but Curtis. In that moment, I loved her more than my own heart. I asked her if she needed anything. When she shook her head, I went in search of coffee. I took the corner toward the cafeteria when a familiar voice caught my ear. I tipped back and saw that Samuel Litchfield had joined the Battle Lake contingent. Behind him was Johnny, bedsheet creases still on his face. I kept walking, like the coward I was. I didn't have it in me to deal with either of them tonight.

I hid out in the cafeteria for an hour, peeking occasionally into the waiting room. The hospital staff eventually had to ask most of the locals to leave, saying they didn't have room for all of us, and besides, there was nothing we could do here. Once Johnny and Samuel were gone, I returned to the waiting room to beg to be allowed to stay. I would have hidden behind a plant or stolen some scrubs and tried to blend in if they'd said no.

Both Theadora and I were allowed to stick around by dint of our closeness to Curtis—Theadora in finding him, and me in being his closest friend outside of the nursing home. Mrs. Berns was a near second, but she let me stay rather than fight it out. She and Kennie each gave me a hug before leaving, and I promised to spread the word as soon as we had news.

◆　◆　◆

A little after eight o'clock in the morning, a nurse with kind eyes touched my shoulder and asked if I was here for Curtis Poling. That "yes" was the most difficult word I'd ever uttered. She must have seen the fear in my eyes, because she immediately shook her head and told me that Curtis was out of surgery. He was in rough shape and couldn't have visitors for at least another day, maybe longer, but it looked like he was going to pull through.

The tears gushed out. I gently shook Theadora, who had fallen asleep on my shoulder. After I shared the good news, I used the hospital phone to dial Kennie.

With the information tree started, I was at a loss. The nurse had gently informed us that there was no reason to stay. I was too wired to go home or to work. I returned to the phone and called Mrs. Berns.

"I heard," she said by way of hello.

"Hi."

"My phone has been ringing off the hook. Are you still at the hospital?"

"Yep. They think he's going to be OK."

"That cat's had more than his share of lives." She coughed on the other end of the phone.

"Are you crying?"

"Are you stupiding?"

"It's OK. I know how much Curtis means to all of us."

I heard snuffling on the other end of the line, then nose blowing. "What was that old fart doing walking behind the drugstore at midnight, anyways?"

173

I had that same question. Not why he was out walking, but why he was walking in an alley. "Theadora said the silent alarm was triggered, but that the police haven't yet found any evidence of a break-in." I thought of what Gary had told me about the booming pharmaceutical market in the region. "Maybe Curtis interrupted a robbery in progress?"

"Like we did in the alley behind the post office the other night?"

"My thoughts exactly."

"Is Curtis talking yet?"

"No. The nurse said he might not even be able to have visitors for days."

"Well, I'll watch the library for you."

"What for?"

"So you can track down who hurt our man and give them back their can of hell."

Chapter 41

I was confident that my two alley-rats, Ray and Hammer, had beaten up Curtis. I also had a hunch that Gary knew the same thing and was on their trail. I intended to help him in any way I could, without him knowing and without me risking my neck.

It would be a delicate dance.

I gassed up the Toyota, purchased a granola bar and a Styrofoam cup of coffee that tasted like burned feet, and got to work, disregarding the sleep-deprived fogginess of my brain and the gravel inside my eyelids.

My first stop was Silver Lake, and specifically the new cabin that had been built on the north side last fall. Sid had mentioned that cabins all around the lakes had been broken into, but that this one had been trashed. It made sense that the gang was using them as a place to squat. Most lake cabins were empty in the winter. Free rent for thieves. That's when it occurred to me that I didn't know how many were in this gang. Gary had made it seem like a lot, but Taunita had made it sound like there were only a handful.

Taunita. I'd need to call her as soon as I reached a phone so I could update her on Curtis. I hoped she and the kids weren't trashing the house. I also wondered when I was going to break down and buy a cell phone. Most everyone I knew owned one, but I wasn't ready to be constantly available. Plus, they were expensive. Times like these, though, it seemed stupid not to have one.

The poplars and oaks lining Silver Lake's shores were frosted with a bright white hoar. I was thankful the weather was good. Cold, but clear, with only a light dusting of snow from the night before. Most of the cabins dotting the shoreline appeared empty, except for one with smoke trailing up from the chimney. I wrote down the address and kept driving. It seemed unlikely that gang members would call attention to themselves by starting a fire, but what did I know from gangs?

I kept driving until I hit the log cabin. It was a gorgeous log A-frame on a pretty little wooded lot. I sometimes drove the long way home and so had witnessed the construction process, the cabin appearing like a grand Lincoln Log project. I was almost surprised when they didn't top it off with a plastic green roof and a little cavalryman to watch over the shores.

It was placed far enough back from the road that I had to pull into the recently plowed driveway for a full view of it, but I didn't need to drive far to spot the damage. The windows facing me had been boarded over, and I had to believe that the gorgeous bay window facing the lake was in the same condition.

I didn't spot any tracks. I stepped out of the car to be sure—fresh snowfall could play tricks on the eyes—but it was clear no one had been here, at least since the previous night's snowfall. The perpetrators, police, and probably owner had come and gone already. The only one left to visit was the insurance company.

I didn't actually want to locate Hammer and Ray. I just wanted to find where they were and pass that information on to Gary. My only other lead was the microbrewery, and that was a long shot at best. It relied on me being sure Aaron was there—which I pretty much was—and that he was tied to the gang activity, even distantly. It was a strong possibility, given his connections to Chicago and crime, not to mention the fact that he'd shown up in town the same time as the Sea Monsters gang. Still, even if those two hunches were solid, I'd needed to coax the honorary Irish staff into giving him up, which was where my plan fell apart.

Maybe it was the giddiness of sleep deprivation that made me forge ahead despite all the long shots. Oh well. I'd worry about that when I got there.

Chapter 42

The fresh snow gave the countryside a fluffy feel, like a loaf of bread just pulled out of the oven. I wasn't in the mood to enjoy it, though. I cruised past Vienna's house, noting that the T. Wrecks tow truck was gone. New snow usually meant new accidents, even during daylight hours. Something about the flakes messes with people's driving skills.

I'd concocted a plan during the drive over. It was brief. Thanks to the bartender's slipup, I was confident Aaron was working and possibly living at the brewery. I also knew that nobody would tell me exactly where to find him. I would chance peeking into the main lodge. If I spotted no one with an eyebrow piercing, I'd feign being lost and leave, my next stop the dorms / fitness center Mrs. Berns had told me about.

I hoped that no one at the lodge would recognize me as that nosy woman from the tour.

I pulled up to the lodge, noting there were no cars in the lot. I checked the front door. Locked. Well, that took care of that. I jogged over to the actual brewery and stepped in. The scent of sour mash washed over me. Two workers glanced up, startled. Neither of them had eyebrow piercings, and neither looked happy to see me.

"Sorry, are there tours today?"

"Not till tonight." The man set down his clipboard and began to walk toward me.

"Thanks, I'll check back!" I smiled and let the door swing shut, hurrying to my car. He stood in the square of the door, watching me pull away.

I veered out the main driveway, cruised a half a mile the opposite direction than I'd come, and found myself in front of a building even larger than the main lodge, though without the charm. It looked like a small apartment complex, boxy, newish, with six large windows spaced evenly apart on both floors. I assumed they had placed it out of view from the main building because it lacked the visual appeal.

I parked between a Toyota Prius and a Chevy Cavalier and walked in like I owned the place. I was surprised at how modern the interior was, though I shouldn't have been. I could see and smell the chlorine tang of the indoor pool, a glass wall separating me from the water and the couple splashing in it. An unstaffed desk was to my left, and behind it were two doors, one marked WOMEN's LOCKER ROOM and the other MEN's LOCKER ROOM.

To my right was a hallway, which I assumed led to the kitchen, other workout rooms, and the "grope room." There also must have been stairs somewhere that led to the second-floor apartments. It was a fantastic setup for a mini-community, and I wondered if they would consider hiring me. Probably not. I had a tendency to burn bridges in situations like this.

"Can I help you?"

"Yes, I'm interested in—" I turned toward the voice and found myself face-to-face with Aaron Offerdahl.

Chapter 43

The photo had been fuzzy, but there was no mistaking the metal stake piercing his eyebrow. The brown hair and eyes matched as well. He was my guy.

I held out my hand. "Betty Fishbacher."

He lifted an eyebrow. He smelled like cigarettes and stale whiskey and had the sallow skin of someone who didn't spend a lot of time aboveground. "Aaron."

I nodded, as if this were all normal. I was about to ask him about a job here when he scratched at his arm, revealing the bottom half of what appeared to be an electric eel tattoo, complete with lightning bolts of electricity zapping out of it. I thought immediately of Ray's stingray tattoo and Hammer's shark ink. *Sea Monster.*

Operation Offerdahl and Cold Case had just merged into one.

While my brain processed all this, my body went a different direction and punched Aaron in the chest. I didn't think about it, I didn't plan it, it didn't even occur to me that I was doing it until I saw him stumble, hand to his heart.

"What the hell was that?"

I glanced at my throbbing hand. *That* was accumulated stress, fear, and anger held in too long. I'd never punched anyone before, at least not like that. His chest had felt solid, and then it had given like wet paper when my force had overridden his, just like they'd taught us in the self-defense class I'd taken the previous month. "You're in the gang from Chicago."

He tugged down his sleeve, covering the tattoo. "Who the hell are you?"

I couldn't remember the fake name I gave him. My adrenaline, out of nowhere, was gushing like a waterfall. "I'm the friend of the old man you shits beat up last night. I'm the person who knows you all drowned Maurice alive and left his two little kids without a dad." I felt dizzy and realized I hadn't been breathing.

To my surprise, Aaron laughed. "Hell, woman, we ain't that. We're just a bunch of dumb punks who like to pretend we're in a gang. We wouldn't hurt anyone. We might smoke a little dope, sure, but that's it. Mostly, I'm clean. I've got this job, right?" He held up his hands and indicated the rec room.

His confidence and unexpected honesty unbalanced me more.

"You're friends with Hammer and Ray?"

"Sure."

"The three of you *didn't* try to break into the Battle Lake apothecary last night and then beat up an old man when he caught you?"

"No." He shook his head, his expression concerned. "That sounds pretty harsh."

And then for a split second, quicker than a blink, his front dropped and I saw his real self. If I hadn't been giving him my full attention, I would have missed it. Behind his friendly smile and easy half-truths, rage boiled like acid. The glimpse was gone, as fast as it had come, replaced by an open smile.

Still, that peek was enough to chill my adrenaline. I suddenly felt shaky and scared. But I wasn't going to make the same mistake he had, so I kept my angry face on.

"Yeah, pretty harsh. What about Maurice?"

Aaron nodded, leaned back on the counter, shoved his hands deep in his pockets, studied his shoes like they held all the answers. "Real sad. We're hoping the police find out what went on there."

He pulled his eyes back up to me, a new light glowing in them. "Hey, are you the detective Ray gave the letter to? Man, I told him he shouldn't have done that. He said you were a hot ride, looked a little like the brunette in *Scream*. What was her name?"

I didn't answer.

"Eve?" he said. "Or maybe Neve? Who knows, but she's easy on the eyes. So maybe Ray went in for that?" He chuckled, and then the chuckle turned to laughter. "What the hell did you lie and tell me your name was? Fishbacher?"

I glanced at the pool. The couple was getting out, disappearing through the opposite door. Had they seen me hit Aaron? Unlikely, or they would have come out already. I listened for other sounds in the building. I didn't want to be alone with this guy.

He pulled a lollipop out of his back pocket, a red one, and peeled off the plastic. He kept smiling as he sucked, still leaning against the front counter as if he possessed all the time and glory in the world. "I was at work here when Mo got offed, you can ask around. I heard he was a snitch who got what was coming to him, but I don't believe it. He was a good guy, a good guy with weird ideas, but man, he didn't deserve to die. You know about Taunita? And the babies? Ray said he called them, let them know about Mo."

I didn't like him being in charge of the conversation. "What do you know about Samuel Litchfield?"

He pushed himself off the counter, his mask falling again. He quickly adjusted. "He's a badass. I'd watch out for him."

I couldn't tolerate his slimy presence for another second. He was a liar, and worse, he was cruel. It was written in the way he carried himself, the tightness in his shoulders, how his eyes always searched for an angle. He was disgusting. I turned without another word, every bit of me listening for him to follow.

"You didn't apologize for hitting me. You sorry, baby?"

I kept walking.

Chapter 44

I dropped a quarter into the first pay phone I found and dialed the Battle Lake Police Station. Diego answered. I told him that I'd located Aaron Offerdahl, that he had a sea creature tattoo, and that he was likely gnawing on a fentanyl sucker. I reported what Mrs. Berns had said about a possible grow room in the brewery dorm as well, and asked him to pass all the information on to Chief Wohnt immediately.

Next I called Samuel Litchfield and told him I'd located the sorry piece of shit otherwise known as Aaron Offerdahl at the microbrewery dorms and that I'd send Litchfield a final itemized bill for my services before the end of the week.

Unburdened of that information and my responsibility to my client, I returned to the hospital to check on Curtis. After much rerouting and waiting, I discovered that he was in stable condition but could not yet receive visitors. Despite this, I saw Bernie from the hardware store, Sid from the café, and Theadora from the apothecary in the waiting room, just in case Curtis woke up and they'd be allowed to visit him.

I also recognized the owner of the Shoreline, whose first job had been working as Curtis's farmhand, the nurse from the Senior Sunset who Curtis had mentioned occasionally sneaked him airplane bottle–size liquors, and the pastor from Curtis's church.

"About time you arrived."

I swiveled to find Mrs. Berns and Vienna wearing matching, swishy tracksuits and fanny packs. Vienna's hair appeared freshly permed, just like Mrs. Berns's, and her pursed lips and stocky build gave her the look of an off-market Martha Stewart.

"What are you both doing here?" I asked, emphasis on "both."

"Wanted to check on Curtis while we were in town buying party supplies," Mrs. Berns said.

Vienna stepped back and abruptly began fanning herself, glancing at Mrs. Berns with an annoyed look on her face. "Baked beans say what? You nearly uncurled my hair with that one."

Mrs. Berns shrugged. "It's your fault I'm eating so many vegetables. I feel like a parade horse. So, are you gonna invite Mira to the party?"

Vienna pulled her hand from her nose. I smelled the same odor she did and thought she was overreacting. Or maybe I'd spent too much time with my pets and elderly friends.

"We're having a party at my house tomorrow," Vienna said. "You're invited."

She didn't seem happy about asking me, like her mom had told her she needed to pick me for the softball team. Was she feeling as possessive of Mrs. Berns as I was? A few more of Mrs. Berns's gas attacks, and she'd likely be cured of that.

"I don't know if that's a great idea, not if there's going to be pot there," I said. "I was just at the fitness center, and you may want to lay low in your neighborhood for a bit."

Vienna drew herself up to her full, impressive height, her eyebrows beetling. "What do you mean?"

Not for the first time, I wondered what Mrs. Berns saw in her. She was a little stodgy, despite her hunter-hunting and her yoga and her faux-hippie lifestyle, and she didn't seem to have much for humor. Plus, Mrs. Berns *hated* to eat healthy.

"I mean the police believe there might be some drug activity at the fitness center where you work and maybe the brewery." I left myself out as the informant in that situation. "I don't suppose you'd know anything about that?"

"I don't draw conclusions," she said archly. "I draw connections."

I looked at Mrs. Berns, my eyebrows raised. *Do you see what sort of person you're hanging out with?* they said.

She raised one eyebrow of her own, its meaning clear: *Don't judge or I'll give you a snakebite that'll make you wish you could smell my fart again for relief from the misery.*

I kept a scowl aimed at Mrs. Berns but spoke to Vienna. "The police know about the grow room at the fitness center."

Vienna crossed her arms, looking from me to Mrs. Berns and back to me again. "How do *you* know about it?"

I shrugged. "There's a gang member working there. He isn't very tight with the secrets. What I want to know: Do the owners of the brewery know he might be using it as a front for drug running?"

She laughed at me, exactly as Aaron had when he realized I'd given him Betty Fishbacher as an alias. "You were talking to Aaron, weren't you? The young man with the piercing above his eye? He's a liar, and a troublemaker, too, if you ask me. I just do the cooking, though, and teach some classes, so it's none of my business who they hire. But no, I can assure you that O'Callaghan's is a legitimate brewery run by decent people. Aaron is a bad apple they think they can reform."

"What about the grow room?"

"It's not even *at* the fitness center. It's just a nickname for an old cabin behind it in the woods where the kids hang after their shifts. They like that it feels secret. I can't guarantee they're not smoking any pot there, but they're certainly no front for a drug cartel." She wiped at her eyes, giggles still bubbling out.

My cheeks were hot. Getting laughed at publicly twice in one day was no treat, but what was eating me was that her story matched Aaron's. Could it be that he *was* just an aimless doper, and that the hard drugs were coming from somewhere else? But no, Jed had told me the Sea Monster gang had the hard stuff, and I trusted Jed. That meant that either Aaron had pulled the wool over Vienna's eyes, or she was in on it, too. I was weighing whether to punch her in the chest or check her purse for drugs when I entertained a thought, one I should have invited a lot earlier.

"Hey, who's watching the library?"

Mrs. Berns pretended to have a great deal of interest in the plant behind her.

"Mrs. Berns?"

She crossed her arms. "Fine. I left the library because I wanted to go out with Vienna. Who reads on Thursdays, anyhow?"

"You just closed it down?"

"No, I didn't *just* close it down." She rolled her eyes. "I got all the people out first."

My head was getting ready to pop when a nurse came over to me, a tentative smile on his face.

"Are you Mira James?" He glanced over his shoulder. "Marnie at information told me."

"Yes." My heart drop-clutched.

"I have good news! Curtis woke up for a few minutes."

I grabbed his arm. "Is he awake now?"

"I'm afraid not. He asked about you and someone named Mrs. Berns, and said something about a tattoo and the sound of a hurt baby animal? And then he was out again."

Chapter 45

I stayed at the hospital until they chased me out well past visiting hours. Curtis didn't wake up again, but the nurse on staff assured me that it was an excellent sign that he had spoken.

Driving home, I couldn't remember the last time I'd eaten. *Was it yesterday?* I was so hungry that my stomach was cramping. I pulled into the Sun Mart Foods parking lot and dipped into the deli to buy some spicy buffalo wings. I ended up leaving with the wings, a grapefruit soda, mashed potatoes with gravy, green beans, and a small bag of salt-and-vinegar potato chips.

When I pulled into my driveway, 97 percent of the food was in my tummy and only 3 percent on the front of my coat and in my lap.

"Where have you been all day?"

Taunita was seated on the couch, Timothy tucked under her arm and Alessa in her lap, reading *The Rainbow Fish* to both of them.

I glanced at the clock. It was 6:28 p.m. "My friend's in the hospital. He was in critical condition, but it looks like he's through the worst of it." Away from the hospital and anyone who really knew me, I began to melt. The tears came first, followed by the kind of crying that made it hard to breathe.

It was embarrassing to be so emotional in front of a near stranger, but she motioned for me to join her on the couch. I'd been doing too much of this weeping thing lately. When my sobs had subsided to whimpering, I wiped at my eyes and saw that Timothy had put his soft blankie across my lap and gone to play with Luna. Alessa was on the other side of her mom, still watching me with her serious eyes, her thumb stuck in her mouth.

"Sorry," I said, pulling away and going for a tissue.

Taunita watched me. "We all need a good cry sometimes. What put your friend in the hospital?"

I told her, starting with who Curtis was and what he meant to me, how he'd become a close friend and honorary grandpa. I counted on him. I needed him. "I guess he woke up for a short bit this afternoon," I finished. "He asked for me, and another friend, and said the guy who attacked him had a tattoo and made a sound like a hurt baby animal."

"Aw shit." Taunita stood and began pacing. "Ray beat up an old man? Outside a drugstore? Shit," she repeated.

Timothy's eyes grew wide. I expected we would hear him trying out that word very shortly.

"Sounds like," I said. "I don't know anyone else with a stingray tattoo. I told the police what Curtis said before I came here."

"But your friend isn't awake yet?"

"He wasn't when I left. He won't be talking to anyone before tomorrow at the earliest."

She glanced at her jacket. "You mind watching the kids for a while? I gotta get out of the house."

Timothy was brushing Luna with a hairbrush that looked suspiciously like my own. Also, a distinct smell had begun to emanate from Alessa's quadrant of the room, and it wasn't chocolate.

"How long will you be gone?"

"Not too long. I need air."

"Fine." The woman had just watched me break down. What else could I say?

Ten minutes later, on her way out the door, she hit me with another zinger. "Oh, and a really hot guy stopped by looking for you. Almost gave me a taste for blonds, except he looked so sad. Said his name was Johnny?"

Chapter 46

"Peeza."

"Your mom said you already ate."

It'd been just the three of us for nearly an hour. For most of that time, Timothy had alternated between saying "ship" (thank goodness he couldn't say his *t*'s well) and "peeza." Alessa hadn't warmed to me yet, but neither was she crying.

I'd spent many of those minutes trying not to think about Johnny. I knew I should call him, but not now. I was busy. I'd think about it tomorrow.

"Peeza."

Had to give the kid points for consistency. "I have string cheese. Do you want some of that?"

"Peeza."

My shoulders slumped. Pizza delivery, like high-speed internet, had not yet found rural Minnesota. A gas station in Battle Lake offered in-town pizza delivery, but I lived three and a half miles *outside* town.

"I'll try." I grabbed the phone. After two minutes of negotiation and "turn left at the Johnson farm"–type directions, the deliveryman agreed he'd bring pizza right to my door for an extra five dollars. I took it as a victory.

Thirty minutes later, Timothy and I were enjoying second supper, and Alessa had allowed me to hold her, though she craned her neck like an owlet so she could watch me while I did so.

"Does your sister ever smile?"

"Dinah-sore!" Timothy dropped his pizza slice, arched his fingers into claws, drew back his lips, and growled.

I was getting ready to check his temperature when I felt the chuckle in my arms. Alessa was laughing at her brother, a deep Buddha giggle that rocked her whole body. It was contagious, calling up bubbling giggles from inside me. The more Alessa and I laughed, the more impressions Timothy did, from fish to giraffe to "monter-bot-a-rawr."

"Hey," I said spontaneously. "Do you guys want to go sledding?"

Timothy stopped in midmonster and pointed at the window. "Dark. Dark out der."

It was indeed night, but a gorgeous full moon glittered on the snow like a promise.

"Moonlight sledding! It'll be fun." I cleaned up the pizza, wrote Taunita a note explaining where we were, changed Alessa's diaper for the second time that night, and piled both kids into their winter gear.

Twenty minutes later, I'd hauled Sunny's sleds out of a nearby shed and pulled the kids to the top of the sledding hill near the house. Luna was at our side, barking her excitement. The three of us slid down dozens of times, snow shushing up at us and the moon smiling down. I was amazed and grateful that Taunita trusted me with such valuable creatures.

They giggled. They begged for more. Boogers ran down both their faces like open faucets, and still they didn't want to stop sledding. I thought of Maurice, and all that he would miss, and I kept on sledding with them until we were all soaked and Alessa's eyes were heavy despite the smile on her face. I situated them both in the sled, Timothy holding his sister, and pulled them gently back.

They were both asleep by the time we reached the house, their cheeks impossibly rosy and vulnerable, their mouths both perfect little hearts. I carried them softly inside, wiped their noses, undressed and changed them, and tucked them into bed without waking them. I fell asleep on the couch so I'd be nearby if they needed me.

Before I drifted off, I had a realization. The night I'd gotten the call about Curtis, I'd been sleeping on my mattress rather than under it. That meant tonight was the second night in a row that I'd slept like a normal person.

Something about having the kids around made me feel stronger.

Chapter 47

I woke to the sound of someone shuffling in my kitchen. I sat up, rubbing the sleep out of my eyes. The sun had not risen, but the murky lavender of the sky suggested it was near morning.

"Taunita?"

"Sh, now. The babies are still sleeping."

I smelled oatmeal and coffee and heard her humming. "Where were you?"

"Stopping a cycle." The humming continued. "Feeding justice. You must have wore out T and Alessa. They never sleep in this late."

I pulled myself off the couch and poked my head into their room. Both were still conked out, Timothy sleeping with his arms sprawled and Alessa curled around a blanket. They looked like chubby angels. Returning to the kitchen, I accepted the cup of coffee Taunita handed me.

"I took them sledding. They're pretty sweet kids."

"Sledding?" she asked. "At night?"

"The moon was full." I sipped at the coffee. It was bitter and delicious. I could get used to these roommates. "What do you mean, you fed justice?"

"Not worth talking about. Can I borrow some money?"

I almost asked her what for, but it didn't matter. I had a rule that I'd lend anyone money once with no expectations of return. That way, I was never let down, only pleasantly surprised. I grabbed my wallet off the counter. I had three twenties. I handed two to Taunita. "Do you know Aaron Offerdahl?"

She shoved the money in her back jeans pocket. "I know the name. He's a drug punk. Maurice met him through a friend in Chicago."

"He's from this area originally and is back here now, working at a brewery."

She snorted. "From what Maurice told me, if Aaron is working a legit job, it's a front to sell drugs. Mo said Offerdahl has bad bones."

Her mention of Chicago stirred a thought. "Have you ever heard of O'Callaghan's? They had a carpet empire in the Chicago area, and now they own the microbrewery where Aaron works. I'm wondering if the whole *business* is a front for drug dealing."

She shook her head. "Nah. Never heard of them. But if they owned an 'empire,' it makes no sense for them to mess with drugs. And why out here, in the middle of nowhere? It's probably just two-bit Aaron doing his business out the side."

"Was Maurice dealing?"

She poured the oatmeal into a bowl. It smelled like apples and cinnamon. She must have brought it with her.

Conflicting emotions chased each other across her face. She took her time answering.

"He said he wasn't," she said softly. "He said he was just here following up on those letters. But then he got himself killed, so I don't know. You're gonna look into what happened to him, aren't you? You said you would."

"Mama?"

We both turned. A tousle-headed Timothy stood in the doorway, his blankie in one hand and a love-worn teddy bear in the other. I wanted to hug him close, but he was studying me shyly, as if he were embarrassed at how well we'd gotten along yesterday.

Taunita walked over to grab him and kiss his cheek. "Hey, baby. I heard you went sledding!"

He ducked his head into the crook of her neck. "Hungy."

She began feeding him oatmeal. I was deliberately ignoring her question. I didn't want to tell her no, but Maurice's death was in police hands now, and with the drugs and recent violence, they certainly weren't going to care about some old letter and a drafty story about a stolen inheritance.

I took advantage of her being distracted and slipped to the phone to call the hospital. No change in Curtis's condition, for better or worse. I ducked into the shower and got myself cleaned and prepped for work. When I returned to the living room, Alessa was awake, too, and eating her share of oatmeal with her mom's help. She put her arms up to me immediately when she saw me, and I felt like I'd just won the Boston Marathon.

I snuggled her, taking over the oatmeal feeding and managing to keep us both pretty clean.

"I'll keep my ear to the ground," I finally said. "But nothing's changed. I still can't promise anything."

Taunita smiled and nodded. She'd been waiting patiently for my answer.

"I've got to go to work at the library, and then maybe run some errands after. I don't know when I'll be home."

"All right," Taunita said.

I'd stop by the Prospect House before work in the hopes of talking with Carter Stone. I'd ask him what, if anything, he knew about Orpheus Jackson. It was the safest way I could think of tracking down information for Taunita.

Chapter 48

It was a beautiful day, icy but clear, the sun sparkling off the driveway with the strength of a klieg light. The air looked and smelled beautifully clean, purified in the bitter cold. I put the temperature at five below zero, but it was only a guess.

I scraped all six windows as the Toyota warmed up, or at least became less frigid. The seat was still rock-cold when I slid into it, hunched forward so I could see through the defrosted circles at the base of the windshield. By the time I reached the end of Sunny's long driveway, I didn't need to hunch. The lower third of the windshield was clear.

By the time I was at the Prospect House, the car was warm.

Oh well.

It was eight o'clock, well before regular hours. I decided to walk right into the kitchen rather than knock. I surprised Carter pouring a mug of coffee, his Civil War–style cap askew on his head.

"Good morning!" His voice was surprised, and he glanced over my shoulder. I followed his gaze and spotted someone disappearing down the stairs that led to the section of the house devoted to the Civil War.

"My wife," he said, by way of explanation. "Going to do some more cataloging. Were we expecting you?"

"Sorry, no. I was hoping you could answer a few questions for me before I go to work. About Orpheus Jackson?"

He leaned into the fridge, grabbed a jug of whole milk, and poured a healthy splash into his coffee. "Who?"

"Orpheus Jackson. He was in the Battle of Honey Hill with—"

"Barnaby Offerdahl," he finished for me. "Barnaby served in the First Artillery. I believe the Union lost nearly a hundred men in that battle. Barnaby was one of 'em." He tapped his chin. "I do recall the name Orpheus, but it's more an old legend than anything. A story, really."

My heartbeat picked up. "Do you mind telling it?"

He shrugged, taking a deep pull from his coffee. "From what I recall, Barnaby didn't mention Orpheus in any of the letters to his brother that I came across, but that's no surprise. Barnaby didn't trust any of his own family beyond his daughter. What I heard, I heard through the grapevine, so I wouldn't call any of it reliable. But there was a story that Barnaby became close friends with a free Black man during the war. It was a bit of a scandal around here, in those times anyhow, because Barnaby spread the word that he was bringing the man back with him to live in Battle Lake."

"Did he ever bring an army buddy home with him when he was alive?"

"Not that I know of. Barnaby only returned to Battle Lake once after he started serving, shortly after the first time he was shot, but he came back alone. He was back in the field again soon after."

"But a free Black man *did* come here."

Carter set his coffee cup on the counter and topped it off. "How do you mean?"

"The hanged man."

"Ah." Carter rubbed his mustache. "That is true."

My heartbeat started humming. I smelled a mystery here, a 135-year-old one. "I don't suppose that hanged man could have been Orpheus, returning with a message for the Offerdahls?"

"Never occurred to me, but unlikely. Why would he have traveled all this way with a message, just to hang himself?"

Excellent question, *if* he actually hung himself. And if what Taunita had said about the return address on the letters Maurice had found was true, I knew for a fact that Orpheus had spent time in Battle Lake. "I wish we knew if the hanged man had any clues on him."

Carter took a big slurp of his coffee. "That I can help with. I found a wooden box of his effects near the attic."

"What? How do you know they belonged to the hanged man?"

"I'm a bit of a historian. Well, more than a bit." He tapped his head. "Plus, the box was labeled 'Hanged Man,' with the date of March 1865 on the box, same month as the body was found."

"What was in the box?" I couldn't contain my excitement. "Anything that would identify him?"

"All I remember is the musket. I keep that on display downstairs."

"Can I see it?"

The words of Orpheus's letter spiraled in my head: *Should anything happen to me, look to the tunnel of justice.* The tunnel of justice! What else could that refer to but the barrel of a gun? For the first time in my life, a mystery was falling into place immediately. I imagined discovering a note from Orpheus tucked in the musket's barrel, yellowed with age but bearing a map to Civil War treasure he'd buried. Taunita and the babies would be rich.

I followed Carter into the basement, fighting every instinct in me to nudge him in the back, forcing him to move faster.

"Libby?"

His wife glanced up from the far side of the room, where she was holding an old handgun in one hand and typing on a laptop with the other. "Yes, love?"

"You remember the 'Hanged Man' box?"

She turned to face us full-on, setting down the gun. Her face was pleasantly lined, her fading blonde hair curling at shoulder level. "Of course. The whole story is gruesome."

"What else was in the box?"

She returned to her laptop, typing in a quick flurry of letters. "Musket 25A, a Bible, a wooden fife, and two quarters, two nickels, and a penny."

"Here's the musket," Carter said, drawing my attention to a nearby table.

He placed the gun into my hands. It was heavy, maybe seven pounds, the dark-brown wood worn so smooth that it felt satiny. The trigger was plated silver, as was the hammer. Metal strips rested on the top and the bottom of the long barrel, three equal-spaced silver bands circling the length of it.

"That's a Springfield rifle musket, a single-shot muzzleloader," he said, reverently. "You see the hammer?"

I nodded, touching the cool silver with my thumb.

"A percussion cap. It fired a .58-caliber minié ball. One of the most accurate rifles of its time."

"And it was found next to the hanged man's body?" I couldn't shake the disappointment. If Orpheus had been murdered, as I believed, surely his gun would have been taken.

"As far as we know. This gun definitely would've been used in the Civil War, so the date on the box is accurate."

I turned the gun around. "No chance this could still fire?"

"None. I cleaned all the rifles myself, made them safe for handling."

"I've always wanted to look down the barrel of a musket." It was a weird thing to say, but less odd than just doing it, I figured.

"Knock yourself out."

I could feel Libby staring at me from across the room. I kept my attention on the hole, angling it toward the light, still nervous about looking down the barrel of a gun despite Carter's assurance. I didn't see anything and so angled it farther, and there it was—a shadow within a shadow.

There was something curled inside the barrel.

I sucked in my breath.

"Well, that's one dream realized," I said, handing the gun back to Carter. I couldn't very well dig out whatever was in there right in front of him. I liked him, but the residue of sleepless nights had me paranoid, and I didn't know whose team he was on.

"All right," he said.

I appreciated that he didn't question weirdness.

Too bad I'd already made up my mind to break into the Prospect House that night and steal the gun.

"Thanks for your time. I better be running," I said, making for the stairs. I walked past a gorgeous corn plant that I must have missed when I first passed it. "Beautiful plant!" I called over my shoulder.

"Thanks," Libby said.

I thought I also heard her say, "Kennie takes care of them," but I chose to block that out.

The Fortune's rich, dark smell of coffee washed over me, trailed closely by the homey scent of fresh-baked rolls. I'd need to cut back on my eating, or at least start eating healthy, but I would think about that next week. Today, I wanted nothing more than a soy latte sweetened with fresh honey and sprinkled with cinnamon powder and a side of Nancy's homemade chocolate chip–walnut banana bread. I swallowed the excess saliva pooling in my mouth and made my way to the front.

The door opened behind me, letting in a gust of icy air, but I was staring at the glass display case like one of Pavlov's dogs. I *could* have a fresh-fried glazed doughnut instead. Or—ohmygod, a new tray had just been slid into the display case—I could order one of Nancy's famous skollebollers, a Norwegian cardamom-scented, vanilla custard–filled, coconut-dusted bun.

They were so fresh that their warmth steamed the glass.

I moaned.

"We have to stop meeting like this."

I swiveled. Mrs. Berns was stepping from foot to foot.

"Do you have to pee?"

"Nope." She tugged off her hat. "Just cold. Whatcha gonna have?"

I glanced back at the case. Could I declare an emergency and budge everyone? "Skolleboller."

"Good choice."

"Why aren't you with your new friend?"

She pulled off her mittens, breathing into her fingers. "I missed you."

I felt my eyes light up. "Really?"

"No!" She grinned. "Ha. You're so gullible. No, I decided there's only room for one gutsy old dame in a gang, and so I dumped her. She was too bossy, anyhow. Speaking of, what's on our agenda for tonight?"

I was ashamed at how happy I was that she and Vienna had broken up. I'd get the details later. For now, I just wanted to enjoy the moment. "Quiet night."

"Hairy liar."

"What?"

"I thought we were stating an adjective and then a pertinent noun. Along those lines, I'm calling you a hairy liar. Not only did I see you pull out of the Prospect House on my way back from the Shoreline, but I also see your eyes are a lighter brown than usual. That means you're excited about something."

Hmm. Maybe she was better at this detective thing than I'd thought.

"I have to run an errand tonight for a friend."

She raised her eyebrows.

I glanced around. Ah, what the heck. There was nothing as fun as a secret shared. I leaned in and whispered into her ear, "I'm breaking into the Prospect House."

She gave a rebel yell. "I'm in!"

"I don't need a sidekick."

She snorted. "And I don't need oxygen. Besides, too late. We're already this generation's Bogey and Bacall. Or at least Bonnie and Clyde."

"I'll think about it."

"I'll save you the time." She gave me two thumbs up. "I'm going with."

"Mira, Mrs. Berns! How're you two doing?"

We were finally at the front of the line, distracting me from my conversation with Mrs. Berns. "Hey, Sid. I need two skollebollers, stat. And a soy café miel."

"Not until you give me some news." She lodged her hands on her hips.

I realized I'd been neglecting her and Nancy. Usually, I stopped in at least once a week during slow times so I could visit. Lately, I'd been doing little more than grabbing a meal and leaving. "Sorry I haven't stayed around to chat much lately. A lot going on."

She raised her eyebrows, waiting for me to tell her more. I didn't mention Taunita and the kids because that would bring up too many questions, and there was a noisy line forming behind me. Instead, I gave her a thirty-second synopsis on Curtis's condition, told her I was researching more deeply into the Prospect House, and updated her on the library business.

"You forgot to mention your Nut Goodie recipe in the paper," Nancy said, coming out to put her arm around Sid. "That was a winner."

"Did you actually make it?"

Sid winked. "Come over later when we're not busy, and I'll let you taste."

She disappeared into the back. Sid began making my order, talking over her shoulder as she did so, filling me in on small-town news—who'd brought the best bars to church, which person had started dating whom, the new hire at the chiropractor. It was comforting.

She had my food and drink ready in a blink. She nodded across the busy main room of the coffee shop while she leafed my change out of the till. "And that's Bad Brad's girlfriend over there. She's met him here for coffee twice this week."

I followed her gaze. All twelve tables were packed, and three women and two men lined the seating counter that faced the main window. "Which one is dating Brad?"

"The one eating a banana."

Mrs. Berns scrunched her eyes in the direction of the window. "Who eats a banana in public?"

I homed in on the woman in question. I was twenty-nine and knew Brad was at least two years older than me. Catriona the insurance agent, however, appeared to be twenty-four, maybe twenty-five, with curly blonde hair. She kept glancing at the front door between bites of fruit. The seat next to her was empty.

"Brad's worried she's cheating on him. Asked me to look into it," I said to nobody in particular.

"Now's your chance," Mrs. Berns said, wiggling her eyebrows at me. She pushed me out of the way so the people behind us could order. She kept nudging me toward the woman. I had no choice but to speak or look like a stalker.

"Catriona?"

She glanced at me, confusion in her eyes. They were slightly wide set and a gorgeous deep green. I noticed she wore sensible shoes. "Yes?"

I held out my hand. "You don't know me. I'm a friend of Ba—er, Brad's."

She appeared confused. "Did he tell you to tell me he was going to be late?"

"I haven't seen him," I answered honestly. "He's mentioned you quite a bit lately, though."

She reached for her coffee cup. "All good, I hope."

Something about her face made me want to tell the truth. "He thinks you're cheating on him."

She did a spit take with her coffee. "Me? Cheating? Why?"

I felt a shove from behind. "No good reason, really. He said you didn't post your relationship status on SixDegrees, and that you don't seem eager to commit." I felt stupid saying it out loud, so I stopped.

She rolled her eyes. "You said you're friends with Brad."

I nodded.

"Then you know what he's like. Look, I love him, though I haven't told him and I won't." She shrugged. "He's a big child. We're having fun now, but he's not husband material, you know?"

It occurred to me that Catriona was around 98 percent smarter than I'd been at her age, or even than I was a year ago, when I'd been dating Brad myself.

Mrs. Berns peeked around my side. "Mrs. Berns," she said, extending her hand. "Pleased to meet you. Pleased to meet anyone with a head on their shoulders, really. Now, let's be honest. You're only with him because he's good in bed, right?"

"I wish," Catriona said.

I could vouch for that as well. Brad subscribed to the McDonald's model of sex: efficient and unvaried.

"So no cheating?" I asked.

"I don't cheat," she said simply. "If I want someone else, then it's time to stop dating the person I'm dating."

I was beginning to think I needed this woman as a friend. Or a life coach. "Thanks," I said. "I'll tell Brad to stop worrying."

"How about I tell him myself?"

I smiled. "An even better plan."

I let Mrs. Berns guide me out the door, where she pinched one of my skollebollers. We parted ways, with her promising to meet me at the end of my library shift. I told her I'd believe it when I saw it.

I drove the short distance to the library, sipping my creamy, cinnamony coffee as I steered down Battle Lake's main street. Except for the spate of crimes that seemed all connected to me, it was a wonderful place to live. I held that thought as I unlocked the library, fired up the computers, and nibbled my cardamom-scented skolleboller, promising myself that I'd learn how to bake them at home so I could eat them in herds.

The library crowd was steady, and the day passed in a pleasant drift of helping people find books, cleaning up computer files, and walking the shelves. I skipped lunch out of deference to my shrinking pants and instead used the time to type a final report on Aaron Offerdahl. I no longer cared why Litchfield wanted to find him or, for that matter, cared about Aaron Offerdahl at all. I was washing my hands of the whole deal. Tonight, I would treasure hunt for Taunita. The police could worry about the baddies.

By the time Mrs. Berns showed up at the end of my shift, I was actually happy to see her. Frankly, breaking into a huge, haunted mansion at night all alone was a scary prospect. Plus, she offered to spring for dinner at the Turtle Stew beforehand. I drove, and we were seated in a booth near the front windows. We both knew what we wanted, and the food arrived quickly.

"What exactly is the plan?" She grabbed the pepper from my hand to douse her plate of gravy-covered mashed potatoes and meat loaf.

I snatched it back to finish peppering my french fries. "We find an unlocked window, sneak in, grab the gun, retrieve whatever's in the barrel, and sneak out. No harm, no foul."

Her eyes widened in disbelief. "Your plan rests on an unlocked window? In January?"

"You have a better idea?"

"Since you ask . . ."

"What?"

"You promise you're not going to ditch me after I share my secret?"

I stole a forkful of mashed potatoes off her plate. *Yum. Homemade.* "We're already committed."

"My friend Ida is a volunteer at the Prospect House. She said they keep a spare key above the inner doorjamb of the garden shed."

I almost laughed out loud with joy. "You are worth your weight in gold."

She grabbed a fistful of my fries. "Tell me something I don't know."

Chapter 49

The gravid moon lent a soft glow to the night. All the lights were off in the Prospect House, but traffic still passed by on 78. Even worse, we could hear people playing a pickup game of hockey near the ice castle on the lake.

We'd left the Toyota parked in the alley behind the Turtle Stew and walked the mile to the house, ducking into the sparse woods circling it when we were certain no one was looking. We'd crunched through the calf-high snow and slipped into the shed. The key was not exactly where Mrs. Berns had said it would be, but with her on my shoulders, fumbling around in the shed's dark interior, we finally located it. Actually, it found us, first plunking onto my head and then hitting the ground.

"Got it!" Mrs. Berns claimed triumphantly.

I helped her down, rubbing at the spot where the key had dropped. My noggin was taking a beating lately.

She scooped up the key, and we stepped out of the shed to consider the house. It seemed to be staring right back at us.

"Eerie, isn't it?" Mrs. Berns asked. "Those two windows up there look like eyes, and the back door is right between and below them, like a mouth."

I recalled the little girl's face in the attic window, the heart-shaped face I'd filed away as Mabel Offerdahl's ghost. Or my imagination. I punched Mrs. Berns lightly on the arm. "Shut up. I'm already scared enough."

"Better git your big-girl pants on, because we're doing this."

Without warning, she took off across the driveway separating the shed from the Prospect House, slamming her back against the wood siding when she reached the house. I was surprised she hadn't attempted a full-body roll on the way over. I wanted to make fun of her, but even more than that, I didn't want to get caught. I copied her moves.

"Suave," she said as we stood with our backs against the house, glancing to the right and left for any sign of movement. Only she pronounced it to rhyme with "wave" because that's how cool people did it.

Instead of responding, I crouched, staying low to the ground until I reached the door. The key fit in the lock like a hot knife in butter, and we stood inside the kitchen in seconds. We caught our breath and let our eyes adjust to the light. I became aware of the clutter, and the shadow-smell of coffee brewed several hours earlier.

The silence in the house was so intense that it almost became a sound itself. I'd snooped around and broken into four, maybe five, places in the past eight months, all in the name of solving mysteries, but it never felt comfortable. The hyperawareness of knowing you were in a place you weren't supposed to be, looking for stuff that people didn't want you to find, was both exhilarating and terrifying. It gave me an intense urge to pee or giggle.

I clicked on the flashlight and directed the narrow beam to the basement stairs. "The Civil War stuff is down there," I whispered.

"You first."

I figured she'd say that. I tiptoed to the top of the stairs and shined the flashlight down the steps. The dusty yellow light landed in a lonely circle at the bottom, something about it suggesting ghost fingers and lurking demons, waiting for someone stupid enough to enter.

"Tell me about your husband," I whispered. I needed something to distract me.

"What?"

"You heard me." I took the first step. Little warning feelers shot like electric bolts down my legs and arms.

"What do you want to know?"

"Did you love him?" I took the second step. Mrs. Berns was so near that I could feel her breath on my neck.

"Sure," she said quietly. "Didn't matter back then, though. He put food on the table. He paid the bills. He didn't hit me. But he didn't live life, he worked it. And he drank too much."

"Your whole marriage?" We were now in the middle of the stairs, halfway between escape and the dungeon. The air felt heavier in front of us.

"You know how when a tree has a good year, lots of water and sunlight, you can see huge growth when you look at its rings? It's the opposite with people. We grow more in our *bad* years. I grew a lot married to Xavier."

Xavier. Xavier Berns. I took another step. Fear crawled across my skin like newly hatched spiders. Any number of horrors awaited us below, hidden among the dusty relics of long-dead soldiers.

Maybe, just maybe, something that would also help Taunita was down there, too.

"Do you miss him?"

"I paid my dues. That was the past. Now I live in the moment. It's the only way to be." She coughed, and I jumped.

"Do you hear that?" I asked.

"What?"

I stopped. Behind her cough, I thought I'd heard a moan. It might have been the wind, yet I couldn't stop the chilly sweat gathering at the base of my spine. We'd reached the bottom of the stairs, large tables standing sentry on each side of the landing. It felt like we were being watched by a hundred leering eyes. I risked panning the room with my flashlight so we could get our bearings.

It lit across uniforms in glass, bayonets, guns, and—

Could it be?

I brought the light back to what had grabbed my attention, my heartbeat thick and terrified.

It was.

On the far side of the room, a little girl, staring solemnly at Mrs. Berns and me.

I screamed and dropped the flashlight.

Chapter 50

"What?"

"I saw a face!"

I fought the urge to charge back up the stairs only because Mrs. Berns was blocking my exit. I snatched the flashlight from the floor, brandishing it like a weapon. That's when I noticed the face was also pointing a flashlight back at me.

It was a mirror.

"Holy crap," I said, gathering my heart from my throat. "I thought it was a ghost."

Mrs. Berns snatched the flashlight from me. "I don't think you are equipped to handle this dangerous tool." She shined it around the room. "Now where's the damn gun? This place gives me the willies."

We held hands and shuffled over to the table where Carter had shown me the musket. I was relieved to discover it lying exactly where he'd set it down. I glanced over my shoulder, still nervous about the mirror, but the space behind us was a dull, blank surface.

"Shine the light in its barrel."

Mrs. Berns complied. "I see it! It looks like rolled-up paper."

"Grab me that poker," I said, pointing at a thin metal pole behind her.

With its cool metal in my hand, I began fishing inside the gun, but my efforts just pushed the paper farther away from us. This wasn't going to work. "Dangit. We have to take this gun apart."

"Don't look at me," Mrs. Berns said. "I fire 'em, I don't build 'em."

I held the butt with my left hand and cradled the barrel in the nook of my right arm. "Well then, it looks like it's coming with us. We'll find someone who knows guns, have them help us remove the paper without hurting it, and return it before Carter even knows it's missing."

That's what I hoped, anyhow.

Rather than question my illegal and ethically murky executive decision, Mrs. Berns led the way toward the stairs, flashing the light in a steady stream. I kept my eyes trained away from the mirror, and we moved as a single beast. We were nearly to the base of the stairs when something caught her eye. She stepped over to a table to the left of the stairwell.

"Look at these!" She took off her mittens and set them on a nearby counter.

"Keep your mittens on! We don't want to leave fingerprints."

She snorted. "This is Otter Tail County, not the Big Apple. Besides, there's got to be a million fingerprints around here." She held up a brilliant blue teardrop necklace. The flashlight's direct beam made it sparkle like a thousand sapphires. "Do you think it's real?"

I couldn't take my eyes off it. The main teardrop was the size of a dime, and the chain of the necklace dripped with pearl-size blue beads. "Probably crystal," I said, hypnotized. "I wonder what it's doing in the basement with the Civil War stuff."

A scraping sound drew my attention, a low, quiet noise on the floor above. It was short and so quick that it might not have happened at all.

"Did you hear that?" I whispered hoarsely.

Mrs. Berns placed the necklace back on the table, clicked off the flashlight, and grabbed my elbow. "Sounded like a one-legged, worm-eyed pirate come to steal our souls."

If my hands had been free, I would have hit her. "Let's get out of here."

I didn't need to tell her twice. We speed-shambled toward where we thought the steps were, and took them quickly, moving toward the lighter patch of darkness that outlined the ground-floor landing above. Even our hair was on high alert, quivering as we strained to hear any more sounds.

We tried to be as quiet as we could, but fear made us clumsy. Mrs. Berns dropped the flashlight, and then I bumped the gun against the wall trying to help her find it. Finally, though, we reached the top of the stairs.

We didn't dare turn the flashlight back on. We'd already made enough noise.

Despite our bumbling, we made it to the back door and locked it behind us, breathing in deep, fresh gulps of winter air. I let my heartbeat slow to a steady pace, infinitely grateful to be out of the house and to have the musket in hand. I tiptoed across the packed snow to return the key to its hidey spot, Mrs. Berns right behind me.

"I didn't know Carter had dolls in his collection," Mrs. Berns said, breaking the silence marked only by our feet crunching in the snow.

My ears were attuned to the potential sound of cars passing. We arrived at the shed.

"I don't think he does." I grunted as I reached up to tuck away the key.

She hitched her thumb toward the house. "Didn't you see that girl doll on the island in the middle of the kitchen on our way out? Looked like she was floating in the moonlight. Creepy. Why people want big old dolls is beyond me."

My blood froze. "There was no doll on the island when we went in."

We swiveled to stare at each other, our faces perfect replicas of fear. When our eyes locked, we squealed and ran, not slowing until we reached my car.

Chapter 51

Before we parted ways, Mrs. Berns reminded me that Johnny's band was playing that night. I knew she wanted to ask if I'd spoken with him since I'd spent the night at Bad Brad's, but she was friend enough not to plant a direct question on me.

I told her I'd think about Johnny tomorrow.

In the meantime, I needed to get this gun to the one person on the outside who could help me dismantle it without destroying it: Curtis Poling. He was still in the hospital, though. I would visit him first thing in the morning, hoping for his sake and mine that he was awake.

Taunita and the babies were up when I returned home, so I kept the gun stowed in my car. I didn't want to raise her hopes unnecessarily, so I didn't tell her about our Prospect House break-in. Instead, we chatted about the day while I helped her to bathe Timothy and Alessa.

She told me that the three of them had checked out the address where Maurice had stayed with his grandma in the summers of his youth. They'd rented a cabin on Silver Lake, though whatever modest structure had originally been there had since been replaced by a modern A-frame.

When I asked, she allowed that it was odd that his family of limited means would vacation on a lake so far from home, friends, and family. She said Maurice had never questioned it as a kid but, as he got older, wondered about the connection between Orpheus and the area.

It was about the time she put Alessa and Timothy to bed that I noticed my house was spotless. Even the plant leaves had been dusted. The air smelled fresh and lemony, and the countertops gleamed. Taunita had been busy.

I wanted to thank her, but the door to the spare bedroom was already closed. I crashed shortly afterward, the postadrenaline letdown hitting me like a cement truck. My plan was to get up at seven so I could make the hospital's eight o'clock visiting hour.

I slept on my mattress.

◆ ◆ ◆

Ron Sims, editor and owner of the *Battle Lake Recall*, beat my alarm clock the next morning. "James."

He'd never been what you'd call loquacious. His wife was the voice of the operation, both in their marriage and the *Recall* offices. They were a decent enough couple, except that if you caught them in a room together, they'd inevitably start making out like two walruses with a limited mating season and only one chance to save the species. It meant a lot of people, myself included, didn't visit the *Recall* offices unless absolutely necessary.

I scratched absently at my arm, standing in the middle of my bedroom and squinting against the promise of sunlight filtering through my blinds. I wondered if I should take the phone off the hook so I could finally land a decent night's sleep. "Morning, Ron. What's the news today?"

"Need someone to cover last night's break-in at the Prospect House. You in?"

I perked up like a gopher, the punch of his words knocking the air and sleep out of me. "Woof."

I actually said that, out loud. It was all I could manage.

"James?"

I sucked in a bit of air. Ron knew the Prospect House had been tossed last night, which meant the police knew. "Yeah. Someone broke into the Prospect House?" My voice squeaked.

"Someone who was not very smart."

Crap. Was he giving me a chance to confess?

"They left their mittens behind," he continued.

The vision was so clear I could have stepped into it. The flashlight catching the glint of the graceful blue teardrop necklace, Mrs. Berns pausing to remove her mittens and never putting them back on.

"What'd they take?"

He grunted. "Impossible to know. It'd be like stealing from a church garage sale. Carter called it in this morning. Said last night he thought he heard noises coming from the house—he and Libby live in the carriage house on the next lot—and he went to check. Found the house sealed tight, everything normal except for the mittens in the basement that hadn't been there when he'd locked up earlier. Plus, footprints leading into the woods."

For the love of Betsy. Had he also spotted the little pee trails we'd left after the ghost scared us out of there? And since when was everyone a detective? Whatever happened to people minding their own business? I was going to jail.

"James?"

"Yeah, I'll cover it. I need to run to Fergus to check on Curtis this morning, but if I can get Mrs. Berns to open up the library, I can stop by the Prospect House after."

If I'm not incarcerated.

"Probably just kids being kids. I'll expect news before tomorrow."

Click.

It was now that much more urgent that I reach Curtis to see what was inside the gun barrel. If I returned the musket before Carter noticed that it was missing, I stood a chance of keeping me and Mrs. Berns out of the pokey.

I speed-showered, told a sleepy Taunita that I'd be back that night, and was almost out the door before I realized I couldn't exactly tote a Civil War musket into a hospital without drawing some unwanted attention. I hurried back to my bedroom closet but couldn't find anything large enough.

I ducked into Sunny's office, where she had piled most of her belongings before leaving for Alaska, and dug through boxes until I uncovered an old hockey stick duffel bag. Perfect. Maybe today wasn't going to be so bad after all. Maybe everything would fall into place.

In fact, maybe pigs were right now flying through a frozen-over hell.

Chapter 52

"Curtis Poling." It was the third time I'd said the name, but still the flustered woman at the information counter couldn't seem to locate him. The heavy black hockey stick duffel lay on the floor next to me like a neon sign.

"Is that with a *C* or a *P*?"

"Is *what* with a *C* or a *P*?" I asked.

"His name."

I wanted to tap on her head to see if her melon was ripe. "First or last?"

"Last name," she said, as if it were obvious.

"It starts with a *P*. P-O-L—"

A deep voice behind me interrupted my recitation. "He's in stable condition. Woke up last night, ate solid food. Still can't have visitors."

I turned so slowly that I could hear my neck creak. No way Gary Wohnt was standing behind me, right? Stolen Civil War musket in a hockey stick bag much?

"Gary! How're you feeling?"

He was not in uniform. Instead, he wore denim jeans that fit him like a friend, a crisp blue oxford, and a green-and-gold patterned tie. He leaned heavily on a cane, but somehow it made him look even more capable.

He aimed one pointed glance at the duffel bag.

I in turn stared at his cane, my eyebrow raised. It was meaningless, but he didn't know that.

"What's in the bag?" Maybe he *did* know that.

"Curtis's favorite hockey stick. I knew he'd want it." Because what old guy doesn't want a piece of wood when he's recovering from a beating? "You said he's alert?"

Gary let the silence fill the air between us. It did exactly that, sniffing around our heads, and it judged me lacking, and then it started pointing at me as if I were guilty. So I threw it a bone. "I'm really worried about Curtis. Can you please tell me more?" I didn't have to fake the pleading in my voice.

It did the trick. "He's going to be OK."

"Did he say anything more beyond the tattoo and the animal-noise comment?"

Gary's eyes narrowed. "What else do you know?"

"That's it. I promise." I raised my hand in what I assumed was Girl Scout's honor. There was nothing like squatting on a bag of lies to make you righteous about a single truth. "The nurse told me that Curtis had asked about Mrs. Berns and me, and that he'd mentioned the tattoo and the same noise I heard when Mrs. Berns and I were attacked in the alley. I told Diego when I called the station the other day."

Gary only nodded.

"Are you questioning anyone in Curtis's attack?"

"What do you think?"

I thought it was time to beat cheeks. "I've got to get to work, that's what. If I can't see Curtis, I'll be on my way."

He stooped as if to help me hoist the duffel, but his cane drew him up short. I lifted the bag myself, trying to flex my muscles only as much as a hockey stick required.

"That looks heavy," he said suspiciously.

I nodded in agreement. "Back in the day, they built their sticks to last."

I didn't look back as I scurried out the sliding doors, but I could feel his eyes boring into me. I'd have to return tomorrow with the gun and hope to high heaven I didn't run into Gary again. For the moment, though, all I wanted was to put as much distance as possible between the stolen item I was carrying and the Battle Lake chief of police. The icy cold scratched at my cheeks.

"Hey. Betty Fishbacher."

I turned toward the hoarse voice, resisting the urge to clutch the gun like the weapon it was. "Aaron Offerdahl."

He'd been standing behind a pylon but revealed himself when I passed. A lit cigarette dangled from his lip in a deliberate attempt at coolness. He kept running his hands through his hair and then patting his pockets like he was looking for his wallet. His eyes jittered, and his mask was gone, open anger laid across his face for all the world to see.

"How's your friend?" he asked.

"You mean the Battle Lake chief of police, whom you shot last week?" It was a blind stab. I knew he was talking about Curtis. The hit scored, though, and his face twisted even more darkly.

He flicked his cigarette at me. I let it bounce off my shoulder. Gary was just inside the hospital doors, talking to the underskilled woman behind the information desk. I could yell for help, and he'd come. I ground out Aaron's cigarette with the toe of my winter boot.

"I didn't shoot anyone," he snarled. "I'm here to tell you that Ray was arrested. Tell Taunita to watch her back, 'cause snitches get stitches."

He stared me down, shoving his hands into his pockets. My first instinct was to punch him in his throat, but then I thought of Timothy and Alessa. I did not want Aaron any madder at us than he appeared. When Taunita had said she fed the justice machine, did she mean putting Ray away?

"What's he in jail for?"

"Taunita knows."

The hospital's automatic doors slid open. A nurse wearing a winter coat pushed a man in a wheelchair forward. A van pulled up at the end of the sidewalk.

When I looked back to Aaron, he'd vanished. I realized it didn't matter why he was threatening Taunita. He knew she was staying with me, and that meant she and the babies were in danger.

Chapter 53

Sid and Nancy were happy to put up Taunita, Timothy, and Alessa in the spare apartment above the coffee shop. Taunita said it wasn't necessary, that she could handle a dumb drug punk like Aaron just fine, but I reminded her that the kids couldn't. Once they were settled, I used Sid and Nancy's home phone to call the hospital. They patched me through to Curtis, who sounded weak but like himself.

"What were you doing scrapping in alleys anyhow?" I asked him, my eyes clouding with tears. I couldn't believe I finally got to hear his voice.

He coughed. "Gary told me to tell you not to mess with them. They're rough people."

I knew he'd been beaten up badly, but that didn't sound at all like something Curtis would say. "Is Gary there right now?"

"I told him you were smart enough to keep yourself safe."

Gary must have been in the room with him, or Curtis would have answered me directly. "Don't let Gary know what we're talking about," I said, "but do you know anything about Civil War guns?"

"Of course I like honey buns. I used to collect them."

I could hear his wink through the line, and it felt like a weight being lifted. They could beat up Curtis, but they could never diminish his humor or wits. "I have one I need you to look at. It might have something to do with all of this, though I have no idea what."

"Bring 'em by," he said. "I'm sick of this hospital food. Now, I've got some people who want to talk to me. You won't want to bring those buns until tomorrow because I'll have a lot of company today."

Message received. "Love you, Curtis."

"That's about right," he said gruffly before hanging up.

I rubbed the back of my hand against my wet eyes. Curtis was out of the woods. Now I had to make sure the same could be said about me.

Mrs. Berns was able to cover my library shift, which meant my next stop was the Prospect House to discover what they knew about the break-in—and the idiots who'd conducted it.

Chapter 54

Turned out, Carter didn't know much, but he did know that the hanged man's gun was missing. I had no choice but to play dumb as he showed me digital photographs of the footprints in the woods, footprints exactly matching Mrs. Berns's and mine. He said the police had confiscated the mittens. The whole time we spoke, I could feel the gun burning a hole in my car's back seat.

At the end of the interview, I returned to run the library to relieve Mrs. Berns—who didn't know that the police knew about the break-in, and whom I had no intention of enlightening—to put the final touches on the Aaron Offerdahl report for Samuel Litchfield, and to write a very brief article about the break-in.

After the library closed, there was nothing to do but go home and wait. Curtis had warned me not to bring the gun to him until tomorrow. My head was too busy to deal with Johnny or Mrs. Berns.

I considered sketching what I knew, but it was so little. Hard drugs had infiltrated Battle Lake about the same time Aaron Offerdahl had arrived. Maurice, Ray, and Hammer had followed shortly after, possibly to help Aaron distribute the drugs; however, Maurice had told Taunita he'd come for a different reason—to claim his inheritance.

If that was true, if there was an inheritance, the proof had fallen into my lap through a convoluted web of history. An inheritance wouldn't erase any illegal activities Maurice had engaged in, but it might help out Taunita and the kids. Also, Aaron had most certainly shot Gary, which made me believe he'd shot and killed Maurice as well. He was a loose cannon, who was now gunning for Taunita because she'd turned in one of his lieutenants for beating up Curtis.

It was danger and confusion, all tied in a bundle and set on fire. All I knew for sure was that I missed having the kids around. Taunita had left behind one of Alessa's blankets, a blue cotton square as soft as duck down. I smelled it. Sweet, clean baby. I couldn't even clean house to pass the time because Taunita had scoured everything, even alphabetizing my seven spices. I finally read until I fell asleep.

Under my bed.

◆ ◆ ◆

The next morning, I was up with the dawn, filled with a rare sense of purpose despite my shame at returning to my nest under the mattress. I was going to check on Taunita and the kids, then bring the gun to Curtis for help dismantling it. We'd find Orpheus's final letter, which would lead us to the inheritance. I'd give it to Taunita, and the debt I owed Maurice would be paid.

I was outside the coffee shop by 6:02 a.m. It was already open. I walked in.

Sid smiled up at me, her eyes tired but bright. "No skolleboller today, but I've got coffee brewing."

"Can I just buy some Long Johns? I'm going to visit Curtis in the hospital."

She began packing them immediately. "Tell him these are on us."

"Will do. Don't suppose Taunita is up?"

"Wouldn't know. She and the kids left with a friend last night."

A cold ball of lead dropped into my stomach. "What?"

"Looked like a punk with that barbell through his eyebrow, but who am I to judge?"

I could hardly push the chalky words past my lips. "She took the babies, too? They all left without a fight?"

"As far as I could tell. Taunita said she'd call you to let you know where she's at. Everything OK?"

I ran all the way to the police station. My chest ached, my lungs feeling like two frozen balloons when I finally reached it. I tore the door open. Gary started to stand when he saw me, but his injury brought him up short. The bags under his eyes and the way his mouth was drawn suggested he'd worked through the night.

"Taunita. The babies. Aaron Offerdahl has them!"

I spilled the story of Taunita's relationship to Maurice, and how she had narced on Ray—and maybe the whole gang—and now Aaron had taken her and her kids.

"They left peacefully?" Gary's eyebrows were arched so close together they almost touched.

"That's what Sid said." I wasn't going to cry in front of him.

"Then there's not much we can do." He turned from me.

I cried out, "Offerdahl is unstable! I think he's the one who shot you."

He shook his head. "I'll look into it. That's all I can promise."

Gary wrote down a description of Taunita and the kids and sent me on my way.

Outside the police station, the cold air cut at my ice-burned lungs. I had no idea where to go. I certainly wasn't going to drive home and wait. I could head to the microbrewery and search for Aaron, but there was no way he'd hide out there with two little kids and a woman. I didn't know where else to dig, so I decided to look online.

I took off on foot, the brisk air cauterizing my nostrils.

I was unlocking the library door when I felt the hand at my throat.

I whipped around to face a very angry-looking Aaron Offerdahl, his pupils the size of pinpricks.

Chapter 55

"I will say this once." His voice was low, dangerous, metal scraping against pavement. "I have Taunita and the kids. I will trade them for the gun."

"What gun?" I wasn't playing stupid. I really *was* stupid. He couldn't possibly be talking about the Civil War musket, which only me, Curtis, and Mrs. Berns knew about. But what other gun was there?

"I know about Maurice's letters. I know the dumbass thought he had an inheritance coming to him. I can't take a chance that he might be right."

"What?" I felt like the world had flipped me upside down and was going through my pockets for change.

His shifty eyes landed on me. "Where exactly do you think this inheritance was gonna come from? Everyone in my family knows the story—that a Black dude showed up pretending to be a good friend of old Barnaby, claiming he had property rights if anything were to happen to Barnaby's daughter. But Barnaby's daughter didn't live and the man disappeared, and so it all went to my great-great-great-grandpa. Not much of it left, but enough, and my dad isn't going to live much longer. I saw your duffel bag outside the hospital. I ain't stupid. You had a gun in there, a big ol' one that matches the one stolen from the Prospect House. I heard it come over the scanner as an update to the break-in."

It was falling into place, but into weird place. "You're not here to deal drugs?"

He laughed. "What is this, a Bond flick? You don't need to know why I'm here. Suffice to say that it's a happy coincidence that I first met Maurice Jackson a decade ago, when he was here visiting his grandma, and that we stayed in touch. And it's an even happier one that he spilled to me about the inheritance he thought he had comin'. How could he know it was tied to the Prospect House? Only people born and raised in Battle Lake know those stories. Crazy world, isn't it? But I need that gun now, just in case there's something to it all."

I swallowed, fear like paste in my mouth. "It's in my house."

"Then you better get it. You think you can find the cabin on Silver Lake, fire number 23470?"

I nodded.

"Good. I'll meet you there in thirty minutes. You show up alone, you hand me the gun, and I hand you Taunita and the snot babies. You tell anyone what you're up to, and the world has three less mouths to feed. I'll be watching you. Understand?"

I nodded again, rigid with fear.

Chapter 56

I raced back to my car outside the Fortune, pushing my sore lungs to take in more air. I didn't see anyone watching me, yet I felt a million eyes crawling across my back as the morning dawned. Plus, Aaron's uncanny ability to anticipate where I was going to be made me feel as vulnerable as a cow in a slaughter chute.

I reached my car and let myself in, trying to think things through as I drove. Thank goodness I'd walked to the library, or Aaron would have spotted the gun in my back seat. My best bet was to drive home exactly as I'd promised him I would, charge inside, and call Gary immediately. Only in movies were people stupid enough to arrive at an isolated location alone for a trade. Who was I, Chuck Norris?

I raced home and tore into the house. Luna and Tiger Pop were both outside, appearing miffed. One glance at them and I knew what I'd find on the other side of the door: destruction.

All Taunita's cleaning was buried under ripped-up cushions and torn-open cupboards. Potato Buds and canned goods were strewn across the floor, furniture tipped over, everything in my bedroom closet thrown onto my bed, the pet door jammed so Luna and Tiger Pop couldn't get back in. At least he hadn't hurt them. Still, I ran from room to room, my breath jagged. In every space, the story was the same.

Aaron had already visited, and he'd left no corner intact.

That meant he knew I'd lied to him about the gun being here. My heart dipped. I hurried to the phone, fear crawling like cold-footed beetles across my skin.

"Calling someone?"

I turned. I hadn't bothered to close the door behind me. Aaron stood there, Timothy on his hip.

"Mee-wa!" Timothy held his arms out to me. Dried tears caked his face, and he was sniffling.

I ran forward, but Aaron swiveled so his body was between me and Timothy. Luna stood just behind them both, her hackles raised and a low growl in her throat. She was confused. She liked Timothy but knew something wasn't right here.

"Thought I'd give you time to call the police, did you? What do you think this is, the movies?"

I would have laughed at the irony if I weren't so scared. A fresh tear rolled through the crust on Timothy's face, and he trembled like a kitten, despite the winter jacket he wore. "The gun is in the back seat of my car."

"Get it."

I hurried past him, trying not to glance at Timothy. He was leaning away from Aaron like he wanted to push off him but was too terrified to do so.

I returned in seconds hauling the black hockey duffel. Aaron closed the house door behind me, trapping the animals outside again.

"Open it."

I followed his orders, pulling out the long gun.

"Is there something inside of it?"

"I can't tell," I said. "It looks like."

"Get it out."

"I *can't*. If I could, I would have already. It's shoved too far in there."

"Then smash it."

"I'm not strong enough." I didn't know if this was true. "Let me hold Timothy, and you can smash it."

Aaron considered his options, then tossed Timothy at me. I caught him just before he hit the floor. He clung to me like a baby koala, trying to crawl inside my coat. I hugged him tight and whispered soothing words, all of them lies.

Aaron picked the gun up off the floor and glanced down the barrel, presumably spotting the same shadow of paper that I had. He raised the gun above his head and smashed it into the doorway. The crash was deafening. Luna began barking.

Aaron swung at the door repeatedly until the barrel separated from the stock. He laughed in triumph when he ripped them apart, revealing a scroll of fragile yellow paper.

He yanked it out and unrolled it, his hands shaking. His eyes moved as he read. He smiled. At least I thought he did.

It took me a moment to realize it was a grimace of fury. "It's a god-damned letter from Orpheus to his wife. It says to look into the tunnel of justice, that she'll find their due in there, just like the other letter."

He moved his glance to me, his eyes bright and dangerous. "You have five seconds to figure out what that tunnel of justice is."

He ripped Timothy out of my arms, dangling the boy by an arm. Timothy screamed and tried to kick at him with his tiny legs, but Aaron didn't flinch. I hated him with a rage I'd never felt toward anyone before. I lunged forward, but Aaron balled his hand into a fist and held it near Timothy's face, his threat clear.

I stopped, the fury burning through me with a white heat. I breathed deeply, forcing my mind to clear, thinking as I spoke. I needed to stall until I could find a way out of this. "How do I know what the tunnel is? It might not even exist at all. Or it might be a place they traveled through, or a . . ."

My breath caught in my throat. I could read Libby's inventory of belongings left with the hanged man as if the words were floating in the air: *Musket 25A, a Bible, a wooden fife, and two quarters, two nickels, and a penny.*

The tunnel of justice wasn't the gun; it was the fife—a battle instrument used to signal victory.

"What is it?" Aaron eyed me suspiciously, ignoring the squirming, sobbing child reaching out desperately for me.

"If I tell you, you'll let Taunita and both kids go?"

"What do I want them for? I just need whatever Orpheus thought he had that would give him what's mine."

I didn't trust Aaron, but what choice did I have? "Orpheus was the hanged man they found by the Prospect House in 1865. He returned from the war with a fife, and I think that's what he meant when he referred to the tunnel of justice."

Whether it would have anything in it, or whether it was what Aaron and I were looking for, remained to be seen.

"Take me to it."

Chapter 57

Which was how Timothy, Aaron, and I found ourselves in the Prospect House's kitchen, talking to Carter Stone. Aaron had warned me that I'd better keep quiet—and make sure Timothy did the same—or we'd never see Taunita and Alessa again.

"Tell me again why you want to see the wooden chest?" Carter directed the question at me, but he was eyeing Aaron.

"We think there might be something inside it to help with the . . . story I'm writing," I said. I was sweating desperation. Aaron had let me hold Timothy to quiet him down, but I was hyperaware of the Offerdahl heir's penchant for violence.

Carter shrugged. "Let me tell Libby what we're up to." He disappeared downstairs and returned moments later, not making eye contact with any of us. Had he felt the terror oozing from my pores? Could he see how badly frightened Timothy was? Had he told Libby to call the police? I prayed to every god I didn't believe in. "It's on the third floor. Follow me."

Aaron signaled for me to trail immediately behind Carter. The hair on the back of my neck prickled, and every animal instinct in me yelled not to let Aaron stand at my vulnerable back, but without knowing where he had Taunita and Alessa or what sort of shape they were in, I had no choice.

As we took the first flight of stairs, Aaron was too amped up to make appropriate conversation but tried nonetheless. "Must be nice to live in a house like this. You get to live here?"

Carter glanced over his shoulder, his hand on the stair railing. The Prospect House was closed for business so the police could continue to gather evidence on the break-in. We were the only ones inside, besides Libby. "My wife and I live next door, in the carriage house."

"This used to be my family's place. I'm an Offerdahl." There was an uncomfortable note of possessiveness in his voice, like he was daring Carter to contradict him.

"You don't say."

We climbed the second set of stairs, this one steeper than the first. I wanted to run, to inform Carter of what was going on, to believe that help was on its way, but I kept myself calm through force of will. My hope was that we would find exactly what Aaron was looking for and there would be no violence.

We ascended the final full set of stairs, the narrowest yet. We had to duck to reach the third-floor landing.

"They must not have had many fat people around when they built this house," Aaron remarked with a snicker.

"Over there," Carter said, pointing across the room. We stood in the only clear area on the landing. Around us was the chaos of uncatalogued items that I remembered from my first visit here—cardboard boxes with scribbled labels, stacks of musty-smelling clothing, old toys, moldering newspapers.

On the edge of the chaos rested a plain wooden box, so old the wood had gone gray. HANGED MAN was written on the side of it, along with the date of March 1865. A stack of newspapers towered behind it, nearly reaching the ceiling. Behind that was one last tiny set of stairs to the attic.

Aaron strode to the box and knelt. He undid the brass latches on the front and lifted the lid, pawing through the contents. Carter, Timothy, and I all watched as Aaron stood and turned, the wooden fife in his hand. It was nearly as long as his forearm, carved out of a blond-gray wood, crudely formed but lasting all these years. Aaron peered through one end as if it were a telescope.

A triumphant smile slid across his face like oil.

"I see it." He dug his finger in. The sound of dry paper riffled through the air.

Behind Aaron, the door to the attic, the unreachable door, began to slowly, deliberately creak open. My heart jumped into my throat. Aaron, oblivious, continued to dig inside the fife. I held my breath, terrified of what would reveal itself on the other side of that door. A zombie ghost in ragged tatters, coming to reclaim his inheritance? A floating girl corpse with maggots for eyes? How bad could one day get?

But then the door was fully open, dusty sunlight trailing in. There was nothing on the other side.

"Got it!" Aaron said triumphantly, holding a yellowed scroll in his hand. He was framed by mountains of papers and, above and behind, the attic door.

"Hi," Timothy said, his tiny voice reverent.

I glanced at him, confused. He was talking to the open attic door. "Hi!" he said again, with more force.

My heart stopped. I didn't see what he was seeing. The doorway was empty. But I did witness the musty tower of newspapers behind Aaron slowly rock, as if pushed by an invisible hand. Reflexively, I opened my mouth to issue a warning, but I wasn't quick enough.

The enormous pile of aged papers fell on Aaron.

He dropped the fife and the paper. Both fell at my feet.

I grabbed the scroll, and Carter snatched the instrument before giving a floundering Aaron a firm push backward into the chaos of papers. He speedily herded Timothy and me down the stairs. He shoved us into a bedroom off the base of the stairs at the second floor and locked the door behind us.

"I'm calling the police," he hollered through the door. "You can explain what's going on when we have handcuffs on that waste of air."

I heard his footsteps race down the stairs. I set Timothy on the bed, pushing aside the gorgeous, yellowed lace dress draped across it. He didn't want to let me go, but I couldn't trust the lock. I leaned into the heavy oak of the dresser to the left of the door, hoping to push it over and seal the entrance. I was grunting and straining when I heard Aaron coming down the stairs toward us. He tried the doorknob, cursed, and kept running.

I raced to the window. The moment Aaron's car sped away, I scooped up Timothy and ran down the stairs. We weren't in the clear as long as Aaron had Taunita and Alessa. Libby was in the kitchen, wondering what was going on. I handed her Timothy and told her and Carter where I was going.

I had no illusions that I could fight Aaron, especially not if he had Hammer with him. I needed to stall for time, though, and I would do that by putting myself in their path. They could be hiding out in one of the cabins, but the police had been watching those carefully since the string of break-ins. They could also be in the rec house of the brewery, though that was next to impossible, as there was no way Taunita would have let Aaron take Timothy without a fight, and the noise of that would have alerted the brewery staff.

That left only the old cabin behind the dormitory, the one Vienna called the grow room.

I drove like lightning, the roads so icy that the front of my car was not always in agreement with the back. I roared past Vienna's, past the dorm, and found the little road behind it leading to the cabin. When I spotted Aaron's car there, relief washed over me like warm water, quickly followed by terror. I had no plan, only a conviction that I couldn't leave Taunita and Alessa alone with Aaron.

I squealed to a stop, tried to breathe around my pained heartbeat, and stepped out of my car.

Puffs of woodsmoke curled asthmatically out of the chimney. Naked oak branches scraped against the snow-buried roof, and the whole unpainted structure leaned a little to the right. Two murky windows stared at me from each side of the door.

Aaron must be inside.

With luck, Taunita and Alessa were as well, and alive.

I felt a muddy mix of helplessness, fear, and anger. Inexplicably, horribly, the image of December's Candy Cane Killer rose into my mind, paralyzing me where I stood. A wave of nausea so strong it felt like vertigo washed over me. I didn't know if I could override my self-preservation instinct and force myself to enter the cabin. How could I?

But then, I heard a baby cry from inside.

Hot tears clouded my eyes, and I sprinted forward, charging into the cabin, hoping that my directions to Carter and Libby had been clear enough, and that the police were on their way.

Chapter 58

My breath was a full second behind me, slamming into my back as my eyes frantically tried to take in everything.

The dirty windows gave the inside of the cabin a smudgy, underwater feel. The single room was bare of all furniture except a pile of wood, a potbellied stove that turned the space into a sauna, and a rickety table surrounded by four mismatched chairs.

Hammer sat in one, Vienna in another.

Niall, my brewery tour guide, was seated in a third. Aaron stood behind them, had probably been pacing before I rushed the scene. Taunita was tied in a bundle on the floor in the far corner, unmoving, her face turned away from me, her hands limp. Alessa was next to her, sucking on a pacifier, a bottle filled with what looked like cola leaned against her chunky little thigh. She had one possessive hand on her mom. Her eyes appeared swollen, and I could smell her dirty diaper from across the room.

Everyone but Taunita looked up when I flew in, their faces a palette of anger and surprise. Vienna moved immediately to the door, slammed it behind me, and leaned against it, her arms crossed.

"You're in on this?" I spat.

She ignored me.

"Who are you?" Niall asked, standing. He wore a white tank, which revealed a deep-purple octopus tattoo curling down his right arm.

Aaron breathed heavily, clenching and unclenching his fists. He must have barely beaten me here. The air was still charged with whatever heated argument they'd been having when I barged in.

"That's the detective I was telling you about. She's got the fife."

Niall shook his head. "You've messed it all up, the whole thing, for a *fife*?!"

"Not just a fife." Aaron tugged on the barbell above his eye. "It's my family legacy."

Niall smacked Aaron alongside the head with enough force that he almost fell into the stove. On the ground, Taunita's form shifted, making me realize I'd been holding my breath.

She was alive. Relief washed over me, making me weak.

"Now what?" Niall asked. "You think about that?"

Aaron held his hand over his bleeding nose. His eyes glowed like dynamite fuses. "Now I go back for the fife. I still have one of the kids."

"Except now both of these women have seen me," Niall said. "Dammit, I knew you weren't worth it, Offerdahl."

"Who told you about this cheap land?" Aaron whined. "Who connected you with all the buyers?"

Was Niall an O'Callaghan, or just someone who had the ear of an O'Callaghan and used his access to convince them to open a brewery here? I inched closer to Alessa, who was still in her footie pajamas. The diaper smell intensified. Poor baby probably hadn't been changed since they'd been abducted. I didn't have a plan, exactly, except to comfort her and her mom until the police showed up. I prayed Taunita was conscious, though I wasn't hopeful.

"You. Brownie. You look familiar."

I stopped in my tracks. "You led a brewery tour that I was on."

Niall nodded before lunging at Aaron again. Aaron tripped over himself trying to get away. It worried me to see how scared he was of Niall, or whatever his real name was.

Hammer watched it all impassively. Vienna fidgeted at the doorway, shifting from foot to foot.

"It's my inheritance!" Aaron repeated.

"Doesn't sound like it," Niall said, matter-of-factly. "And you're the reason I now have to kill all three of these people. Or, I should say, why *you* have to kill them. If you hope to walk again, that is. We've got too much money riding on this. Those drugs don't grow on trees, you know? There's investors I got to pay off. Hammer, you guarantee he does what he's supposed to do. Chop the bodies up, for all I care—just don't leave a mess here."

Niall grabbed a black ski jacket off a chair and strode toward the door, his cold authority chilling me. "Oh, and her, too." He tossed a glance at Vienna.

"What?" Her voice was a yelp. "I didn't do anything wrong."

"Except tell people about this place. You had one job, and that was as lookout, not hostess. You messed up a good thing, sweetheart."

She opened and closed her mouth like a landed fish.

"Don't look so stupid," Niall said, brushing past her. "Aaron said he saw you showing some old lady around. Had to be how Brownie here found us, right?"

He glanced at me. My poker face gave me away.

"That's what I thought." He slipped out the door, slamming it behind him.

I started talking fast, the sweat running down my spine. "You're not guilty of anything right now, Aaron. You kill us, though, and you're a murderer."

He looked at me blearily. "Shit, I'm already a murderer. It should have ended at Maurice, but then that damn backwoods police chief almost catches me with a trunk of Oxy. Plus, now I got this little kidnapping. What's four more bodies?"

He reached into his waistband and pulled out a gun, a sleek black semiautomatic, glittering and efficient. "If I don't do it, I can't live nowhere nohow. That shitstain has eyes everywhere. You watch the front for me, Hammer."

The giant was emotionless. He strode to the door, pushing Vienna toward the table. She was as pale as winter, her eyes wide circles of shock.

My voice was hoarse. I felt like I was choking on words, not sure which to choose, knowing that four lives rested on me picking correctly. "Kidnapping carries a shorter sentence than murder."

"I don't plan to be caught for either."

I shook my head. "I don't believe you can shoot us in cold blood."

Aaron snorted, aiming the gun at me sideways, gangster-style.

"Dang, Eel," Hammer growled, his first words since I'd charged into the cabin. "Dude said not here. Then we just got a mess to clean up. Go do it out back, in the woods."

I wondered if this was what Orpheus's last moments had been like, fumbled between inept crooks trying to steal what was rightfully his. As long as we were talking, though, we weren't dying. I twisted the skin under my arm to give me something to focus on other than the panic. "Let me get Taunita up. I'll carry the baby. We can walk to the woods. It'll be quicker."

I hurried to Taunita's side before he could argue. I was grateful to find that she was not only conscious but had no visible wounds other than deep bruising over her right cheek and a black eye. I didn't know how much longer we had, but her being conscious increased our odds of survival from zero to around a tenth of a percent.

"Keep her hands tied," Aaron warned.

I unknotted the rope around her ankles and helped her to her feet. Her eyes were grateful but bruised. "The police have Timothy," I whispered. "He's safe."

A sob escaped her, and she fell into me.

"Hurry up!" Aaron pushed us with the butt of his gun.

I made sure Taunita could stand before I scooped up Alessa. She felt soggy and light, her tiny body hot and wiggly in my arms.

"Hey, sweetheart," I said. It was all I had. I opened my jacket and zipped her inside, where she squirmed and whimpered and stank, only her head visible through the neck of my coat.

I gently held Taunita's elbow to steady her. "I'll lead the way," I told Aaron.

My words sounded brave, but I felt like I was floating above myself, looking down to see our sad little trio marching to our death. I kissed the top of Alessa's head and held her tight, the honey scent of her baby shampoo thick in my nostrils, laced with the sour reek of urine.

Taunita leaned into me. Alessa's grubby little fists bunched up my shirt.

We stepped into the glare of the sunlight, the brightness blinding after the cabin's murk.

Something even brighter than the diamond glint of the sun caught my eye, and then again, from a different angle, followed by a third glare from a new angle.

I had only one second to guess what it was.

I pushed Taunita down, curled Alessa into my arms, and fell over them both.

The raging thunder of a gunfight rained over our heads like judgment.

Chapter 59

"I knew she was no good," Mrs. Berns stage-whispered. She was wearing her cap guns—had, in fact, told me she hadn't taken them off except to sleep since her grandkids had arrived two days earlier, coincidentally the same day I'd charged into the grow room. Apparently, they appreciated Mrs. Berns exactly as she was.

"You knew no such thing," I argued, my voice significantly quieter than hers.

Because of her grandkids' arrival, we hadn't had a chance to speak since the shoot-out, an Old West–style gunfight of Battle Lake's finest against Hammer and Aaron. Gary hadn't seemed happy, exactly, when he'd first spotted me stepping out of the cabin, but at least he hadn't shot me.

Aaron had taken one in the elbow and another in the shoulder. Hammer had not been so lucky and now sported a toe tag. Vienna, using her finely honed hunting instincts, had ducked about the same time as me and gotten away without a scratch.

Once taken into custody, Aaron refused to go on record for killing Maurice, though Kennie informed me that Ray was in the middle of negotiating a deal, narcing on Aaron, and admitting to robbing cabins and thrashing Curtis when the old man had caught him and Aaron trying to rob the apothecary. In return, he'd been offered leniency on drug possession charges.

Niall—whose real name was Bill—had already been extradited to Chicago for a whole raft of drug-related crimes he'd left behind. For now, the O'Callaghan's brewery was set to reopen once the police were done thoroughly investigating the premises. It remained to be seen whether anyone in the family knew about the drugs being dealt right under their noses. If O'Callaghan's could be traced back to the influx of OxyContin and fentanyl into Otter Tail County, they would go down hard.

I kind of hoped they weren't in on it. The world needed more ice castles and chocolate stout.

"Did too," Mrs. Berns said. "That's why I dumped her. I don't roll with criminals."

"She's not going to be rolling with *anyone* for a while," I said.

Vienna was currently awaiting trial on assisted-kidnapping charges. Her ties to the OxyContin trade were not yet clear, but it appeared as though Bill had hired her to be his eyes in the woods, keeping track of anyone who wandered the property. She might have done some dealing, too.

"Shh."

I glanced down at Timothy, who sat next to me in the pew, and I blushed. There was something about having to be shushed by a toddler that truly mortifies, especially since we were at the funeral of a man likely to be his great-great-great-great-grandfather.

It took Barnaby Offerdahl's notarized will—retrieved from the hanged man's fife and naming Orpheus Jackson executor of his estate should anything happen to Barnaby and heir to the estate should anything happen to Barnaby's daughter—to convince the county coroner to exhume the hanged man's grave.

It would take weeks to verify through DNA that he was indeed Orpheus Jackson and that Timothy and Alessa were his direct descendants. My money was on a happy ending.

If all went as planned, the children stood to inherit the land surrounding the Prospect House. Given that most of it was lakefront property, it was worth over half a million. At least, that was what Samuel Litchfield told me when I spilled the whole story.

Turned out he'd hired me to find Aaron because Aaron's father, Gregory, had been hospitalized for a stroke the previous week. Gregory was still hanging on but looked like he wouldn't last through the month. As per his will, which Samuel Litchfield had drawn up, Aaron was to be contacted and informed if his inheritance became imminent.

Because the Prospect House had been rightfully bought and sold at least four times since Orpheus's death, it was unclear what would happen to the structure, though Taunita said she and the kids had no interest in it. If lineage was established, she would now be executor of the estate for her children, until they were old enough to decide if they wanted to sell the land or keep it in the family.

In the meanwhile, Samuel Litchfield was able to uncover some liquid assets of the Offerdahl estate. He promised to work on obtaining a loan for Taunita with the assets as collateral so she had money to raise the kids until all the legal aspects were worked out. He was also the one who'd helped her to organize today's funeral for Orpheus, and tomorrow's for Maurice, both at the Battle Lake Lutheran Church. He said it was the least the town could do for the two men.

I might have pegged Samuel wrong.

For the time being, Sid and Nancy had offered Taunita and the babies the apartment over the coffee shop rent-free and given her a temp job as a barista. She paid back the forty bucks she'd borrowed from me after her first shift. As a bonus (for me, anyhow), I'd agreed to watch the babies at night until she could make other arrangements.

I sincerely hoped she would not be able to.

Taunita sat on the other side of Timothy during Orpheus's service, bright tears streaming down her face, Alessa in her arms. She'd lost Maurice. He'd been her whole family, other than her kids. She didn't have anywhere to go and, I'm sure, had mixed feelings about staying here until everything was straightened out. I wished I could ease her loss, but only time had that power.

At least there'd been a good turnout for today's funeral, and I knew there'd be even more tomorrow. A few of the attendees were ambulance chasers, but most came because it was the right thing to do. Barnaby Offerdahl's brother had stolen Orpheus's inheritance and likely his life.

His descendant had then done the same to Orpheus's, and very nearly gotten away with it. Justice had finally been done, possibly with the help of Mabel Offerdahl's spirit. Carter and I had spoken about the opening attic door and the falling papers since Aaron had been arrested. Neither of us had actually seen a ghost, but we weren't willing to write off the possibility that the Prospect House had an otherworldly protector.

As my eyes took in the full pews, I couldn't help but notice how ridiculously glossy and gorgeous the plants lining the window wells were looking. I felt the familiar jealousy burn.

Kennie.

When the service was over, we filed toward the basement for the funeral meal. I passed Kennie talking to a particularly perky-looking fern in the hallway. She was wearing all black, but Kennie-style: leather pants and a fur coat, plus sky-high stilettos. Atop her head rested a demure hat with netting and sleek black feathers.

"What're you saying to that plant?" I demanded.

She turned, a guilty expression on her face. She quickly wiped it off. "Why, Mira! You just can't accept that you're not the only one in town with a green thumb."

For some reason, her comment made me glance at her thumb, which was presently *blue*. I grabbed her wrist and yanked back the loose sleeve of her fur coat. There it was. A catheter bag strapped to her arm, the hose leading to her wrist. It was filled with a Smurf-blue liquid.

I sniffed it.

"Miracle-Gro! I knew you were up to no good."

She put her hand over my mouth and dragged me into a corner, smiling and making *everything is fine here* faces to the people walking past.

"I am a plant healer," she hissed into my ear.

"You're a plant *liar*," I squeaked through her fingers.

She pressed me against the wall, glancing right and left. Her expression grew calculated. "Have it your way. But if I'm not doing my plant and animal psychology, I might go back to renegade makeovers. Or home bikini waxes." She glanced at my crotch area, her eyebrows raised. "You'll never know when I might drop by."

I pushed her hand away. "Fine," I said, exasperated.

I didn't want her to know I was actually happy. In fact, I was thrilled to find out she was not an actual plant whisperer. I still wore a smile on my face as I stepped down the church basement steps and smack into Johnny.

And his blonde girlfriend.

My heart cracked.

I glanced from one to the other, for some strange reason feeling guilty even though *he* was the one who'd technically cheated. It didn't help that Johnny was as gorgeous as ever, wearing a light-green button-up shirt and dark tie.

The woman I'd seen him embracing in Bonnie & Clyde's alley was as strikingly blonde as he was, her features carved out of ivory. Probably they were perfect for each other. I turned, ready to head back up the stairs. I'd taken about as much pain as I could for the month. I didn't want to be broken up with in a church basement.

I felt a gentle hand at my wrist.

"Mira, have you met my cousin Corinne? She was at my practice last week."

I turned, all my emotions on high alert. "She's your cousin?"

Up close, I could see the resemblance: the same hair, stunning blue eyes, and plump, curving lips. She was a knockout.

He nodded. I couldn't read his expression. Was he mad? Disappointed? And why was he getting on one knee?

Chapter 60

Before my thoughts could organize, he gently leaned his shoulder into my stomach and stood, hoisting me over his shoulders in a fireman's carry. He began walking up the steps, and the entire basement erupted in a cheer.

He kept walking, opened the door, and stepped outside into the ice crystal–perfect day, before heading away from the church and toward his house. The smell of winter air filled my nostrils, and the cool lemon sun glowed overhead. People were staring, some of them laughing and pointing, others looking at me with something like admiration, still others acting like it was just another day in the life.

"I imagine you've guessed that Mrs. Berns told me what you *thought* you saw," he finally said, only a little winded. "I'll make a deal with you."

I didn't say anything, just enjoying the ride on his shoulders. It'd been that sort of week.

"If one of us wants out of this relationship, we tell the other," he said, raising his voice so it carried. "No cheating. No lying. No drama. Because you know what? I'm always going to treat you well. But if you take me for granted, or assume the worst about me again, I don't know if we can make this work. Understood?"

He set me down on his front stoop two blocks from the church. Before I could answer, I felt his mouth on mine, hot and seeking. His hands followed, and then his hips pressed into me, pinning me against the door.

He kissed me deeply, then pulled back abruptly to open the door, throw me back over his shoulder, and lock the door behind us.

He carried me to the bedroom. His house was strong and neat, with guitars leaning against the wall and books lining the shelves.

It smelled like vanilla.

Johnny threw me onto his bed. The down comforter held me like a cloud, and sparkling sunlight filtered in through the curtains. I'd been to his house a handful of times, but never in his bedroom. He tore off his jacket, then stripped off his tie and shirt. He never dragged his eyes from me except for the brief moments when cloth separated our gazes.

"I love you," he said, earnestly. "I want to be with you. I want you always. Nod if you understand."

I nodded.

At least I think I did.

My whole body had been taken over by a buzzing sound that started between my thighs but had since spread to every centimeter of my body, a warm, honey-liquid feeling that warned me I was about to have a really, really good time.

He knelt on the bed. The sun shone behind him, lighting up his curly blond hair like a halo, perfectly outlining his sculpted shoulders and arms. His hands were gripped into fists. He had been worried, angry even.

But he hadn't left me.

In fact, he'd come after me.

I sat up and yanked him on top of me, both of us falling back into the covers in a passionate, laughing, hopeful pile.

In that moment, I vowed to reconsider how much better it was on top of the bed than under it.

And with Johnny than without.

Acknowledgments

Terri Bischoff, this series would have ended at *September Mourn* if not for you. Thank you for being an intuitive, kind acquisitions editor and a genius friend. Cheers to many shared projects in our future. Thank you also for lining me up with Nicole Nugent, an editor whose eye for detail is surpassed by only her organizational skills. In other words, she's the type A kinda editor this writer needs. Courtney Colton, I'll miss your publicity skills, but I appreciate all the help you've given my writing career. Victoria Skurnick, thank you for being my agent and my friend, and for taking me out for the best Greek food of my life. Barbara Moore, thank you for giving me my first break.

Jessica Morrell, I've said it before, and I'll say it again: you make me a better writer every time I work with you. May you live a long and healthy life. Christine Hollermann, your support and friendship mean the world to me. Same to you, Dana Fredsti, Linda Joffe "We'll Always Have the Metro" Hull, Aimee Hix, Catriona McPherson, Cindy Pederson, Shannon Baker, and Erica Ruth Neubauer.

Zoë and Xander, none of it would be half as much fun without the two of you.

About the Author

Jess Lourey writes about secrets. She's the bestselling author of thrillers, rom-com mysteries, book club fiction, young adult fiction, and non-fiction. Winner of the Anthony, Thriller, and Minnesota Book Awards, Jess is also an Edgar, Agatha, and Lefty Award–nominated author; TEDx presenter; and recipient of The Loft's Excellence in Teaching fellowship. Check out her TEDx Talk for the true story behind her debut novel, *May Day*. She lives in Minneapolis with a rotating batch of foster kittens (and occasional foster puppies, but those goobers are a lot of work). For more information, visit www.jesslourey.com.